D1114436

The Zaharoff Conspiracy

by

Toby Purser

METHUEN

Published by Methuen 2014

1 3 5 7 9 10 8 6 4 2

This edition first published in 2014 by

Methuen
35 Hospital Fields Road
York, YO10 4DZ

www.methuen.co.uk

Methuen Publishing Ltd. Reg. No. 3543167

ISBN: 978 0 413 77754 6

A CIP catalogue for this title is
available from the British Library

Printed and bound in the UK by
CPI Group (UK) Ltd, Croydon CR0 4YY

Typeset by SX Composing DTP, Rayleigh Essex

For Cerys

'All men dream: but not equally. Those who dream by night in the dusty recesses of their minds wake in the day to find that it was vanity: but the dreamers of the day are dangerous men, for they may act their dream with open eyes, to make it possible.'

T. E. Lawrence
Seven Pillars of Wisdom

Toby Purser read Modern History at the University of Oxford (Mansfield College) and holds a PhD in medieval history. Toby has taught in a range of schools and colleges across the United Kingdom and is currently a university lecturer. His teaching and research has taken him to Prague, Vienna, Budapest, Berlin, Istanbul, Normandy, Jerusalem, Jordan and the battlefields of France, Belgium and Gallipoli. Toby is married to opera singer Cerys Jones and they live in Gloucestershire with their three young children.

Other works by Toby Purser:

Fiction:

The Devil's Inheritance

Non-fiction:

Medieval England 1042–1228

The First Crusade and the Crusader States 1073–1192

Raiders and Invaders: The British Isles c.400–c.1100

Power and Control: Kingship in the Middle Ages c.1100–c.1500

Further details can be found on the author's website www.tobypurser.org.uk and his Facebook page 'Toby Purser Author'.

Acknowledgements

No man is an island, and the writing of this novel has been made possible only with the support and inspiration of many people and places. The original ideas sprung partly from the Society of Genealogists, and the Bodleian Library and Shiplake College made wonderful writing environments. Recently, the friendship of Jim and Claire at The Ebrington Arms has offered a unique bolthole to complete the final edits, so much so that I have become the 'pub author.' Trips to Prague and Vienna with my former teaching colleagues, including the inimitable Philip Pedley, Keith Hannis, Martin Collier, Dan Connolly, Richard Mather and Max von Habsburg, are remembered with great fondness and sparked so much that has gone into the book, along with the countless conversations continued long after the chimes at midnight in bars, restaurants and trains across central Europe. To Sarah Gillard, who read the first draft with a critical eye and with such enthusiasm and to Jane Anson, who first edited it brilliantly, I owe huge thanks and of course to Methuen which has shown enormous faith in the manuscript while seeing it through all the stages of publication with tremendous professionalism. To my family I owe a debt for the unconditional support over many years; to my mother and Martin for providing a home, without which it would never have been finished the way it has been – and to Bill, Gill, Kyffin and Bryce for their unquestioning love and encouragement and to my three young sons, without whom it would have been finished a lot earlier. To my father, who first taught me history, and instilled in me the confidence to ask 'why?'. But most of all to my wife, Cerys, who has lived with and put up with Septimus Oates, George Rex and Hannah Lightfoot for more years than she deserves, never doubting the novel through its many forms and always being its main champion – to her, this book is dedicated: you are my sky.

Toby Purser
Gloucestershire
February 2014

1759

17 April 1759

Kew on a wet, windy April afternoon. Far from the bustle of the narrow, noisy streets of the city of London, the genteel denizens of Kew go about their business. Married couples stroll side by side, wearing the latest fashions from Paris. Men on business walk with greater urgency. Carriages rattle along the cobbles. Shopkeepers stand confidently on their doorsteps, nodding at customers who stop to exchange views about the health of King George II and the news from North America, where the King's army, under the brilliant young General Wolfe, is campaigning against the French. In a few months' time, Wolfe will win a momentous victory at Québec, a victory that the shopkeepers' anticipate will propel Great Britain to the forefront of the commercial world.

A carriage stops unobtrusively alongside St Anne's Chapel. A young woman steps out gingerly, assisted by a distinguished gentleman, and walks inside. Some moments later, another carriage draws up, and three gentlemen – cloaked and gloved – descend and walk quickly up the steps. The people of Kew have not noticed that a coat of arms on the door of the second carriage has been covered over. They walk past without a glance.

Nobody recognises the young woman's escort. A minor

commotion would have erupted had they done so, for it is Mr William Pitt, senior minister in Parliament, and the genius behind Britain's astonishing victories over France. Furthermore, one of the young gentlemen is none other than George, Prince of Wales, heir apparent to the throne of Great Britain.

Anyone in Kew who paused to observe the visitors' arrival outside the chapel might have seen the Rector standing at the entrance, and wondered whether a marriage was about to take place.

This was indeed the case. Twenty minutes later, the small, anonymous party leave the chapel. The rain is coming down in a steady shower. People hurry by.

Rather than get into a coach together, the newlyweds touch hands and kiss so briefly that it may never have happened. The bride climbs into her carriage and is whisked away. The Prince of Wales stares after the coach and, for a moment, his face is a mask of despair and grief. Then, at Pitt's insistence, he draws his gaze away from the rapidly departing coach and steps into his own.

He does not look back.

1914

12 June 1914

If Septimus Oates had known he was to witness a murder that Friday afternoon, he would have thought twice about answering the tentative knock at the door. He hadn't long changed into his subfusc – the formal Oxford academic dress of a dark suit with white shirt and white bow tie – in readiness for lunch. He was giving a lecture that afternoon in the Examination Schools entitled *The Patronage of Pitt the Younger* and word had it the dons who had been appointed to examine his Fellowship thesis would be in attendance. Septimus stood in front of the mirror for a moment to check if his tie was straight. It was a dark-haired and rather good-looking young man, clean-shaven with serious green eyes who stared back. Septimus pushed his long hair behind his ears and raised an imaginary glass to the photograph of his parents on the mantelpiece next to the mirror. It had been taken in the summer of 1902 in the Lake District, by a thirteen-year-old Septimus with his new camera – a Sanderson regular popular, which he still owned – and they had smiled out at him ever since, frozen in time: his father, Harold, a provincial solicitor with small round glasses, relaxing in tweed slacks and an open-necked shirt; his mother, Florence, in a flowery dress, looking radiantly happy.

Tragically, Septimus had been orphaned the year after the photograph had been taken. His parents, whilst on holiday in Belgrade, had been knocked down and killed by a motor car. Not just any car though, but the very vehicle leaving the royal palace after the brutal assassinations of the King of Serbia and his family, driven at speed by the perpetrators. Everybody agreed it had been bad luck to be in the wrong place at a terrible time. Despite his loss Septimus had continued his studies at Winchester College, a place where academic merit was everything. He flourished, and his visits to the home of his guardian grew less and less frequent. At seventeen he won a scholarship to Christ's College to read History and quickly settled into its quiet quadrangles, playing croquet and cricket, and joining societies devoted to wine and philosophy. He was awarded a First and a junior research fellowship which enabled him to remain at Oxford to write his thesis, which he would soon present for examination in order to become a full Fellow of College.

Whenever Septimus saw the photograph of his parents – and he looked at it at least once a day – he queried the wisdom and the faith of the religion his school and college had taught him, privately wondering how any God could allow such a thing to happen to ordinary, harmless people. Privately, because although he could be elected to a Fellowship without taking Holy Orders, the traditions still ran vigorously amongst the elderly dons and if he voiced his bitterness it might count against him. Better to bemoan how fate had placed his parents in the path of some Balkan madmen bent on murdering their king.

'Here's to you,' he said, and it was then he heard the fateful knock on the door.

'Come in!' Septimus shouted as he glanced at the clock on the mantelpiece. It was twenty-five to one. Lunch was about to commence. This had better be brief. Irritatingly, the door opened so slowly Septimus had to go and open it himself, almost pulling the unexpected visitor into the room as he did so.

A wiry, slightly built man with dark hair and a sallow complexion stood in the doorway with an apologetic expression on his face.

'Mr Oates?' he asked, hesitantly.

'Yes.' Septimus looked at his visitor impatiently, trying not to snap at him. Four years' worth of work on the thesis could not be jeopardised now. 'Can I help you?'

'I must speak with you, Mr Oates,' said the stranger, in heavily accented English. 'There is a matter of extreme urgency you should be made aware of. It involves historical papers. You are an expert on the eighteenth-century are you not?'

'I am, yes, but there are others better qualified than me.'

'I was advised to seek your assistance.'

'Well, what is it?'

Septimus peered at the visitor, trying in vain to place him. Perhaps he was a regular from the Bodleian Library, or maybe he'd come across him at the reading rooms at the British Library or the Public Record Office?

'May I come in?' he asked nervously. 'I am not able to talk openly out here.'

At Septimus's nod, the man entered the room, closing the door behind him.

'My name is Karl Hahn,' he began. 'There are some papers you must see. They are of vital importance and will change everything you believe to be true about the descendants of George III and even your present monarch, His Majesty King George V.'

'What do you mean? Where did you find these documents?'

Despite his pressing afternoon engagement, Septimus was intrigued. How could he not be? Who could ignore the possibility of newly discovered historical material?

'I'm unable to tell you where they come from, but I believe you'll find them of significance.'

'Where are these documents?'

'I don't have them with me,' Hahn explained, licking his upper lip nervously, 'but I can show them to you later today.'

Septimus snorted derisively. This was beginning to sound like a waste of time.

'You must leave. I have to go to lunch.'

'Please,' Hahn begged as Septimus opened the door and started to usher him out. 'At least let me show you the papers. You really should not overlook this opportunity!'

Something in the stranger's tone made Septimus hesitate.

'Bring them to me later today or send me a message via the College. I'll give it some thought.'

Hahn gripped his hand in gratitude. His eyes blazed with a fervour which was almost religious and Septimus found he couldn't hold the stranger's gaze for long.

As his visitor began to descend the stairs, Septimus heard him utter the words which in the coming days he would have bitter cause to remember perfectly clearly:

'You're most kind. You will not regret your generosity.'

The sun glistened on the paving stones in the quadrangle, following one of those short, sharp summer showers that soaked everything within minutes. This was typical June weather for Oxford; one minute the sky was black and purple, the next, steam was rising from the paving slabs in the heat. It was what made the lawns verdant and the quadrangles so welcoming in the golden light. Centuries of storms had battered and bruised the stones, but the serenity of the College remained intact throughout all time, unimpressed by the autocracy of Charles I, the bacchanalian antics of Shelley or the controversies of Newman.

As Septimus reached the foot of his staircase he spotted Hahn disappearing past the lodge and out of the College. What a strange business – still, it might yield something interesting. Documents did crop up every now and then, and it was always the historian's unspoken ambition to find them and present them to the world with a new interpretation. More often than not, however, they turned out to be some sort of elaborate fraud perpetrated by deluded would-be historians.

The gong sounded as Septimus walked up the dining hall steps. Hahn and his strange collection of documents, real or imagined, would have to wait until later. An early-morning dip in the Isis followed by a morning's research in the Bodleian Library had sharpened Septimus's appetite considerably. A glass of sherry in the Senior Common Room before lunch and several glasses of sauvignon blanc to accompany the mushroom soup and roast chicken served to remind Septimus that life was good, so there was no reason to suppose that pudding would be a disappointment. It was not, so another helping was perfectly in order.

Lunchtime conversation at High Table ranged from the ridiculous – how the June thunderstorms made the cobbles extremely slippery – to the sublime, as two young dons, Claude Larkman and Herbert Gilbert, argued vociferously over Freud's latest publication. Septimus naturally inclined towards the Freudian debate, but found himself excluded by their technical expertise.

'I suppose one might imagine, or even dream the past,' he suggested, during a pause in the debate.

'You can't do that,' protested Larkman, the younger of the two, his long face pinched with dismissal. 'You historians gather facts; facts are what make history, not imagination.'

'But what is a fact? Merely a statistic or an event which we choose to assign significance to.'

'Facts are the recognised data,' said Gilbert, between mouthfuls. 'All facts can be catalogued. History is a science. The past is there to be mapped with precision.'

'But one can't travel the past with a map!' Septimus retorted. 'It isn't signposted with directions. You'd be lost within minutes.'

'That is for you to rectify. Ours is the luxury of hypothesis.'

The discussion wound its way back to Freudian specifics and Septimus turned his attention to a conversation between the Master of the College, Lord Trevelyan, and the Senior Tutor, Amos Brereton, who were engaged in an earnest discussion about Ireland and the threat of terror from the Irish Volunteers.

'They have to be dealt with,' Trevelyan boomed, unable to converse with the person opposite him without the rest of High Table hearing. 'After the disgrace at Curragh we all know it's got to stop and soon.'

'You talk as if they were a crowd of undergraduates jumping into the Cherwell on May Morning, Master,' replied one of the oldest and most distinguished dons at the table. 'This is a problem going back to Oliver Cromwell, even to Richard Strongbow who invaded Ireland in 1168 on Henry II's orders. It will not just disappear overnight.'

Septimus waited for Trevelyan's response. The elderly don who had spoken so querulously was his tutor, Reverend Professor Bertram Battiscombe – the most senior, and much-loved and respected, of the College Fellows – who had been at Christ's for almost fifty years. His acerbic comment matched his spartan appearance; those around him hushed to hear if Trevelyan, a florid-faced, blustering civil servant, would use one of his notoriously blunt put-downs. Trevelyan judged the moment correctly.

'I understand what you're saying Battiscombe but action must be taken. You historians have the luxury of hindsight, the wisdom of generations from which to judge, but we politicians have to seize the moment. The problems facing us in Ireland today are the greatest in our Empire, and they lie right in our backyard.'

'I would contest that,' said Amos Brereton. 'The threat from Germany is much more severe.'

'Nonsense, Brereton!' Trevelyan snapped, on surer ground now. 'I suppose you will be telling me next that Oxford is infested with German spies. We mustn't forget the Kaiser is half-English. The old Queen died in his arms.'

The conversation moved on and people drifted into the Senior Common Room. During coffee, the weather broke again. Thunder and lightning cracked down and the rain hammered into the uneven medieval gutters of the quadrangle. Septimus remembered that he had forgotten to close his windows: the carpets would be soaked. Groaning inwardly, he hurried out of the Common Room. The short dash to his rooms left him drenched and panting for breath, and he'd almost fallen flat on his face. Perhaps the conversation at High Table about wet cobbles was more pertinent than Freud's latest theorems after all.

The rain ceased as swiftly as it had begun but Septimus wasn't taking any chances. He closed all the windows – there wasn't too much damage done – and decided to take a stroll around the quadrangle. It would calm his nerves and help him concentrate on his lecture. It was due to commence in half an hour and it was essential to make a good impression in front of his audience of Fellowship examiners.

'Message for you, Mr Oates. Said it was urgent. I popped it in your pigeonhole,' Travers, the College porter, called out as Septimus walked past.

Septimus diverted into the Lodge and swiftly rifled through supper and drinks invitations and a couple of cards wishing him well for the lecture before he came across a small envelope upon which was inscribed *MR OATES. URGENT.* He ripped it open. It was from Karl Hahn, the curious stranger who had called on him before lunch. His heart sank. He'd forgotten about Hahn and the last thing he needed was some crackpot pestering him. The letter, written in childish block-capitals, begged for his help:

Certain papers have been brought to light which have significant consequences for not only the history of the period but for the events of the last one hundred and fifty years . . .

Possibly . . . possibly not, thought Septimus dismissively. The letter went on:

These papers threaten to change the way we govern our country. They are extremely dangerous in the wrong hands.

Surely this was an absurd claim? Hahn had moved from vague historical assertions to hysterical rambling. The letter ended with a request to meet at half past two by the old college gate in New College Lane. Septimus dug in his pocket for his watch – once his father's – and flipped it open. It was almost that now. The lecture was at three. He decided in that instant that he would meet Hahn. There was just time to see the man and get it over with before the lecture. Septimus felt compelled to honour his promise to him earlier that day. He was curious, too, and why shouldn't he be? It was his calling as an academic to be inquisitive. But it was a curiosity that would almost cost him his life.

Nestled within the medieval walls, New College Lane, one of the oldest streets in Oxford, meandered through the middle of the old university, beginning at the Bridge of Sighs by the Bodleian Library and Old Schools Quadrangle and zigzagging through New College, Hertford, All Souls and Queen's before joining the High Street opposite the Examination Schools. It was a long, narrow, twisting street, usually deserted and well out of the way of the main routes along the High Street and Broad Street. Halfway along the lane was the old gatehouse and entrance to New College. The high walls either side of the lane were blackened with age, the cobbles too decayed for safe passage of any motor cars, with room for only one horse-drawn delivery cart at a time. Rarely in sunlight, pools of water, manure and other effluence lay stagnant in the gutters. It was not a place to walk through at night with any degree of confidence, although the new gas lamps had made it a safer place for undergraduates. By day, it remained the silent artery running through the city centre, long forgotten by the bustle of the High Street, and a perfect meeting place for someone who didn't wish to be seen.

Christ's College was situated to the south of medieval Oxford, across the High Street. It would take Septimus no more than five minutes to reach the old gatehouse by New College. Leaving Christ's, he walked briskly down Merton Street. It was the last time he would leave College with a carefree mind. Oxford – his life, his whole world – was about to change forever.

What were these documents Hahn kept referring to? Could they be of any value? He recalled the words of his old Winchester history master, Mordecai Quayle, one summer years ago: 'The past is like a darkened room, full of people. Occasionally, a light flares and we catch sight of their faces momentarily before the light fails and darkness returns.'

Perhaps Hahn knew something that would cast light onto that darkened room. Maybe not – probably not – but what did Septimus have to lose?

Crossing the High Street, he marched up past Queen's and St Edmund Hall, following the road up left towards New College. Several weeks ago, during the height of the examination season, the streets would have been teeming with undergraduates on their way from Finals. Now it was almost deserted. Puddles from the thunderstorm had all but evaporated. The narrow street was in heavy shadow; the sky had cleared to a brilliant blue and the sun beat down mercilessly on the honeyed walls. Septimus was grateful of the shade as he turned another corner towards the old gatehouse. Directly in front of him, about twenty yards away, he could see Karl Hahn, recognisable in his grubby linen suit and white, open-necked, shirt. He was standing under the gateway, half in the shade, smoking a slim cigar. Drawing nearer it became obvious that Hahn was constantly looking over his shoulder. As he saw Septimus approach, Hahn stubbed out the cigar and stepped into the road, holding out an outstretched palm. In his other hand he clutched a bulky brown package.

'I don't have much time. I have an important lecture to give this afternoon. You'd better be brief.'

Septimus shook Hahn's proffered hand. It was warm and sticky: Hahn was sweating profusely. There was something unnerving about the stranger's demeanour.

'Thank you for coming,' said Hahn. 'Take these,' he added breathlessly, thrusting the package at Septimus. 'For the good of what is right and truthful, take these and help me do my work.'

Right and truthful . . .?

'What exactly do you mean? And what's in here?'

Hahn swallowed nervously. 'I can't tell you. They'll come for me soon. They follow me everywhere.'

'Who follows you everywhere?' Caught between irritation and suspicion, Septimus restrained himself from provoking Hahn into further paroxysms of nerves.

'You must go – now. Read the papers. They are of vital historical significance and will change the way we understand the past.'

As he spoke, Hahn repeatedly turned to glance over his shoulder.

'I must warn you that the information is a danger to the present, also. But you're an expert. You will know what to do with the papers, and . . .'

'What is it?'

'They're coming for me, I know it!'

Septimus followed Hahn's increasingly frantic glances and tried to hide his frustration. What was the man talking about? With the exception of a rapidly approaching dark-suited, bowler-hatted individual redolent of a college porter – or perhaps a bank clerk – carrying a newspaper and briefcase, the lane was deserted. Even the bustling traffic of the High Street had dimmed to a low hum. A door slammed in the tower above them, the tuneful whistle of a college scout doing his rounds abruptly cut short.

'They follow me everywhere,' Hahn repeated. 'I am not safe. It is why I need your assistance.'

Hahn fumbled as he lit another cigar. He was drenched in sweat. Septimus noticed with distaste the dark sweat-rings spreading from his armpits.

'Why should I help you? And who is pursuing you?'

'You must. I . . .'

Backing away, his eyes popping with fear, Hahn left the sentence unfinished. Septimus looked past his agitated companion. The clerk – now less then five yards away – had discarded his newspaper and levelled a revolver directly at Hahn.

'Get down!' Septimus heard somebody shout, just as two gaping holes appeared in Hahn's chest. A large red stain spread across his white shirt. His cigar hit the pavement before Hahn himself silently crumpled into a heap.

Septimus dived to the ground. Somebody screamed. A third bullet whined past his ear and ricocheted off the wall behind him. Hahn grasped at the young man as he fought for air. Septimus took his hands and held them tight but he was powerless to help. When he looked over his shoulder the murderer had vanished. He could taste blood. His blood: he'd bitten his lip in the fall. A tidal wave of bile rose in his throat and his heart was racing so quickly he thought it would burst out of his ribcage. Much later, he would notice how sore his knees were, where the skin had been badly grazed.

Some primitive instinct of self-preservation kicked in and Septimus heaved himself from the ground – still gripping the package – and forced himself to run back up New College Lane, under the Bridge of Sighs and, with a flash of inspiration, he then took a right turn into St Helen's Passage, a tiny walkway a yard in width and in total shadow which gave him respite as he came to a standstill. He leant against the wall and gasped for breath.

His legs were shaking and he crouched down in the gutter. A wave of nausea came over him. He pulled a handkerchief from his pocket and wiped his lip. The blood was drying already. Gathering himself, he straightened up and walked further down the passage round the corner to the Turf Tavern, which nestled snugly under the ancient city walls, in a courtyard cluster of seventeenth-century cottages.

The pub was quiet with just a few students drinking at the wooden tables. Nobody looked up. In spite of this, Septimus felt conspicuous as he wove between the tables and through the passageway between the cottages before emerging cautiously onto Holywell Street, using the shadows as cover. He continued walking, keeping the package close to his chest, but as he looked back, he could see the anonymous assassin had materialised again. Septimus started to run, blundering past people, ignoring their shouts to stop, instead dashing left into Mansfield Road. He collapsed against the wall. He hadn't run anywhere that fast for years. Septimus gingerly peered around the street corner. Nothing. Then without warning the murderer appeared out of a doorway and started walking towards him. The man had just shot dead Karl Hahn in cold blood but was strolling down the street without a care in the world.

Septimus turned and walked quickly down the road but it stretched ahead of him for around five hundred yards and offered no obvious place of refuge. His mouth was dry, and every instinct screamed at him. *Run! Run! Run!*

But Septimus forced himself to walk rapidly, tearing great breaths out of the air. The road ahead was empty. Septimus glanced behind and stifled a scream of terror. The assassin had broken into a trot and was gaining on him. He was still armed.

Septimus started to run but years of sedentary study in libraries and idling in pubs now caught up with him. The taste of lunchtime wine swirled unpleasantly in his throat and threatened to overwhelm him as he staggered down the street. He could hear footsteps behind. *Give in* a voice calmly spoke to him. *Give him the package!* But then in his mind's eye he saw Hahn's twitching body in the gutter and made a great effort to run faster along the street. He dared not look behind now. A motor car pulled out in front of him. A taxi. Septimus stepped into the path of the oncoming vehicle, waving like a man drowning, which he was in a way, in his own despair. He scrambled into the back of the car, sobbing, still clutching the package.

'Where to sir?'

If the driver noticed his distress, he paid no attention. His passenger glanced out of the rear window.

'Do you want to go somewhere or not?'

'Christ's College please.'

The taxi jolted forward as it accelerated. Septimus lay on the back seat, holding the door handle tightly. As the taxi swung onto Holywell Street, he peered out of the window. There was the killer. Septimus shrank back into the seat, stifling a whimper of fear.

'Are you all right, sir?' the taxi driver asked, belatedly acknowledging his passenger's agitation.

'Fine, thanks,' he muttered sitting up, wiping a sheen of sweat from his brow. Septimus said nothing as the car drove up Broad Street, down the Turl, over the High Street and along the narrow lane towards Christ's. 'Just here, please.'

As he reached for the door handle he froze. Blood rushed to his brain. Christ's looked no different to any other day or time he had known it over the years. And yet there was something sinister about the shadows under the arched gateway. The thought occurred to him that the murderer had probably followed Hahn to Christ's earlier that day, and may even have watched him cross the quadrangle and enter the staircase to Septimus's rooms. He would know, therefore, where to find Septimus. If not now, then maybe later, under the cover of darkness, slipping past the diligent Travers, revolver concealed in the folds of an overcoat, treading softly and swiftly up the stairs. A ruthless assassin who gunned down Hahn in broad daylight would hardly hesitate to kill again under cover of darkness.

'Yes or no?'

'No.'

In his hands he had the package; Hahn had died giving it to him. He was holding a death sentence.

'Take me to the police station, please. As quickly as you can.'

Police Inspector Albert Coppard carefully observed the young gentleman seated across the table from him. The subfusc and gown gave him away as a 'varsity man, who was clearly exhausted and under severe nervous strain. If he weren't so pale and wide-eyed he'd be a handsome young blighter. The Inspector had heard the excitable fellow enter the station and report a shooting in the city and immediately despatched a couple of his men to New College Lane to investigate. Once the desk sergeant had escorted the gentleman to Coppard's office, and provided tea and biscuits, the Inspector was able to start to interview his witness, who by now seemed a little calmer.

'How would you describe the victim, sir?' Coppard's pencil hovered over his notepad.

Septimus cleared his throat.

'I would say medium height. Perhaps five foot five, with a sallow complexion and of foreign extraction.'

Coppard wrote down the details.

'And the alleged assassin. Can you describe him?'

'He looked like a college porter. Like a clerk. Dark suit. Bowler hat. Quite innocuous. At least, until he shot Mr Hahn.' As the events of the past hour flooded back, Septimus felt a rush of blood to his head and the sweat on his upper lip. He accepted the Inspector's cigarette gratefully.

'Feeling better?' Beneath the elaborate side-whiskers, Coppard had a kindly face.

'Yes, thank you.'

Coppard returned to his notepad.

'Can you tell me what happened next, Mr Oates?'

Septimus closed his eyes. In the room next door a typewriter tapped and clacked rapidly. Further away a cell door clanged. There was the newspaper, yes, he saw it now; folded, then discarded, the revolver coming up . . .

'We were partly in the shadows, under the walls of New College and at the back of Queen's.'

'What happened next?'

'There were two cracks, like a car misfiring, and a third, the one which almost got me . . .'.

But somebody had shouted. He remembered that; a warning, perhaps?

'And then . . .?'

'Hahn fell to his knees, gurgling blood.'

Then running away with the package in his hands. Should he tell the Inspector about the documents or not? He should –

'Do you think he pursued you with the intention of killing you?'

'Most certainly: yes.'

Coppard continued writing. A clock ticked on the wall. It was half past three. Little over an hour ago Hahn had been alive. Now he was dead, his body lying in New College Lane in a pool of blood. Inspector Coppard closed his notebook.

'If you would wait here I shall put out an alert for this man,' he said as he rose from his chair. 'It appears we have a murderer loose in the city.' As the Inspector went to the door it opened suddenly, after the briefest of knocks, and a police sergeant entered.

'What have you got to report, Wickes? Have you kept the public out of the way?'

'No, sir.'

Coppard's expression changed to one of concern, and then anger.

'Why ever not? We can't have everyone trampling all over the corpse.'

'There is no corpse, sir. In fact, there's nothing to report whatsoever, sir. No sign of a struggle, no blood or clothing left at the scene. We talked to some passers by but there was nothing, sir. We had a look down the street, checking all the corners and lanes around, but no body.'

Coppard must have seen the colour drain from Septimus's face.

'Are you sure? This gentleman says he's just witnessed a shooting in broad daylight. Where's the body?'

Wickes shrugged.

Coppard asked: 'Is it possible that the victim was only wounded and managed to crawl away Mr Oates?'

Septimus thought for a moment but then shook his head.

'There was a lot of blood. He was hit in the chest twice at close range and fell at my feet.'

Coppard frowned and consulted his notes again.

'Had anything to drink at luncheon, sir?'

Septimus felt his mouth go dry. What was this? Didn't they believe him?

'Only the customary glass or two with my meal.'

'A customary glass or two?' Coppard's manner was no longer benevolent. 'Long luncheons in College are often well served with wine.'

Wickes suppressed a snigger.

Septimus got up from the chair so abruptly it almost tipped over. His legs had regained their strength but his head was swimming with anger and confusion.

'I assure you, Inspector, everything I have told you is true. A man was shot dead in front of me not half an hour ago and his killer then pursued me.'

Coppard closed his notebook decisively and walked to the door.

'This had better not be one of your 'varsity jokes. It is the silly season, now that the examinations have ended. Wasting police time is an offence. I have your name and College.'

'This is ridiculous!' Septimus snapped angrily. 'I don't have time to indulge in end of term japes. The victim handed me this package of documents minutes before he died. He said they were of vital historical importance!' Septimus held up the documents, still sealed in the envelope, for Coppard to see.

'Have you read these papers, sir?'

'No, I haven't – not yet, anyway.'

Coppard cast Wickes a sideways glance and opened the door.

'I was due to give a lecture at three o'clock. Dozens of people have been let down. Years of my work have been jeopardised. You have to believe me!'

The desperation in Septimus's voice caused Coppard to hesitate. Perhaps there was something in what this witness was telling them after all.

'We'll put out an alert and search the city tonight. I suggest you return to your rooms and get a good night's sleep Mr Oates. Please remain at College where we can contact you if need be.'

The finality of his tone indicated there was no point in Septimus protesting any further, and moments later he found himself on the steps outside the Police Station, nervously scanning the street for any sign of the killer. He began walking back to College but after a few steps he stopped. He couldn't face it. It really wasn't safe. Oxford wasn't safe any more. He couldn't go back to College, despite Coppard's insistence that he remain there.

But he knew where he could find a place of safety.

❖ ❖ ❖

There was a train departing for Winchester from the platform over the bridge and Septimus had just three minutes to catch it. Pushing impatiently through the evening crowds he took the steps at a run, wrenching open the carriage door as the guard blew his whistle. The compartment was almost full but he squeezed in between a buxom lady with a spaniel on her lap and a pipe-smoking clergyman. The train pulled out with a shuddering roar. Septimus apologised profusely as he stepped on the clergyman's toe, the baleful glare through pipe smoke serving as a reminder of his exile. The spaniel licked his hand and he wiped the drool on his gown, thankful at least for some sign of friendliness, even it it was from an overfed pet.

Septimus was surrounded by people but he had never felt more alone. The brown package in his hand was a sickening reminder of what was happening to him. He had yet to open it. He couldn't bear to. The image of Karl Hahn in his cheap linen suit dying in front of him came to him each time he closed his eyes.

He changed trains at Reading and found an empty compartment. The train rattled through Berkshire and into Hampshire. On arriving at Winchester, he headed for the tobacconist on the main platform and bought a packet of cigarettes. His hands trembled slightly as he lit one. He inhaled and almost groaned with the pleasure of it. It more than made up for the thumping headache he was now nursing. The smoke gave him clarity of thought for the first time since Hahn's murder. He spotted a wastepaper basket on the platform and without hesitating dropped the package in. He finished the cigarette and walked out of the station and towards the taxi rank.

'Where to sir?'

'College Street please.'

Another taxi, another town, but he knew he was safe here.

Drawing away from the station Septimus sank back with relief. Winchester. His second home. After graduating, Septimus had taken a teaching position at the College before returning to Oxford to work on his research and pursue an academic career. And it was here where the man who had offered him so much friendship as his teacher and later, as his colleague, would shelter him in his hour of need. Quayle would rescue him from this nightmare. The familiar streets rolled by, places he knew, man and boy: City Road, Southgate Street, Canon Street.

'Stop the car,' he shouted suddenly.

What was he thinking? He couldn't leave it in a bin, undiscovered and unread. Hahn had died giving it to him.

'Do you want to get out?'

'Can we return to the station please? I've left something behind.'

The driver manoeuvred the car expertly and was soon back at the station.

'I won't be a minute,' Septimus said, clambering out of the car, cursing himself for his moment of stupidity. What had he been thinking of? Supposing it had vanished? He ran onto the platform. Through the steam of a departing train he caught sight of the station porter pushing a heavily laden trolley to the storeroom.

'Excuse me!' he shouted, running after the porter. 'I dropped something in one of the bins on this platform by mistake,' he spluttered breathlessly.

'Try this.'

The porter opened the bin. Septimus could see that not far

27

from the top of the heap of rubbish lay the now familiar and deadly package.

'Yes, there it is,' he said, seizing it with relief. 'Thank you for your trouble.'

'Not at all, sir. Worse things happen at sea, as they say,' said the porter, but Septimus had gone.

'Got it!' he said, collapsing into the back of the taxi.

'Smells like it, too,' said the driver, hurriedly dropping the latch on the window.

'Sorry,' said Septimus. 'It was in the bin.'

'It can't be anything much, to have been left in a bin.'

'I've no idea.'

'Haven't you opened it yet?'

'No.'

The driver turned to Septimus.

'Go on, then.'

'What, here?'

'Why not?' grinned the driver. 'You've got me wanting to know now.'

Yes, why not, thought Septimus. He was safe here in these streets. He pulled at the string and a bundle of what appeared to be letters, faded and coloured with age, cascaded onto his lap. Septimus instantly recognised the eighteenth-century handwriting. They weren't just letters, however. Deeds, wills and various cuttings were there amongst the pile. Not all were antiquated documents; there were recent newspaper cuttings in amongst the manuscripts, and a small, leather-bound book.

'What have you got, then? Anything that sets the world on fire?'

'Not really,' said Septimus. 'Just fragments of historical documents.'

'History, eh?' said the driver. 'All those dead people. I mean, what's it got to do with us today?'

'Quite a lot, actually,' said Septimus absent-mindedly as he stared at a dusty, dirty piece of manuscript which had been at the top of the bundle.

The handwriting on the manuscript was old-fashioned, but quite legible. Septimus had trawled through thousands of similar documents at the Public Record Office while researching his dissertation. Looking more closely Septimus could see it was a fragment from a marriage certificate which had been torn from a register. Dated 17th April 1759, it recorded the marriage of Hannah Lightfoot to a George Hanover. Nothing special about that, Septimus thought to himself.

Except for the fact that in October 1760 'George Hanover' became George III, King of Great Britain, Ireland and Hanover, following the death of his grandfather George II. And this same George III had married Princess Charlotte of Mecklenberg-Strelitz in 1762 and their children were the direct ancestors of the present royal family, including His Majesty King George V, King of Great Britain and Emperor of India since 1910.

Septimus tried to remember what Hahn's message had said. *Certain papers have been brought to light which have significant consequences for not only the history of that period but for the history of the past one hundred and fifty years. These papers threaten to change the way we govern our country. They are extremely dangerous in the wrong hands.* If George Hanover was indeed King George III as Septimus supposed, then he had contracted a secret marriage never before revealed to the outside world. And if Hannah Lightfoot was still alive in 1762, then George III's marriage to Princess Charlotte was bigamous and therefore illegal. The children of George and Charlotte would have been illegitimate and should not have inherited the throne and neither should their descendants.

If . . .

Septimus's head thumped with the effort of comprehending

the ramifications of the document in front of him. The current monarch, His Majesty King George V, was a descendant of that supposedly bigamous marriage. That would make his position on the throne illegal.

If . . .

The evidence which proved such a thing was clearly dangerous. Hahn had died in front of him, handing Septimus precisely that evidence.

Fact.

Quayle lived just off College Street. Set behind the Cathedral Wall and Kingsgate, College Street was a delightful serendipity of late Georgian and early Victorian redbrick and flint cottages. A narrow lane, no more than a rutted track, led mid-way from the street to Spurlings Cottage, Quayle's house. Septimus approached Spurlings gingerly. It was well over a year since he had last seen Quayle and the man was notoriously difficult to communicate with; he didn't possess a telephone and acknowledged letters sporadically – and only then if he was not away on one of his many foreign walking tours.

But Spurlings was Septimus's only refuge.

Nothing had changed. The house was overgrown with rose bushes and ivy; any attempt to cut them back would probably have brought the wall down. The front door was almost totally obscured. Successive postmen, having long ago abandoned their attempts to reach it, now left the post in a tin box by the gate. The garden was a riot of wild flowers and weeds.

Septimus peered through one of the small, mullioned windows. There was no sign of life inside. Anyone unfamiliar with Quayle's chaotic way of life would think the house was deserted. Piles of books lay on the dining table, dusty old prints lined the cobwebbed walls and several cricket bats lay scattered on the floor. The complete sets of Gibbon's *Decline and Fall of the Roman Empire*, Macaulay's *History of England* and several copies of *Wisden* gathered dust on the shelves as they had always done. Leaves nestled around the books and the fireplace contained the remains of a fire that burned out months ago. A leather-covered desk was relatively tidy – a pile of class reports lay unfinished in the centre, fountain pen alongside – but the back of the chair pushed against it was broken.

The familiar chaos of the house sent a wave of relief through Septimus. But when he knocked on the front door there was no reply. That was hardly surprising; Quayle would never be inside on a sunny day like this. Septimus made a mental note of the day: Friday. Lessons would have finished at five that afternoon. No cricket today, so Quayle should be around, unless there was a match with one of the local villages. Otherwise, it was the bar at the Wykeham Arms.

'Oates!'

Mordecai Augustus Quayle, late Captain of the Rifle Brigade, sometime scholar of St John's College, Cambridge and Senior Master at Winchester College for ten years, trudged up the track clutching a large pile of books. He was an arresting figure; tall, slender, but for the stomach, with a fine head of unruly hair swept back from a high forehead. A pair of horn-rimmed spectacles perched precariously on his beaked nose and his chin jutted imperiously upwards with a permanent air of enquiry. He was immaculately dressed in gown, morning coat, pinstriped trousers and wing-collar, an outfit that contrasted sharply with the parlous state of his house. A gold chain glimmered at his waistcoat, dancing on the substantial bulge which even the finest tailor in Jermyn Street could no longer disguise.

Septimus spun round, his nerves shredded after the events of the day. Relieved by his friend's arrival, Septimus found himself gabbling.

'Thank God you're here. I need to talk to you. Something terrible has happened. I've stumbled upon some astonishing evidence – and someone's been murdered . . .'

Quayle dropped the books on the garden table and dug deep into his pocket for his house keys.

'Are you listening?'

Over his spectacles the schoolmaster fixed a baleful eye on Septimus.

'Let me get the door open and we'll have a drink. You might talk some sense then. Go and sit in the garden and I'll be right back.'

❖ ❖ ❖

Quayle blew out a stream of cigar smoke into the golden sky and poured his guest another glass of wine.

'Why didn't you return to College after leaving the police station?'

'I panicked,' Septimus said.

'Of course you did. But later. When you were on the train. When you had calmed down and had a chance to think. You could have changed at Reading and gone back.'

'I had to keep going and get away from Oxford as quickly as I could.'

'You're fortunate I'm here today. I've recently returned from a walking tour in the Lake District and term finishes next week, you know.'

'I didn't think,' Septimus said shaking his head. 'You could have been anywhere. You can see how important it was for me to see you.'

Quayle grunted.

'Thank God you are here. I don't know what I'd have done otherwise.' Panic welled up inside Septimus again, turning his wine sour. 'What am I going to do? Hahn was shot dead in front of me. The police have my address and when they eventually find Hahn's body they'll arrest me. Inspector Coppard's probably watching the College, searching my rooms even now . . .'

Septimus rose from his chair and began pacing the long grass. Hahn was there before him in the garden, the crack of the pistol in his ears, the documents thrust into his hands, Hahn gasping his last words. He tried to light a cigarette but couldn't.

'Calm down, Oates, calm down!' Quayle opened another bottle of wine. 'Think. *Think*. Who else was in the street, apart from you, Hahn and the assassin?'

'Nobody.'

'That's what you suppose. But that doesn't matter at the moment. Just try to recollect what you have witnessed this afternoon.'

Septimus slumped back in his seat, closed his eyes and forced himself to envisage the sunlit street again. The door slamming, the whistling servant, a delivery cart. Had there been someone cowering in the shadows? Had anyone raced down the street after the shooting? No, he couldn't recall anything out of the ordinary.

'No one leaving the College by the old gate?' Quayle wondered breaking into his thoughts. 'Any students up in their rooms overlooking the street?'

'Possibly.' Septimus passed a weary hand over his face. He had forgotten the multitude of rooms that faced the street. At this time of year windows would have been open and any number of people – undergraduates staying up, College dons and summer visitors – could have been gazing out into the lane.

'Do you remember hearing the gunshots?'

'Of course,' Septimus protested. 'The man died right in front me, didn't he?'

'But that doesn't mean the shots were heard by anyone other than yourself. The lane is very narrow with high walls. A gunshot would reverberate off the walls for several seconds. People would hear it and come to their windows to see what was happening.'

Septimus looked at the schoolmaster with relief. The truth was beginning to dawn on him.

'Yes, absolutely, which means . . .'

'. . . someone else saw what happened.'

'Someone else saw what happened . . .' Septimus repeated slowly.

Quayle rose from his chair.

'I think that pretty well puts you in the clear. Coppard and his men will track down the witnesses in good time. Now, finish your wine, and I'll get us another bottle. Oh . . .'

'What?'

'When I come back, I want to know what the devil is in that package you were clutching. After all, it's what's got you into this.'

Septimus poured himself another glass of wine and began to sift through the papers.

The first document he looked at was a short statement to the effect that the marriage 'of these parties' was solemnised at Kew Chapel and signed by J. Wilmot, George P and Hannah. Then he looked again at the certificate he had first seen in the taxi. He passed both certificates to Quayle, who had returned from his cellar and placed a bottle of 1905 Château Canon Saint Émilion on the table.

'These mean very little by themselves. "George P" could be anyone. Who is Wilmot?'

'Look at the second witness.' Septimus leant across the table and prodded one of the certificates. 'You'll know that name.'

'"W. Pitt". Not Pitt the Elder, Earl Chatham?'

'It could be.'

'Who is Hannah?'

'Someone you wouldn't come across unless you had a detailed knowledge of George III. She's something of a footnote in the history of this monarch, but she always pops up here and there. The story goes she married George when he was Prince of Wales, but there has never been any evidence to link her with him.'

'Until now?'

'Until now. Hannah was supposedly a Quaker's daughter – she was known as the "Fair Quaker" – and may even have had children with George.'

'But that's preposterous!'

'Read this document. It's far more specific.'

Quayle took the third certificate and read aloud: '"I conducted the marriage of George Prince of Wales to Princess Hannah his first consort, on 17th of April, 1759, and that two princes and a princess were the issue of such a marriage." Good God!'

'And in this one Wilmot certifies that when Hannah died, she left two sons and one daughter "lawfully born in wedlock".' Septimus passed over the fourth paper.

Quayle scratched his jaw. His hair, once a luxuriant black, was now flecked with grey and Septimus realised with a slight shock that he must be close to turning fifty this year.

'Well, what do you think?'

Quayle placed his spectacles on the table and refilled their glasses. He held his up to the evening sunlight, the wine ruby-red, and took a mouthful.

'You're the expert on George III, Oates, not me. But this whole business of a secret marriage and children seems a rum do. Which these papers seem to prove.'

Septimus took the documents from Quayle and read through them again.

'But didn't he marry Charlotte of Mecklenberg?'

'Yes, because he was German royalty and was obliged to marry a lady of his station and nationality. The strange thing is that George and Charlotte married for the *first* time in 1762.'

'What do you mean?'

'A second ceremony was conducted two years later which was supposed to be all dressed up as some midsummer festival. Queen Charlotte herself insisted upon it.'

'Perhaps suggesting she was aware that George was already married and she knew she had entered into a bigamous contract?'

'Yes, it's possible they "remarried" because Hannah had died. Look at the fourth paper where Wilmot refers to Hannah's death. The manuscript is unclear. That might read 1764.'

'So if Hannah and George were childless, and George and Charlotte remarried after Hannah's death, their marriage was legitimate as were their heirs.'

'That's right, and George and Charlotte's younger son, Edward, Duke of Kent, was the father of Queen Victoria. He was born three years later.'

'After Hannah's death.'

'Assuming she died in 1764.'

'And assuming she remained childless. But these documents prove there were children from George and Hannah's marriage.'

'Which means these children were the legimate heirs to the throne.'

'And that our current monarch is not legally King.'

Quayle's words fell like a sword between them, slicing through the dusk. Neither man spoke for several minutes, each thinking the

37

same thing. Their line of thought had careered on like an express train out of control, before crashing at full speed into the buffers. Both men knew the significance of Quayle's last utterance. It had been nothing less than treason: and from a former British Army officer, at that.

The sun was setting behind Spurlings. Septimus took another drink, and loosened his tie. It was a balmy evening but he felt a chill run down his spine.

'If that is the case, and let us imagine that it is so,' Quayle continued eventually, refilling their glasses and lighting another cigar, the match flaring in the twilight, 'the implications are enormous. Thirteen of George III and Charlotte's children survived infancy and from these the nineteenth-century royal families of Russia, Germany and Britain are descended. Queen Victoria was George III's granddaughter and her grandchildren include King George V, Tsar Nicholas II of Russia and Kaiser Wilhelm of Germany, all of them cousins . . .'

'And don't forget the Kaiser's mother,' said Septimus, warming to his theme. 'Vicki – Queen Victoria's eldest daughter – suffered from a crippling form of porphyria, inherited directly from her great-grandfather George III. If all these people were not legally monarchs, how different would history have been?'

Quayle laughed.

'What if . . ., what if . . .? Everything that happened occurred in the context of a mass of possibilities. We can only understand the actuality if we look at those possibilities. How far back do you want to unravel the past? What was it Voltaire said? "History is no more than accepted fiction".'

'That was no fiction I witnessed today, Quayle, accepted or otherwise. A man was murdered in front of me. These papers have to be worth more than simply tricks we play on the dead. Look at these.' Septimus picked up the newspaper cuttings and peered at them in the fading light. 'Where do these fit in? The first is a report from 1889 into the death of Crown Prince Rudolf, heir to Emperor Franz Josef, found dead at his hunting lodge at Mayerling with Baroness Vetsera, believed to be suicide. The second is a report about the assassination in Geneva of Empress Elisabeth of Austria, stabbed to death by Italian anarchist Luigi Lucheni. It's dated 1898.'

'Sisi,' murmured Quayle. 'The darling of the Hungarians. I remember it well. The Mayerling affair was very suspicious. But what's the connection between these cuttings and the certificates recording George III's secret marriage to Hannah Lightfoot?'

Septimus drained his glass.

'The first rule when using historical documents without a context is to authenticate them.' He passed over a slim leather-bound volume from the table. 'This may well do that.'

'What is it?' Quayle took the book gingerly.

'As far as I can gather,' said Septimus, 'this is the memoir of George Rex, eldest son of George III and Hannah Lightfoot, his first – and secret – wife.'

1759

It is time now to commit to paper all that has happened in my long and adventurous life. What I write here is the truth and it is this truth that will shine like a beacon into the darkness of lies and deceit. Whosoever reads this shall become party to my secret life and with that knowledge shall have great power. Power to destroy Kings and Emperors; power to bring down Governments and power to freeze the blood of all the Princes and Premiers of Europe – most especially the realm of Great Britain – at the word of my story.

I was born in England in 1759, one month after my parents were married. My mother was Hannah Lightfoot, the daughter of a Quaker. The Prince of Wales, as he was then, had taken a fancy to her as he made his way to the theatre one evening and wished to establish her as his mistress. He was so much in love with my mother, and he was a man of honour, so much so that he insisted upon marriage when she fell pregnant. The Prince loved England and the English so much that he thought that when he became king he would announce his secret marriage to the world and everyone would respect him for it.

Poor man, to think it would be so easy! When his grandfather

King George II died in 1760 and the Prince acceded as George III, he was forced to put away his wife, who was denounced as his mistress. Those in power at court, including Lord Bute, had total control over the twenty-one-year-old king. My mother was forbidden to come to Windsor, or Kew, or to St James's, or anywhere where the King was in residence. I know he managed to visit my mother secretly several times, and she bore him two more children, James and Sarah. But in the year 1762, the King was forced to marry a German princess, and never saw my mother again. My father had married Princess Charlotte Sophia of Mecklenberg-Strelitz. He was bound by duty, and advised that his marriage to my mother was not recognised by Parliament.

Dutifully, he produced fifteen children by the horse-faced Charlotte. Although their marriage was fruitful, their first four children failed to produce any heirs who survived to adulthood. The eldest son of that marriage was George IV – my half-brother – who died without issue. His younger brother William IV followed him on the throne but he too died childless, and was succeeded by his niece, the young daughter of the Duke of Kent, Queen Victoria, crowned just two years ago. Some whisper the girl is illegitimate, and was smuggled into the bedchamber after thirty years of childless marriage. So not only am I George III's eldest legitimate son, but I have outlived all the sons by his second, bigamous marriage! And now a slip of a girl sits on the throne of England.

My mother was sent to live in Bruton, a small town in Somerset, as a widow of means. The government paid her a pension and we were comfortably off. She was not allowed, and neither were the children, to ever approach the royal court or the presence of the King. My mother was happy enough, but always seemed reticent about our father, who she claimed to be John Rex, a wealthy distiller of Goodman Fields, Whitechapel, who had died of a heart attack a week after Sarah's birth. My mother was an orphan, brought up by the Quakers and married to John Rex by arrangement.

I had two younger siblings, James and Sarah. We were very close in age, the three of us, and played together all the time. We had a private tutor at home and enough servants to do the housework. Ours was the largest of all the houses on the High Street in Bruton, opposite Hugh Sexey's Hospital and School. It was a privileged and sheltered life. My mother had grown up in London and often talked wistfully of the hustle and bustle of the streets and the great buildings of St Paul's and Westminster, but the furthest we ventured was to Bristol to see the ships bringing in cargo from the West Indies.

❖ ❖ ❖

When I was thirteen years old my life changed. I had been tutored at home with our governess until that time, and considered myself quite well educated. But on the day of my birthday, my mother received a visit from three well dressed gentlemen who arrived in a barouche. We children were ordered to go upstairs and lock ourselves in the nursery, but I disobeyed orders and crept out onto the landing. The door to the drawing room was slightly ajar and I could hear voices, which were gradually increasing in volume as the argument grew more heated.

'Madam, you must heed what we are saying. The King has commanded that you listen to his wishes. You must tell the boy who he is and you must allow him to come with us.'

'The King forsook me over ten years ago to marry his German princess so that his royal heirs would be truly royal,' I heard my mother say, with such venom I had never heard from her before. 'Our vows remain unbroken by myself. It is why I am unable to

45

marry again and must live in this state of perpetual loneliness. You will not take the boy away from me!'

Vows, what vows? I recall my thirteen-year-old mind attempting to work out. What on earth was my mother talking about? Why had the King forsaken her?

'You will allow the boy to do as the King commands or you will be cut off without a penny and turned out of this house!'

This came from a different, mature voice, which spoke with greater authority than the first man.

'The King would see me a pauper, then?' My mother's voice grew faint at her predicament.

'He would see his eldest son educated properly, as befits one of his birth,' came the response from the authoritative man, slightly less harsh than he had been. 'You will continue to enjoy all your privileges, as before.'

'And after his schooling, what will he do? What then, my lord?'

I craned forward, straining to hear what this lord, as my mother called him, would say in reply.

But instead, the door was flung wide open, and the three gentlemen marched out of the room. I shrank back onto the stairwell, hiding behind the banister. Through the banisters I could see them taking their hats and coats from the maid. There was one who was very elderly and walked with great difficulty. He turned at the door and, when he spoke, his words sent a chill through my very soul and made sense of what I had heard:

'He is the King's first-born son and he will do what the King desires.'

Later that evening, when James and Sarah had gone to bed, my mother summoned me to the drawing room. I will never forget how she sat by the fire and took my hand, and said, with a trembling voice:

'Your father is the King of England. He was not John Rex from

Whitechapel. I married the King when he was the Prince of Wales, because we fell in love. He was a man of honour, and married me so you would not be born a bastard.'

I nodded. It all made sense to me now. I decided not to tell my mother about how I had overheard her discussions with the three gentlemen.

'I am not supposed to tell you this. It should be a secret that I take to my grave, but I have been so burdened by it these past years, I cannot tell you how difficult it has been. The lies and the deceit – to my own children!'

Tears coursed down my mother's cheeks as I held her in my arms.

'Those men who came today were powerful men, George,' my mother explained. 'They control our lives. One of them, the elderly one with the limp, is William Pitt, Lord Chatham. When I married Prince George, Mr Pitt was a senior minister in Thomas Pelham-Holles' government. He witnessed our marriage and he knows that the King's marriage to the German princess is all a sham. The other gentleman was the Lord Chancellor, Lord Apsley. Between them they have destroyed the evidence which proves I was ever married to Prince George. But the secret is still with us. The King and his Ministers are bound together by the secret which they know could destroy us all.' My mother released me from her grasp. 'You will have to do as they say, my darling boy, and leave me tomorrow.'

The carriage came for me at seven, and I dressed bleary-eyed. I had no knowledge of where I was going or whether I would see my mother, brother and sister ever again as they waved to me tearfully from the front door of the house that had been my only home.

❖   ❖   ❖

I sat alone in the coach with my belongings piled on the seats around me. We rattled at top speed up to Bath, only stopping long enough to change horses, and then continued on to Chippenham, where we spent the night. It was the furthest I had ever been from home and the rain hammered mercilessly on the shutters, keeping me awake for hours; eventually I cried myself to sleep. The next day, we were to change horses three times more, for the coachman drove the creatures on remorselessly. Everything was paid for. The coachman never said a word to me, but he had a large purse of coins fastened to his waist along with a pistol in case of any highwaymen. He never let me from his sight. When I asked where we were going, he merely grunted.

On the evening of the second day, just as the sky was darkening and the rain easing, we approached a small town set upon a hill. As the coach climbed the slope, I leant from the window and could see far below us many church spires of the city sprawled for miles. This, I discovered the next day, was London. Early evening lights flickered in the dusk, and smoke from many thousands of chimneys drifted into the twilight; dogs barked and I felt homesick for Bruton.

We did not go into London. Instead, our destination was Windsor. The coach took me past the walls of the great castle and towards the gatehouse of a school. Boys everywhere were scurrying hither and thither in their gowns, clutching books. We halted at the lodge, where a schoolmaster in gown and mortar board opened my carriage-door. I was sore and shaken after the journey, but before I could demand to know where I was, he beamed at me.

'Welcome to Eton, Master George. This is your home for the next five years.'

❖　❖　❖

And so passed the next years of my life, which I will not fill these pages with. Tedious years of schoolroom drama: endless Latin and Greek and savage beatings from the older scholars and masters; poor food, no heating and criminal neglect. Those were my years at Eton. My mother had charged me never to tell anybody the secret of my birth, not even my brother and sister who died without knowing their true parentage. I never dared to tell anyone, and when James came to the school after two years, I almost began to tolerate it. I certainly looked after him and ensured he did not receive the beatings I had suffered.

The one event that stood out during my time at Eton was the visit to the school by William Pitt, the son of Lord Chatham, in my last year. Pitt was a brilliant young scholar many years ahead of all of us, who had gone up to Cambridge aged only fourteen. He came to the school to speak to the boys on a matter of politics and he seemed so much wiser than his sixteen years. Little did I know then that my fortunes would be inextricably intertwined with his own. After supper Pitt came to my study to seek me out.

'George.'

Unusually in a school where one was normally addressed by one's surname or a nickname Pitt called me by my first name.

'Mr Pitt.'

I showed my respect for one so clever and for his rank as the son of the Earl of Chatham, one of England's most revered statesmen. Little did we know then that Pitt the Younger would become much more of a household name than his illustrious father. Pitt leant against the bookcase, assuming a proprietorial air over me, which would become all too familiar in the years to come. It was not an attitude I was comfortable with, but I could never find the courage to confront him over it.

'My father informed me of your true parentage, George. I know who you really are. You are the son of the King. His first born.'

I said nothing. I felt that I knew this moment had been coming ever since I heard that the son of Chatham was to visit Eton. After all, how could my special status remain a secret forever? And who else but the son of Pitt would have knowledge of the secret?

'Fear not,' Pitt went on, but his next words shocked me out of my complacence. 'I shall not tell anyone – at least, not at present.'

'You think telling people will help you in any way?' I snapped, my mask of deference beginning to slip. 'Your father was party to an illegal marriage involving the heir to the throne and connived to conceal the knowledge that the King has married bigamously and that the current Prince of Wales is actually a bastard!'

Pitt coughed. He was not a healthy young man, and his illness caused him to leave Cambridge prematurely.

'I have no intention of making any grand announcements, George, as I would most likely be charged with treason. There is no evidence of your parents' marriage – except you, of course.' Pitt smiled wryly. 'Just remember me if you have need of any advice, or assistance, that is all. I have intentions of a political career and may be of some use to you in the future. That is all I wished to say.'

I saw that I had perhaps misjudged him. He wanted to offer help. He knew that my financial support was based upon money from the Crown paid to my mother as a royal pension. That money might not last forever.

'Thank you. You have been most thoughtful, Mr Pitt.'

I rose from my desk and held out my hand. Pitt shook it. I knew then that our dealings with one another were far from over. But I could not have anticipated just how much more we would have in common.

❖   ❖   ❖

I left Eton in the summer of 1777 and went up to Oxford. My mother had hopes of my securing some sort of position in the law. James, a year younger than me, had left Eton at the same time as me to seek a career in the Army. The same source of my mother's income provided James with professional patronage and he found a position in the Royal Engineers, a less fashionable regiment that would not attract attention. Our choices of career were still determined by the Earl of Chatham and his powerful allies. Thankfully, I enjoyed my time at Oxford. After the brutal bleakness of Eton, three years at Christ's College was unbridled joy. I had a set of rooms, a generous allowance and very little work to do. Oxford dons seemed to spend most of their time drinking port or visiting London, where they discarded their clerical robes to indulge in pleasures of the flesh. Those who were conscientious about their parish disappeared for months on end, only to reappear and affect not to know me.

I spent my allowance wisely, though Heaven knows I could easily have sunk into the same sewer of drink-induced dependence as so many of my contemporaries. I felt different from them. I was not an aristocrat with a title or a great inheritance as so many of my school and university friends were. I was a gentleman from Somerset of relatively modest means, although I knew that I was of more exalted birth than any of them. If only they had known!

I wrote often to my dear mother, and went into Somerset during the university vacations. I also spent holidays travelling across Europe on what they used to call the Grand Tour. I often heard from my brother James, whose career in the Army was progressing well. By the time I left Oxford he had joined his regiment in India. Sarah had remained in Somerset with a private governess and became engaged to marry a young doctor named James Dalton.

I went down from Oxford with my degree – unusual for my

generation, for unless one was going to become a clergyman, schoolmaster or lawyer, most young men simply did not bother – and had already decided to pursue a career in the legal profession. I duly enrolled as a member of the Society of the Middle Temple. I diligently carried bags for my pupil-master Mr Witherspoon and prepared his papers for the coming trials, and so was granted a desk in one of the upper chambers in Middle Temple to carve out my legal career. Like most young men in that profession, I had an allowance – not as much as many, but it was sufficient. I had no intention of making any claims on my birthright and when the payments continued uninterrupted after Chatham's death, I assumed that it would continue for the rest of my life.

All this changed, however, in the winter of 1783. Now firmly settled in my chambers in Middle Temple and beginning to make some money on top of my allowance, I was not entirely immune to wider events in the world of politics. This was particularly so because in the summer of that year, Great Britain had signed a treaty with France, Spain and the United States of America. Yes, the United States! For since the rebellion, a whole new country had been formed. From Eton to Oxford I had eagerly followed the events of the war, from the Boston 'Tea Party' to Bunker Hill and Burgoyne's ignominious surrender at Yorktown.

It was not the disaster for the country that some people think. When the rebellion began, the mood of the nation was bellicose to say the least. But as the campaigning ground on, and the French came in, popular opinion turned steadily against the war. Let the colonials have their independence, people on the streets of London murmured. Perhaps one day we should have ours? It was strange to think that the one person most affected by the loss of America was my father – the King. It was also to affect me. The loss of prestige for the king and the country had a great impact upon the leader of the government, Lord North. In the autumn his government fell from power – North resigned despite the King's pleas and it looked as if Charles James Fox, republican, inveterate gambler and supporter of the perpetually bankrupt Prince of Wales, would lead the government, much to the King's disgust. However, against all the expectations of the day, the King appointed a different leader of a new government: William Pitt, son of Lord Chatham. Pitt was precocious, and the son of a very great politician, but he was only twenty-four years of age when the King appointed him First Lord in December. He had been an MP for a mere two years and I had often seen him scurrying from his rooms at Lincoln's Inn, where he too practised law. The Commons laughed when he took his seat on the front bench and his government was nicknamed the 'mince-pie administration' because it was widely expected not to last beyond Christmas. He was the sole member of his cabinet and suffered defeat after defeat. It was the support of the House of Lords – persuaded by the 'King's friends' – that allowed him to remain in power; Pitt's refusal to dissolve Parliament bought him time. The continued antics of Fox – who was too drunk or too busy gambling to take his chance – enabled Pitt to build his power-base.

It was at this time early in the New Year when I received a handwritten invitation to Number 10 Downing Street. I had always suspected my encounter with Pitt at Eton wouldn't be the last time our paths crossed. Ever since his father Lord Chatham had browbeaten my poor mother all those years ago, our fates had been linked.

I arrived after supper, during quite a dark and stormy evening. Pitt was a bachelor and lived alone at Downing Street. He still faced tremendous opposition in the Commons and was about to dissolve Parliament and begin the fight for his political life, which was to result in his supremacy in the House for the next twenty-two years. He was not yet twenty-five.

'George.'

The same polite, but distant, greeting. A brief, limp handshake. He took my coat – he lodged rarely in Downing Street and did not appear to have any staff – and led me through to the withdrawing room where a small fire flickered in the grate.

'Take a seat, George.'

Pitt poured me a large glass of port. He was rumoured to imbibe several bottles of the stuff a day.

'How's business?'

'Good, thank you.'

I sipped my port, fully aware that Pitt had not asked me here to talk law.

'Glad to hear it.'

Pitt shovelled some coal onto the fire. How many First Lords of the Treasury did that, I wondered.

'George, I have to tell you that I intend to win the majority of the Commons and secure my premiership at the forthcoming elections.'

As he spoke, Pitt's head twitched from side to side. He was a person of brilliant eloquence and extraordinary speed and clarity of thought. Physically, he was ungainly and his clothes did not fit too well, despite what must have been excellent tailoring. Anyone who came anywhere near him could not but sense that the magnetism within his small frame was extraordinary.

'People laughed at me when I was appointed by the King, but I have the support of the Lords and His Majesty. Your father.'

Pitt looked at me and smiled, but his smile was as cold as the winter wind outside.

'I told His Majesty that if he did not appoint me First Lord of the Treasury then I would expose his marriage to Queen Charlotte as a sham and all his children by her as bastards. And you, George Rex, as his firstborn, would be revealed to the world. It is fortuitous that you are working and living in London. We know where you live and whom you work for. How lucky for you that we instructed Witherspoon to take you on in his chambers.'

Pitt laughed at the surprise on my face.

'Do you really think you would have been given a position without my instruction? My dear George, you truly have the Hanoverian brain. You're a decent chap, but there's not a great deal up here, is there?'

Pitt tapped his forehead and, as he reached for the port, my temper flared.

'Damn you, Pitt! Have I not a degree from Oxford? Have I not studied the law diligently? We cannot all be blessed with your brilliance!'

'I grant you that you have plodded dutifully through the established rites of passage: school, university . . .'

'That's more than you managed!' I spluttered, sure of my ground at last. In spite of his brilliance – or perhaps because of it – Pitt had been tutored at home and left Cambridge after a year due to illness.

'Which is why I intend to be the greatest First Lord since Walpole. My father was denied that high office, even though he was the most brilliant politician of his generation. Those fools Newcastle and Fox stood in his way when he led the nation to victory over France. Then he was too ill to return to the power he so richly deserved. And now I intend to defeat the son of Fox and consign him and his rabble to the political grave.'

55

I saw it all now. This was the last hand in the deadly game between two generations of the Fox and Pitt families. Henry Fox had deserted Chatham to take high office and make a vast fortune as Paymaster-General where he made his name in political bribery and corruption. His son Charles James had made his name as a gambler and leader of the dissolute life and was well on the way to spending his father's fortune.

'My father believed in good government for the people,' Pitt was saying. 'Government without corruption and bribes. And I'm going to give it to them. I'll abolish the rotten boroughs, kick out the Tory squires, and who knows, maybe even abolish slavery?' Pitt downed his glass. 'And your father the King has no option but to support me and keep me in power for as long as I need to do these things. I know his secret. With that knowledge, I could ruin him and bring down the monarchy.' Pitt stared at me with piercing coldness, adding, 'We all know there is still a King over the water.'

'You would not dare?'

'People's memories are short. And the English so love a hero, especially a tragic hero.'

It was decades since the doomed Jacobite rebellion when Bonnie Prince Charlie had landed in Scotland and claimed the throne. The Forty-Five had panicked the court and got as far as Derby before 'Butcher' Cumberland had slaughtered the highlanders at Culloden Moor. But the return of a Catholic monarch would plunge Britain into civil war once again. As far as I knew, Bonnie Prince Charlie was still alive and, even as an old man, his name might be enough to provoke rebellion.

'You would never allow that to happen?'

Pitt smiled.

'No, probably not. But the threat is there, isn't it?'

I had to agree, yet my head grew hot at the thought of this

precocious creature threatening my father, even though it was never to be my inheritance.

'What have you said to the King?'

Pitt handed me a piece of paper. 'I merely presented him with this.'

It was the marriage certificate, dated 17th April 1759, of my mother, Hannah, and my father, 'George P'. As I read it I tried not to tremble so that Pitt would not see me in a moment of weakness, damn his eyes.

'I was under the impression that this had been destroyed by your father, Lord Chatham.'

Pitt took the document back.

'My father thought it prudent to keep a single copy. The individual who officiated at the marriage, John Wilmot, has, shall we say, been well looked after. And the legal business is under the management of the Lord Chancellor, now Baron Thurlow, who will be returned to office when I win the election. So you see, we have the evidence and we can always produce Wilmot to provide affidavits.'

Pitt was right. I knew that, legally, he had my father in a tight position. The King, who had not wanted North to resign, had been forced to back this evil young genius to form a government.

'What shall you do if you lose the election?'

'We shall not lose. The King will use his influence in the Shires to win the votes for me.'

'And yet you claim to be a man of pure conscience in the matters of government?'

'One has to win power before one can exercise any principles, George.' Pitt waved an arm impatiently. 'Enough of this. I have the full support of the King and I will win the election. I brought you here to tell you that your allowance will continue if you keep your silence. If not, then you will find your burgeoning legal career cut short, your ageing mother without a pension, your brother's brilliant army career inexplicably damaged by some sort of scandal and, who knows, your sister tragically widowed.'

He had us where he wanted us. Watched and controlled. What could I do at that moment? Precisely nothing, though my hatred of him was so intense I had to restrain myself from seizing the poker from the fire and beating him senseless with it.

'You have my word, Mr Pitt,' I said instead. 'We shall keep our counsel. We have made no mention of it for over twenty years, so why speak out now.'

'Because the stakes are higher than ever before,' Pitt snapped, his expression betraying a rare flash of the overwhelming political greed which drove him on.

'You have my word on it,' I repeated.

I reached for my coat, not wishing to linger another minute in his presence. We shook hands at the door, but as I walked back to my lodgings, I prayed I would never encounter Pitt again.

Pitt won the election with a resounding victory over Fox. He had clung to office with support from the King and the Lords, turning down lucrative sinecures in search of honest government (I alone knew the real source of his hold over the King) and gained the backing of the country at the hustings. The people wanted Pitt, they wanted trade and prosperity with the new United States and so they supported the King.

I was drawn away from all this political excitement by a family death, which hit us hard: my dearest mother, Hannah, passed away. She had been taken ill in the winter with a fever and I made the familiar journey back to Bruton for what was to be the last time in the summer. I stayed with her, and so did Sarah; James was in India and had no knowledge of her illness. After her death, we cleared the house of her belongings. At the reading of the will, the local lawyer was attended by a black-hatted gentleman from London. I knew from his look that he was one of Pitt's men, come to ensure that nothing untoward was revealed in the proceedings.

I was the executor of her will. She left the three of us £3,000 each – a far from modest sum which would leave us reasonably well off. She also left me a bundle of papers and a ring. This ring, which I examined by myself, was evidence of the love between my mother and the King, if I ever needed it. It was a solid gold band and on the inner side was inscribed 'Hannah – *À mon soul désir* – George R.' By signing himself King George, here too was the evidence that the King continued to communicate with my mother when he was King. I loved his name, too, for that was my name – George Rex.

Four years passed. I was happy in my work, and continued to accept the allowance from Pitt's government in return for my silence. My brother was promoted to Colonel in the Engineers. My sister was now married to Dr Dalton and they had moved to his native Carmarthen, where they started a family.

In the winter of 1788 my own life changed for the good. I was now courting Catherine Meadows, the daughter of another barrister, and I sincerely hoped I might be able to propose marriage before very long. I was succeeding at the bar. Pitt's hurtful comments still echoed in my ears but increased my determination tenfold. The money my mother had bequeathed me had been invested and I had made more, enough to support a wife and family in the future. I intended to seek out Catherine's father over Christmas and make my feelings for his daughter clear.

Catherine was a dear girl. Not yet twenty, she was blessed with clear skin, wonderful dark hair and bore herself with a grace and beauty I did not deserve. We met at a summer ball in Lincoln's Inn Fields, and I was in love from the very first moment I set eyes on her. She seemingly returned my favours, and we danced several times that evening, enough to set some tongues wagging amongst members of the Bar. But the talk was encouraging and the gossip excitable and not in any way malicious. It would be a good match for both parties, it appeared, and there was no objection to my affections. I took Catherine to the theatre and we walked in Hyde Park on Sunday afternoons as often as we could during that summer and autumn. I was the happiest soul alive when Catherine hinted broadly that my affections were returned with equal, if not more passionate, force and that any future I might imagine together was a certainty.

Three evenings before Christmas I was in my lodgings in Lincoln's Inn Fields when I was paid a visit that was to set my life on a path that I could never have desired. Even now, after so many years, I wish that I had not been at home when they came. But I was, and the housekeeper, Mrs Greenaway, did not answer the door, so I took it myself.

Three black-cloaked and hatted gentlemen stood in the doorway, breathing clouds of frozen air.

'Mr Rex?' asked the one in the centre.

'That is I.' I wondered if they had a pressing case for me for the Christmas period and fervently hoped not.

'We come from Mr Pitt. He seeks your urgent presence.'

It was news that I dreaded and had hoped never to hear.

'What does he want?'

'He requests your presence at Downing Street tonight.'

'Why?' I asked belligerently, making no attempt to invite them in.

'He said to show you this.'

I took the sealed letter, broke it open and read: *Your father the King is grievous sick. He has gone mad. He is asking for you. Come without delay. Pitt.*

My mind was filled with conflicting emotions, including anger. Yes, it had come to me after all these years. I was to meet my father; he had summoned me. But did I wish to see him after the way he had treated my mother and condemned her to a life in exile? I truly did not know the answer, but with Pitt's men standing there, I did not have to make up my mind, for it was done for me.

I glanced at the men on the doorstep and resigned myself to my fate.

'Permit me a moment to gather my coat and boots.'

Pitt was waiting in the hallway of Downing Street. With him were Lord Thurlow, the Lord Chancellor, and a slight, bewigged clergyman whom I took to be an attendant of some sort.

'We must hurry,' Pitt said without preamble. 'The King is at Kew. The coach is ready for us.'

The three of us climbed into the coach, accompanied by the attendant. Pitt must have seen me look at him, for he added: 'How remiss of me. Let me introduce Dr John Wilmot, the man who married your mother to the Prince of Wales.'

Wilmot shook my hand.

'Your mother was a true friend to my daughter Olive.'

So this was the mysterious Wilmot. He seemed a decent enough

61

fellow, but I wondered what his reward had been for keeping quiet about my parents' marriage. No doubt he had done as well as Pitt in some way or other.

The coach rattled though the streets of London to Kew. It was bitterly cold and the four of us had no conversation. Pitt passed round a flask of port, which warmed our bellies a little.

As we approached the palace at Kew, Pitt leant towards me and for the first time I saw a glimmer of fear in his eyes.

'Fox and his wretched rabble have already put forward a motion in the House to have the King declared insane and to establish the Prince of Wales as Regent. The motion was defeated by sixty-four votes, which was sixty-four votes too close for comfort. If Fox has his way, my government will fall.'

'Is the King really mad?' I asked, more concerned for my father than for Pitt and his blasted political machinations.

'He raves and foams at the mouth,' said Wilmot. 'He talks for hours non-stop and rages foul oaths and refuses all medicine. He runs away from his doctors and his legs weep blood and pus from open sores. He . . .'

'Enough!' snapped Pitt, as the carriage came to a halt. 'The King is not mad. He has an illness none of these damned quacks at court can deal with. I have sent for somebody special.' Pitt grasped my arm as we climbed out of the coach. 'But the King has asked for you, George. Nobody must know who you really are. You must see the King and tell him to keep his mouth shut about you. You must calm him down. But no one must know about you,' Pitt's hissed as his grasp on my arm tightened, 'otherwise the consequences will be unthinkable. We could have anarchy, civil war or even revolution. And your life would not be worth a bottle of gin. Do you understand?'

I saw what he meant. For better or worse, the two of us were now bound together by the deadly secret of my birth. If I could not calm the King, then his ramblings would give me away and my happy, quiet life would be held up for any revolutionary or radical to make play with, and the fall of Pitt's government would plunge the country into crisis.

Colonel Greville met us at the door and ushered us through a series of dimly lit ante-rooms, drawing rooms and corridors. There were few staff in the building. The King had been brought here under guard and under duress, Wilmot whispered to me. Away from his wife and away from the prying eyes of the court and the press, who were baying for a good story.

Then, after another corridor, Pitt paused at the door of the next room. Slowly he opened the door and put his head inside the room. A few muttered words, then he jerked his head at me.

'Wilmot, Thurlow. You come too.'

I was finally to meet my father the King. I had seen him from afar once or twice during the state opening of Parliament through the press of the crowds, but never before had I been in his presence and spoken to him. Would he even know me?

We stepped through the door, Pitt close behind us. Wilmot nudged me into the room and there, seated in a plain wooden chair, was my father.

As I moved into the candlelit room I saw, through the flickering shadows, that he was not merely seated in the chair, but firmly strapped to it. His legs were wrapped in bandages and I could see the blood and pus seeping through. His mouth was gagged.

I felt anger quicken my heart, despite my lifetime of disinheritance. Here was my father, my flesh and blood. Furthermore, he was the King. How could they treat him this way?

Beside me, Wilmot gave a rapid intake of breath.

'You are his very image. My God, if people could see the two of you together . . .'

'Go to him,' Pitt hissed, his hand on my back.

I stepped forward but before I could say anything, a voice from behind the King spoke:

'Do not come too close, Mr Rex. And do not make any sudden movements.'

It was Dr Willis, the mad-doctor from Lincolnshire. I had no knowledge of Willis then but discovered much later that he had once been in holy orders and was sometime vice-principal of Brasenose College, Oxford. His fame for curing the sick of mind would spread far and wide.

I moved close to my father who was watching me with a calm eye. Willis removed the gag from his mouth.

I spoke to my father, my mouth dry.

'I am your son. I am George.'

The King lifted his head and stared at me with sad eyes.

'You are Hannah's son, then?'

'Yes. I am Hannah's son. I am your firstborn.'

'You are the son I never had – better than that fat useless fool the Prince of Wales!'

Willis put his hand on the King's shoulder and my father closed his mouth. Evidently such familiarity with the monarch was part of his treatment.

'And James – how is he? And Sarah? Married, I believe?'

'Yes. They are happy. We are all happy.'

I wondered if he knew about my mother but his next words confirmed that he did. He drew himself up in the chair as best he could with his arms pinioned the way they were and said,

'And Hannah, God rest her soul. I loved your mother so much it broke my heart. But I wish to God I had never set eyes on her and caused all this distress.'

'Sire, do not trouble yourself.' Willis spoke quietly from behind the chair.

'She led a good life,' I said. 'She was well looked after. We all were. You should not reproach yourself.' As I spoke I realised that I did not feel any bitterness towards this man. He had loved my mother and married for his kingdom. He had ensured that we were financially secure – far more so than most.

'Release me,' the King said to Willis.

At a nod from Pitt, Willis untied the rope from my father's arms.

'Come to me, my son.'

As he held me tight for that moment I felt his love surge through me.

Then we stood back from one another and I was ushered from the room and I knew in that instant that I would never see him again.

The rest of that night has always remained a blur in my memory. Pitt took me back to my lodgings and helped me to my rooms. I was numb with shock. Pitt was muttering about the Regency Bill, anarchy and Fox, but I did not care a damn. I had met my father in his worst moment – too many years too late. He had chosen, in a moment of lucidity, to summon me after all those years of exile. All those years of not acknowledging me, his firstborn by his love Hannah. My life was a grubby secret, my existence an embarrassment and shame. It was as if I, and not all those children by Charlotte of Mecklenberg, had been illegitimate. We were the bastards, James, Sarah and I, fruit of the king's overactive loins. The world seemed turned upside down. Our legitimacy was false. The German wife and her German children were the true heirs of the King in the eyes of that upturned world. Pitt left me that night with a bottle of port, which I gulped down greedily before collapsing into my bed in a drunken stupor, weeping myself to sleep, alone and unloved.

◈ ◈ ◈

I did not go to my chambers in the morning, or the next morning. I went in on Christmas Eve and was received with stony silence from my colleagues. I claimed a touch of gout and spent the morning working through my papers for the forthcoming trials early in the New Year. After lunch at the Cheshire Cheese Inn, I picked up some fine wines to take for Mr Meadows for I had been invited to Christmas dinner with his family.

I realised in the grey dawn on the morning after I had met the King that I was neither alone nor unloved. Although I had only a belated and minimal recognition from my father, it was to the future that I looked on that Christmas morning. I considered the meeting with the King as the end of a chapter, and now it was time to start afresh with Catherine. I had bought her some rather delightful lace and I was looking forward to spending the evening in Islington with the family and asking her father for her hand in marriage after dinner.

As I approached the ornate front door of the Meadows household I was calm and collected. I had met my father and was glad to have done so. I hoped our meeting would help his illness. Whatever I felt for Pitt (and it was not much), I did not want his government to fall and plunge us all into anarchy. So it was that I knocked confidently at the door, clutching my presents with hope in my heart for my new life with Catherine. Evening was upon us and it was cold enough to snow.

The door opened but instead of Charlie, the cheerful young doorman, there stood a large, fleshy character whose eyebrows met in the middle and whose mouth was fixed into a large snarl.

'You're not welcome here,' he said.

'What do you mean?' I asked. 'Is this some sort of joke?'

'Get him away from this house!'

Wilfrid Meadows had appeared at the side of the doorman. He was red in the face, dressed only in his shirtsleeves and looked as if he had been drinking heavily. I was astonished. Wilfrid was a mild-mannered man who loved chess. Here he was standing on his own doorstep screaming at me.

'Get away from here! How can you come here when you have brought such shame on this house?'

'What shame? What are you talking about, Mr Meadows?'

I took an involuntary step away from the door. Something was happening over which I had no control. I glanced up at the windows, wondering whether I had come to the right house.

'Do you think we don't know about your filthy secret?' Meadows yelled, spitting at me in his rage. People in the street were now stopping, turning round to look at the scene. 'And to think I might have granted my daughter's hand in marriage to you. You rascal!'

I heard a woman's sobbing behind him. It was this that snapped me back to the reality of the scene before me.

'Catherine!' I shouted. I threw my gifts at the oaf at the door who instinctively went to catch them, and barged past him into the hallway. 'Catherine, my darling, what is happening? What is your father thinking of?'

Normally so delighted to see me, Catherine staggered back from me, her mouth working silently. Her bedraggled hair hung in knots and wisps over her tearstained face but before she could speak, rough hands grabbed me and hurled me into the street. I crashed onto my back, seeing the thug in the doorway raising his belt to thrash me.

'Leave him,' spoke an ice-calm voice, used to issuing orders. From the ground I saw Catherine's brother, Lionel, step to the fore. 'He has impugned my sister's honour and there is a better way to deal with him.'

67

Without another word he stooped and slapped my chest with his glove before dropping it to the floor. As the door slammed in my face I realised I had been challenged to a duel, yet I was entirely ignorant of the reason.

There was one person I could turn to that Christmas morning. Not any of my London friends, for they had left for the country and their families. Not my sister, for Sarah was with her husband and children in Carmarthen. Not my brother James, who was still in India with his own family now. There was one person I could call on in the bleak dawn of Christmas before anyone was awake.

He was there, as I knew he would be. Doing some government business or other before leaving for an afternoon off, if he would allow himself even that. He probably hadn't even slept, working at his red boxes throughout the night, a couple of bottles of port to keep him going.

Pitt himself answered the door to Downing Street. How typical, I reflected, even in the state I was in.

'George . . . What a surprise!' For once, Pitt's suave omnipotence abandoned him. A look of shock followed by panic flashed across his face. It lasted a mere second but he knew I had seen it. Then his expression passed from irritation to a concern so false that neither of us pretended to dwell on it.

'Mr Pitt, I must talk to you.' Hoping the house was empty, I all but pushed past him. 'I have been challenged to a duel.'

'A duel, you say? My dear man, how exciting.'

'It is not a matter of amusement,' I snapped.

Such rudeness to Pitt would have been unthinkable yesterday. Things were different now. I was a hunted man. Pitt beckoned me into the drawing room. The embers of a fire glowed in the grate.

Candles burned low in their holders, globules of wax overflowing everywhere. I was right: he had been working. Pitt poured me a glass of port.

'Who has called you out?'

'My . . . my intended's brother.'

'Your intended? Good Lord, man, you're engaged to be married? Congratulations. But why . . .'

'I have no idea. None whatsoever.' I helped myself to more port. Desperate as I may have been to keep a level head, I still needed a drink. I had spent the night going over and over my meetings with Catherine, wondering whether our conversations could have been overheard or our glances and notes misconstrued in some way. I had walked the empty streets of London for hours, racking my brains for a solution. There was nothing. Try as I might, I could not think of anything I had done to compromise her position as a maid and as the daughter of a gentleman. I was resolved to get to the bottom of it, but I needed a man of intelligence and resource on my side. After all, Pitt owed me.

Pitt listened in silence as I told him of my last visit to Catherine's house. I also briefed him on my courtship with Catherine. I could almost hear Pitt's great brain humming as he worked out my options.

'Your courtship seems entirely conventional and honourable, George.'

'It is. There is nothing out of order.'

'I take it that you have not told anyone of our little visit to Kew?'

'No – absolutely not.'

I met Pitt's piercing gaze.

'Then you must accept the challenge. In order to keep it quiet, to satisfy honour all round. Grass before breakfast, as they say.'

'Are you mad? He'll kill me.'

I was horror struck at Pitt's decision. Was this the best he could come up with?

'Listen.' Pitt sounded almost sympathetic. 'It is your only chance of getting Catherine back. If you run away from this, your good name will be ruined. You'll never practice at the Bar again. You clearly cannot visit the Meadows household. But if you accept the challenge and go through with it, honour will be satisfied. You can get to the bottom of it all after the duel.'

'But he is an army officer. He'll be a good swordsman and a crack shot. What chance have I got?'

It was true. I had fenced at Eton but had not concentrated well enough to get further than the basics. I had, however, shot a good deal at home in Somerset amongst our small social set and considered myself not a bad shot. But I knew from my brother's experiences and the contents of his enthusiastic letters that 'not a bad shot' was not good enough to face an army officer at twenty paces.

'I'll act as your second,' Pitt said. 'I'll send a man round immediately and arrange a time and a place. I suggest today.'

'Today? My God –'

'And I recommend you choose pistols over swords. It is your right as the challenged to decide your weapon. But don't worry. With me as your second, everything will go as we wish.'

'What if anything should go wrong?'

I dared not say what I meant – what if anyone should get killed. Namely, me?

'With the First Lord of the Treasury acting as your second, this Meadows fellow will point his pistol in the air unless he wishes to hang for murder, or attempted murder,' Pitt corrected himself hastily.

I realised the enormity of Pitt's offer: he had saved me. I was elated. There was no way Meadows would dare harm me with

Pitt present. Duelling was legal, but if there was a fatality, then murder charges could be brought. Meadows would never take the risk.

'Go to your lodgings.' Pitt laid a firm hand on my shoulder. 'Await my message and be prepared to come out this afternoon.'

❖ ❖ ❖

Snow was settling on Hyde Park as I trudged through the park gates with Pitt's messenger. The winter sun had never quite risen that Christmas Day and the afternoon light was fading fast. I had my best coat on and a scarf wrapped closely around my neck. It was not the cold that made me shiver. Four figures in the distance gradually came into focus as we crossed the park. I recognised Pitt, stooping slightly, stamping his feet in the snow. Clouds of frozen breath drifted in the air. Captain Lionel Meadows stood with the person I presumed was his second, who looked likely to be another military type. Pitt was exchanging words with the fourth man, who was clutching a leather case. He must be a doctor. My hands clenched at the sight of him. I hoped to God that Pitt was right about Meadows firing into the air to satisfy his honour so we could both go home alive. I took the flask Pitt handed to me and swallowed a mighty draught of port.

'Dr Kettwood,' Pitt gestured at the doctor, then turned to Meadows and his second, who stood grim-faced in the gathering gloom.

'Captain Lionel Meadows of course, you know, and his second, Major Calthorpe.'

Neither man offered to shake my hand – but then, I had made no such offer.

'Now, to business.' Pitt was brisk. 'Captain Meadows has agreed to the use of pistols. If you accept then you may fire at twenty paces. Major Calthorpe and myself will mark out the paces and place a sword in the ground at the spot where you will stop. At my signal – which will be the dropping of my handkerchief – you may fire. First blood drawn is honour satisfied. Agreed?'

Lionel and I nodded. Pitt and Calthorpe ceremoniously drew their swords – Pitt was awkward and ill at ease with his, Calthorpe athletic and confident – and measured out the twenty paces, placing their sword points into the snow.

'Funny old business, eh?'

The doctor swigged heavily from his own flask. His mottled red face and heavily veined bulbous nose were clearly not caused by the cold. I reflected that even Pitt would be hard-pushed to find an honest, sober quack to patch up any duelling wounds at such short notice as this, and on Christmas Day. Meadows and I ignored him and waited for Pitt and Calthorpe to return. Calthorpe had with him a case which he set down on the ground. He lifted out two duelling pistols and with Pitt loaded and checked them.

'Gentlemen. If you please.'

Calthorpe gestured to the ground between the two swords. Pitt handed me my pistol, which seemed unnaturally heavy. My hand shook. My breath was coming in short, frozen gasps.

'Keep steady, Rex,' Pitt hissed, squeezing my wrist. 'Remember what I said. Wait for him to fire into the air first.'

I nodded, desperately trying to hold the pistol still. I walked towards Meadows, who avoided my gaze. We squared up, back to back. It was growing dark. I resisted the urge to turn and beg Meadows to tell me what I had done and why we were there with loaded guns in this God-forsaken place.

The moment passed. At Calthorpe's nod, we began walking apart, each towards the sword in front of us. Pitt had his white handkerchief in his outstretched arm. I reached the sword. It had taken seconds, minutes, I did not know. I turned, saw Pitt waiting, Meadows facing me, turned to his side so as to minimise his body in my sights. I did likewise, the pistol to my side.

Pitt dropped his handkerchief.

I raised my arm. It was shaking so much I thought I must be having some form of seizure. Meadows raised his arm, perfectly steady. The end of his pistol magnified into a grotesque black hole, as if it would swallow me. I blinked and tried to focus, but my vision was blurred, the thumping of my heart making it all the more monstrous. I realised at that moment that Meadows was not going to fire into the air. He was going to kill me. My hand became still. My breathing slowed and then stopped.

The explosion of powder cracked through the park. There was another roar, and then silence. Meadows remained where he was, his arm outstretched, smoke gusting from the end of the pistol barrel. But his silk cravat was no longer cream coloured. Blood was running freely from his neck. Meadows coughed and dropped the pistol.

There was an exclamation. It was either Pitt or the doctor. Meadows fell to his knees, his hands to his throat. His breath was rattling and gurgling. The doctor was running to Meadows, with Pitt and Calthorpe close behind. Meadows was now on his back, writhing. Blood stained the snow, pumping steadily from his neck. I walked towards the group, still holding my pistol. The doctor was wrapping a cloth round Meadows's neck, but it did no good. As I approached, Meadows tried to sit up and speak but no sound came out. The musket ball had taken him full in the throat and ripped through his vital arteries. He was pointing to Pitt, but looking at me. He was trying to tell me something. He was dying but there was a message for me. His attempt failed. He fell back into Calthorpe's arms, coughed again and lay still.

We stood there, looking at Meadows lying in Calthorpe's arms for what must have been several minutes. We were oblivious to the cold.

Calthorpe's hard eyes bored through me in the dusk.

'You have killed him, Rex. The agreement was only first blood – not death. You fired first. Meadows missed you. It's a cut-and-dried case. You'll hang for this.'

I looked at Pitt, but Pitt was shaking his head. I backed away. The doctor was hurriedly packing his bag, wanting to be as far away as possible from this scene of tragedy. Meadows's blood was already freezing in the snow. Calthorpe got up and carefully placed his cloak over the body.

In the gloom the sound of horses' hooves and the jingle of harness signalled the arrival of a coach.

We all stood fixed to the ground, even the doctor.

'Who goes there?' came the shout from the coach.

Men were climbing from the coach. They carried truncheons and had badges on their coats: they were constables from Bow Street. I felt numb. This was justice. Calthorpe was talking, pointing to me and to Meadows's corpse. Pitt kept out of the way, saying nothing.

As the men approached me I held out my hands in surrender.

1914

13 June 1914

Septimus was running.

'Wait!' Karl Hahn shouted, 'I must talk to you!' His chest was bloodied with the bullets that had torn through him. 'Take the memoir!'

Septimus, his mouth open with terror, ran down New College Lane and under the Bridge of Sighs. He raced onto Hertford Street and into Old School Quadrangle, towards the entrance of the Bodleian. Glancing behind, he could see that the assassin had taken Hahn's place. Septimus screamed, but nobody heard him. He burst through the library doors and entered the staircase to the reading rooms. Sweat poured from his forehead and his chest was pounding. Halfway up the stairs he ducked into Duke Humfrey's Library, the hallowed inner sanctum of the Bodleian, where visitors were not permitted. The ancient manuscripts were stored in medieval galleries to the sides of the central oak-panelled passageway.

Septimus was safe here. The silence was absolute. He slowed to a walk, conscious that his presence might disturb the scholars at their work. He reached the end of the long gallery and looked back. Hahn's murderer was at the far end, walking towards him slowly and deliberately.

'No –'

Septimus reached the end of the gallery and made his way up a small, spiral wooden staircase. He climbed to the top, where there was a narrow seating area. There was somebody sitting at a single desk, with his back to him. Septimus looked down into the library. The assassin hadn't seen him. He crept to the end of the gallery and the person at the desk turned to face him.

'Who are you?' Septimus whispered.

The figure smiled. He was dressed in a black frock coat, breeches and a dirty white stock. He wore a wig: his face was powdered and scattered on the desk in front of him were sheaves of paper covered in familiar spidery handwriting.

'You know who I am.'

The assassin stood at the top of the staircase.

'I am George Rex.'

The smoke from Septimus's cigarette curled and drifted through the open window and out into the trees in the garden. On the floor beside the bed lay the leather-bound memoir. The bed itself was slightly damp. In fact, the entire upper floor of the house was damp; the wallpaper was peeling and a large hole in the ceiling on the landing, which Septimus had first noticed last year, was still visible.

Septimus was in the 'Swiss Room', so called because Quayle had long ago taken to putting up maps of the Alps around the room, along with postcards, recording his summer visits to the mountains. He stubbed out the cigarette, climbed gingerly out of bed and reached for his shirt. He had fled Oxford in the clothes he was standing in, and he groaned. Heavens above, what a dream. So vivid, so real: the Bodleian Library, where he had spent so many hours; Hahn's killer, still on the loose. And George Rex . . .

Septimus flicked through the yellowing pages of the memoir. It retold the events of 1783 from a different perspective. Pitt had attained high office not as a consequence of his precocious talents, nor because of a lack of suitable candidates for the post, but by devious manipulation. Pitt had blackmailed George III and secured his appointment as Prime Minister to keep the bigamous marriage secret. This meant Septimus would have to rewrite his Fellowship dissertation. But then, such a sensational piece of evidence would make his name in the academic world and beyond.

Assuming the memoir was authentic.

The door swung open, and Quayle walked in, dressed resplendently in a maroon silk dressing-gown, a cigar clamped between his teeth. He set two steaming cups of tea down on the bedside table and picked up the memoir.

'Wonderful.' Septimus slurped at the tea greedily. His mouth throbbed with dehydration from last night's wine. 'The memoir's dynamite, Quayle, pure and simple.'

'That's one way of putting it. I have my doubts, however. Haven't you heard of the Journal of Julius Rodman? It fooled the United States' Senate!'

'But that was Poe. He was a novelist and hoaxer. This memoir is convincing. The characters – Pitt, Chatham, King George – are very convincing. And it explains so much, not least Pitt's appointment at the age of twenty-four. How else did he become Prime Minister? It was considered extraordinary at the time and it's never been explained adequately by historians.'

'Yes, there's plenty of circumstantial evidence.' Quayle shut the memoir and replaced it on the bed. 'But we need to prove this is genuine before we take it any further.'

'But . . .'

'No buts. Historical research comes from years of painstaking effort and not blundering guesswork. You know that better than anyone. I've arranged to visit the College library today to see if I can track down any additional information about this secret marriage.'

'What shall I do then? I'm not keen to return to Oxford.'

Quayle finished his tea and replaced the cup firmly on the saucer.

'You, Oates, are going acquire some new clothes, and then we can meet for breakfast in town. Agreed?' Quayle's stern glare brooked no argument. 'Good. And here's some money. I won't take no for an answer. Then you're going to the Public Record Office in London, to see what they have on these.'

'I'm not showing them the certificates!'

'There's no need to do that. Just sniff around and see what you can locate in the catalogues. Ask if they have anything. Right, I'll see you in one hour at Café St Gilles. You know the place. By the Butter Cross.'

Septimus knew it well. As schoolboys he and his friends had nicknamed the café Fat Arnold's in honour of one of Winchester's ancient masters who was grossly overweight and often drunk.

'I'll be there,' he said.

'What we should do,' Quayle continued through mouthfuls of devilled kidney, 'is to establish the provenance of those certificates and that memoir. Is this whole thing an elaborate hoax? See what you can find at the Public Record Office. I'm going to grill Hargeaves about eighteenth-century marriage laws and acts. It's the kind of tedious thing he'd be proficient in.'

'Is he still the archivist?' Septimus remembered Percival Hargeaves only vaguely from his school days; a giant of a man, quite bald, with little beady eyes and a booming voice.

Quayle paused, his fork in mid-air.

'Yes, has been since the 1880s.' A slow smile spread across Quayle's face. 'And do you know where he was before Winchester?'

'Of course not.'

Refreshed by tea and kippers, Septimus spoke without rancour. Quayle had the annoying habit of pretending other people knew as much as he did, when he knew perfectly well they didn't.

'Windsor Castle.'

Septimus swallowed his mouthful of toast abruptly.

'You're joking?'

'I'm certainly not.' Quayle was grinning like the Cheshire Cat. 'By Jove, it's only just occurred to me. Hargeaves will know all about Hannah Lightfoot and any secret marriage. Come on, Oates, we can't hang about.'

They returned to Spurlings via the Close, which was already busy with day trippers enjoying another fine summer's day. As they entered the kitchen Quayle stopped so abruptly that Septimus nearly bumped into him.

'I've been burgled.'

Septimus followed Quayle into the drawing room wondering how he could tell. Everything looked as it always did: a complete mess.

'What do you mean . . .?'

Quayle held up his hand and stood perfectly still for a moment. Then he walked to the front door, which he never used, and picked up a book from the floor.

'This book was on the shelf here, by the door. They came in here and knocked it off. They wouldn't know I always come in the back. Otherwise it's very clever. Very subtly done.'

Septimus frowned.

'Are you sure? I mean, there are enough books lying around the place.'

Quayle looked at Septimus over the top of his spectacles.

'I'm positive. And you know what they were after, don't you?'

A chill crept over Septimus. This time, he knew the answer to Quayle's question.

'My God: the memoir. I left it upstairs with the marriage certificates. Damnation!'

In three bounds, Septimus reached the landing and burst into his bedroom. The documents had vanished. He stumbled out of the room in a daze. How could he have been so stupid?

'I'm such an idiot.'

'No, you're not,' Quayle said unperturbed. He held up his battered leather briefcase. He'd had it with him at Café St Gilles, but because he never went anywhere without it, Septimus hadn't questioned it. With a flourish, Quayle pulled out the memoir and the certificates. 'Eh, voilà! Remember, Oates, the golden rule of historical research: never let any other swine steal your sources.'

Awash with relief, Septimus lit a cigarette.

'So I was followed from Oxford. They know I've got the memoir and they know I'm here.'

'They do indeed. Somebody – most likely the person who shot Hahn – needs these documents.'

'They could be back at any moment.'

'Maybe. Maybe not. How could they know you're here? You took a taxi to the station, then you boarded the train. You didn't see this assassin at Oxford station?'

'No, nor on the train . . .'

'. . . where you were an easy target.'

'So there are others who want these documents?'

'Possibly. They are pretty contentious, after all.'

'Why me? Why not Professor Battiscombe, my supervisor? He's the doyen of eighteenth-century politics. Why not give him these wretched documents?'

'I don't know.' Quayle shrugged. 'What I do know is that there is a purpose to all of this. It will become clear at some point.' He fumbled on a shelf above his desk and pulled out his battered Bradshaw. 'Now then,' he whistled tunelessly, 'the trains up to town are pretty frequent.' Quayle inspected his pocket watch. 'You should be able to catch the ten thirty-three in plenty of time.'

Whilst Quayle was talking, Septimus thought about the number of times he had travelled to the Public Record Office from Oxford in the course of his research. After the Bodleian, it was his second home. It would be good to get out of Winchester for the day, too.

'Oates?'

Quayle affected the look Septimus used to receive at school when he hadn't been listening for some time.

'Take some paper – I have some around here somewhere – and a pen. I'll keep the documents and I'll read the memoir while you're up in town. Whoever broke in here this morning will never get into the College library. We'll meet at the Wykeham Arms at seven o'clock for supper and some beer. Right?'

Septimus met Quayle's firm stare.

'Right.'

Where to start? A secret marriage was unlikely to be listed in the main collections of Chancery, State Papers or the General Register Office, and Septimus searched through the catalogues without success. Possibly in the Special Collections? Nothing. After two hours painstakingly checking the comprehensive catalogues, followed by a nasty pie at The Seven Stars public house, washed down with a half-decent pint of beer, Septimus admitted defeat and decided to ask Arthur Gooch, the eminent and most feared desk clerk in the building. Gooch wore a frock coat cut to a style that must have been at least forty years out of date. He was very tall and stooped, with a cadaverous appearance. Septimus had pestered him many times during his research and had much to thank him for, but always approached him with trepidation, wary of the explosive temper Gooch unleashed on hapless academics, young and old, notable or insignificant, who had failed to complete the rudimentary – or sometimes less obvious – stages of research before seeking help from the highest.

'Secret marriage?'

As Gooch gave him a baleful glare over his pince nez, Septimus was convinced he was about to receive one of those famously withering dispatches.

'I very much doubt there was any such secret marriage you refer to, young man. It's certainly not something I have ever come across in my time, but since you're here in the name of research – and that I would not obstruct – I'll try the acquisitions for you.'

Gooch went to a large cabinet behind the desk and spent several minutes examining the acquisitions catalogue. A muted exclamation of success raised Septimus's hopes. He watched as Gooch filled out a green slip of paper in his immaculate copperplate handwriting and rang a bell. A short while later, a young assistant in a tailcoat bustled out of a small door to the left of the gallery and took the paper from Gooch.

'We have a reference for what you require. I suggest you resume your seat whilst we wait,' said Gooch.

Septimus returned to his seat and tried to find other papers to read, but his eyes strayed to the large clock in the centre of the room as the hands crept unbearably slowly around the circumference. Ten minutes passed, then twenty, then thirty but eventually the side door opened again and Gooch beckoned him over to show him what the assistant had uncovered.

Septimus approached Gooch with his heart in his mouth,

only this time it was the scent of the chase in his nostrils, that familiar, heady taste of one's quarry not quite in view but most certainly within reach. Would these certificates establish that those in Quayle's care were forgeries? Or would they be identical, suggesting the copies were genuine?

But Gooch's expression had softened. It was not a look Septimus was familiar with. It was one of sympathy. That was not right, for sure.

'I'm sorry, Septimus. The reference is correct but we do not have the documents.'

'Where are they?' Septimus was dumbfounded.

Gooch shrugged his shoulders, for once at a loss.

'They're missing.'

It was ten to three and Septimus didn't want to return to Winchester empty-handed. Things did go missing from the Public Record Office from time to time but it didn't automatically mean they had been stolen. It was more likely that they had been misfiled or were in transit somewhere in the system. Gooch was apologetic and assured him that he would look into it, and since Gooch had been at Chancery Lane for over forty years, there was not much he missed.

Even so, it was suspicious. Was it possible that Quayle was holding the only genuine certificates? But there was another place to look. The secret marriage between George and Hannah had taken place at Kew. The parish records would now be archived at Somerset House on the Strand.

Septimus decided to walk. The bright sunshine cleared his head after the hours spent in the stifling air in the reading rooms at Chancery Lane, even though a London summer was never going to be very healthy. But it was good to get out, to feel so completely anonymous after the familiar – and now perhaps deadly – streets of Oxford and Winchester, in amongst all the many thousands of swarming clerks, tradesmen, shoppers, day trippers and tourists bustling along the Strand.

It took ten minutes to walk to Somerset House and a further ten to establish that the parish records for Kew 1714–1845 could not be located.

Why were they missing? Nobody knew. But at the end of the catalogue entry, there was a note: see file C/459/3/6. Septimus handed this to the collections desk and within minutes a small box was brought out for him. He took it to a desk in the far corner and opened it, but all that was inside was a newspaper cutting from *The Times*, yellowed with age, dated 26th February 1845:

On Saturday February 23rd a little before nine in the morning the pew-opener found the vestry unlocked, went in and missed the iron chest from its accustomed stand on two wooden blocks. It is thought the thieves scaled the wall and picked the lock of the door. The iron chest contained all the parish records from 1717 to the present time. Plates, surplices, academic robes were untouched and no attempt had been made to enter the church.

Septimus copied the report into his notepad. It accounted for the missing registers at Somerset House. Somebody had wanted the Kew registers removed from the public domain. What was the significance of the year 1845? That was decades after the secret marriage. Then there was George Rex's memoir, written as he was dying in 1839 and a mere six years before the theft of 1845. But somehow against all the odds the marriage certificates of George and Hannah had survived and found their way to Chancery Lane before being stolen. Had Hahn stolen them? Or others? Whoever had taken them from Chancery Lane, they were now in Quayle's briefcase in Winchester.

The thought of his old friend reassured Septimus that he had done enough for one day. Given the missing registers from Kew, the newspaper article and the fact that the Public Record Office hadn't got them on file – and maybe not in the actual building – it was probable that Quayle had the original certificates with the memoir in Winchester.

And he was the only other person who knew about these documents.

Documents Karl Hahn had relinquished moments before being shot dead. Septimus felt chilled to the bone. He had to get back to Winchester before Quayle became another victim of the secret marriage.

The Wykeham Arms was already half full even at twenty past six. Septimus walked to the pub directly from the station, sensing that Quayle would already be there – probably on his third pint by now – and deciding it wasn't worth calling in at Spurlings.

The Wykeham wasn't a large public house, but it had several small rooms and corners, which were easy enough to hide in when the pub was filling up with College masters, local tradesmen on their way home and tourists who were lodging nearby. In the evening the pub served excellent sausages with mustard, a favourite with the regulars, including Quayle, who rarely had to bother returning to Spurlings for supper. He was sitting in his usual corner, in the snug by the great fireplace. Taking over two pints, Septimus manoeuvred himself alongside him.

'Quayle!'

He looked up from the papers he had spread across the table. Septimus's relief at seeing his friend was tempered with annoyance: he didn't seem to be remotely bothered about the danger he might be in. Quayle took the beers from Septimus and placed them carefully on the table. Septimus noticed there were two empty glasses.

'Hargeaves has joined us,' Quayle said, by way of explanation. 'Bring another beer over, there's a good sort.'

Septimus tried and failed to conceal his irritation.

'Do you have any idea what we're involved with here? Why have you brought Hargeaves into this? Presumably you've told him everything about the documents?'

Quayle's slow smile served only to increase Septimus's concern. 'He knows nothing about Hahn – merely that the certificates were left in your pigeonhole at Christ's.'

Still worried that Quayle's eagerness would make it all too complicated and involve too many people, Septimus got another beer and when he returned the College archivist was firmly ensconced behind the table. Hargeaves took the beer and gave Septimus's hand a damp squeeze.

'Good to see you again, Oates,' he said in the booming voice Septimus remembered so well. Hargeaves hadn't aged a day. Still the same sheen of sweat on his forehead – the man detested warmth and had been known to sit at home in a cold bath when the summer days grew too oppressive – the black suit, white shirt and black tie, as if dressed for a funeral. Only the expanding waistline acknowledged the passing of the years.

'Now then,' Quayle said, smacking his lips and replacing his pint on the table with a firm thump. 'What have you got, Oates?'

Dropping his copy of the 1845 newspaper article on the table, Septimus began to recount his day. Hargeaves and Quayle said nothing during his account of the missing documents and the Somerset House parish records, but both raised eyebrows at his discovery of *The Times* article reporting the thefts at Kew.

'You've done well,' said Quayle. 'What you've deduced today suggests that the documents we have are genuine. They're the ones missing from the Public Record Office and also those missing from the parish chest at Kew. Somebody wanted them sixty years ago and collected them all together.'

'But why, given that George Rex died in 1839?'

'Because in 1866 it all came out in a case heard in the Divorce and Matrimonial Courts in June of that year,' Hargeaves explained.

'What case . . .?'

Septimus's question died in his throat. Quayle's raised arm was enough. As usual, their relationship reverted to schoolboy and master. But his grin indicated that he was just as excited by the whole business as Septimus, who knew damned well that Quayle hadn't waited patiently for Hargeaves to tell the tale earlier in the day.

'In 1866 . . .' Hargeaves began, drawing himself up, savouring his moment of importance, '. . . a woman called Mrs Lavinia Ryves set out to establish the legality of her grandmother's marriage to the Duke of Cumberland, brother of George III. The Duke apparently married a certain Olive Wilmot but later married another commoner, Anne Horton, much to the King's anger. But the Duke managed to get her accepted as a duchess, possibly because he blackmailed his brother over George's own bigamous marriage. If Lavinia Ryves had been successful, not only would she have been entitled to around one million pounds of financial claims, but it would also have brought down the monarchy. This was because Mrs Ryves had all these documents at her disposal and was prepared to use the secret marriage of George III and Hannah Lightfoot as a stick with which to beat the establishment. She had already used the new Legitimacy Declaration Act to prove that she was the daughter of John Thomas and Olive Serres. It was Olive's mother, Olive Wilmot, who had allegedly married the Duke of Cumberland. At the hearing she presented these documents.'

Septimus took the three scraps of paper Hargeaves passed across the table and read them quickly.

'I take it Henry Frederick is the Duke of Cumberland?'

'Correct,' said Hargeaves.

'And Chatham is of course William Pitt the Elder, Earl of Chatham given the date of the certificate?'

Hargeaves nodded.

'It's the third paper that's the most interesting,' said Quayle.

'It's this chap Wilmot again,' said Septimus. 'Wilmot conducted the marriage of George and Hannah and presumably this Olive Wilmot was related to him. Perhaps she was his daughter?'

'Look at the other side.'

Quayle, wreathed in cigar smoke, couldn't contain his triumph. Septimus turned the papers over and sifted through what he had first read in the taxi yesterday: the certification by Wilmot of the marriage between Hannah and George, Prince of Wales and that two sons and a daughter were the issue of the marriage.

'Good God, this must have upset the apple cart at the hearing.'

'That's putting it mildly.' Hargeaves took a swig of beer and wiped his mouth before going on. 'The hearing was before the Lord Chief Justice, the Lord Chief Baron, the Judge Ordinary, and the Attorney General responded in person with the Solicitor General and two Queen's Counsels. Mrs Ryves was represented by a junior barrister – a chap called Smith – and his assistant, who remains nameless.'

At this minor digression Quayle snorted with impatience and Hargeaves quickened his pace.

'The Lord Chief Justice informed Mrs Ryves that she would never inherit the legacy because even if she proved that her grandmother had married the Duke of Cumberland, this had not been authorised under the Royal Marriages Act, which was hardly fair, because the act came into force in 1772, presumably to prevent any further irresponsible marriages in the first place. And we can include George III's own secret marriage in that.

'It certainly frightened the judges. The Attorney General believed Mrs Ryves's case amounted to no less than a claim to the throne and he boasted that he would demonstrate that this fraudulent fabrication would be exposed. However, it didn't start too well when the handwriting expert, a Mr Frederick Nethercroft, declared the documents genuine. The Lord Chief Justice declared them to be "rubbishy bits of paper" and "gross and rank forgeries." Nethercroft, however, stuck to his guns. He compared Wilmot's signatures in the registers of Trinity College, Oxford with those on the marriage certificates and declared them a match. He also attested that the signatures of George III were genuine. But the Lord Chief Justice was equally determined to ensure these signatures were recorded as forgeries.

'This was reinforced by the Attorney General, who was interrupted by the foreman, who said the jury were all agreed that the documents were forgeries. Smith then pointed out that the entire proceedings were prejudiced from the start because the Attorney General had made it appear as if Mrs Ryves was making a claim to the throne, which she most assuredly was not. Smith's address to the jury was interrupted by both the Lord Chief Justice and the Attorney General. The authorities were so desperate to conceal the marriage of George III to Hannah Lightfoot that they had to brutally crush Mrs Ryves's case, even though it was sound enough.'

Quayle drained his glass.

'She never stood a chance against those blackguards.'

Septimus, who had listened intently throughout Hargeaves's exposition of the trial, asked, 'What happened next?'

'Well, that's the funny thing. The Court ordered that all the documents be impounded. Why do that, if they were such obvious forgeries, written on "rubbishy bits of paper"? Why not return them to Mrs Ryves or insist they were destroyed?'

'Because they were genuine.'

As he said it, Septimus felt a shiver run through his spine. The secret marriage between a youthful prince and an unknown girl reached out to him from the past, ready to take hold of him. The cover-ups, the pay-offs and the injustices from 1759 to the present day, when murder had been committed in a quiet Oxford lane, demanded answers.

'Because they were genuine,' Hargeaves repeated. 'And that was the opinion of the time. The previous Lord Chief Justice, Sir John Bayley, was heard by his daughter to comment that the Lavinia Ryves claim was just and fair. His daughter had been acquainted with Mrs Ryves for ten years. And, when the *Morning Post* ran a series of articles investigating Mrs Ryves's claim, and that of her mother, Mrs Serres, it concluded that there existed a case of grievous and flagrant wrong. This was only three years after the break-in at Kew. The newspaper seemed to have examined a great deal of documentary evidence in its investigation.'

'What happened to Mrs Ryves?'

'It's rather sad, really. Her appeal was dismissed and she died three years later. Her grandmother, Olive Wilmot, had been spirited away back in the late eighteenth century, but her daughter and granddaughter fought to have their royal connection recognised without success.'

'And the secret marriage of George and Hannah rippled across the royal lake until it vanished with the Ryves case,' said Quayle.

'And now it has resurfaced,' said Septimus. 'But these legal cases and claims are all within living memory –' he broke off, thinking about Gooch in Chancery Lane. What did he know? Had his expressions of surprise been entirely genuine, or had he managed to manufacture his look of sympathy whilst concealing deeper knowledge as to the whereabouts of Septimus's requests. If so, who was Gooch answering to, if not the honesty and search for truth his profession demanded.

'Oh, we all knew about it at Windsor,' said Hargeaves. 'I had to call in one or two favours to obtain the documents but it's common knowledge – or an open secret, I should say – amongst archivists. The King – Edward, that is, not our current sovereign – came to have a look at them years ago and he thought Olive and Lavinia had been hard done by. Also covered up in the trial was the fact that, in the 1830s, the Duke of Kent was sending four hundred pounds a year to Mrs Ryves. These payments continued for decades, sanctioned by his daughter, Queen Victoria. There was never any credence lent to the marriage certificates, so the monarchy didn't feel threatened.'

Until now, thought Septimus.

'So who stole the parish records from Kew?' he asked.

'Could have been anybody – members of the royal court, journalists working for the *Morning Post,* people employed by Mrs Ryves – any one of a number of people. Once the King had passed away and, more importantly, once George Rex was dead, it was open season.'

'But how did people know that George Rex had died if he was supposed to have vanished into obscurity?' asked Quayle.

'Perhaps he didn't vanish into obscurity,' said Septimus. 'After all, the memoir is clearly unfinished.'

'You mean there's more?'

This time Hargeaves was the one visibly excited.

'I don't see why not. I imagine you've had time to read it today . . .'

Hargeaves nodded.

'. . . so you'll agree with me that it obviously doesn't conclude with the death of Meadows. And we assume that the rest of the memoir will tell us what happened to Rex and whether he married . . .'

'. . . and whether or not he had children . . .'

'. . . who would have been the true heirs of George III.'

Septimus lit a cigarette in the silence that followed. Quayle folded his arms and shook his head slowly.

'The circumstantial evidence for the authenticity of the memoir is seemingly overwhelming. Set alongside the marriage certificates it could prove devastating. But we need internal proof.'

'We need the rest of the memoir,' said Hargeaves.

'Wherever it is,' said Septimus, watching the smoke from his cigarette curl upwards. He picked up his glass and gestured towards Hargeaves. 'Your round, I believe, Mr Hargeaves?'

'Telephone for Mr Oates!'

The barman's voice cut across the conversation in the busy pub. Septimus looked at Quayle.

'Who knows I'm here?'

Quayle shrugged, but spoke warily, and looked around the bar as he did so: 'I know not.'

Septimus caught the doubt in Quayle's voice and walked to the bar with a sense of unease. An intruder had broken into Spurlings that morning. Hargeaves now knew all about the documents and the memoir – although he had proved very informative – and the entire pub was aware of Septimus's whereabouts. He took the telephone from the barman before he could bellow his name again and spoke loudly into the telephone, hoping his nerves wouldn't betray him.

'This is Septimus Oates.'

The voice was difficult to distinguish above the hubbub of the bar, but Septimus followed the clipped public-school accent well enough.

'Mr Oates, you have something which belongs to us. A memoir. We suggest it will be to your benefit if you were to return it to us.'

There was real menace in the caller's tone but Septimus wasn't going to surrender to threats just yet.

'Who are you? Did you break into Quayle's house this morning?'

'That is of no consequence. Just meet us and we can come to some agreement.'

'Why should I?' Septimus sensed hesitation at the other end of the telephone and suspected his defiance was working.

'Let me see. You're in the Wykeham Arms at the moment. You've been sitting with your friends Quayle and Hargeaves.'

'How do you . . .?' Septimus's confidence deflated in an instant. They'd been under surveillance the whole time. He forced himself to turn round slowly and scan the pub. There were at least thirty people standing at the bar and sitting in the alcoves, chatting, smoking and drinking. Who had been watching them? It could be anyone. The voice on the telephone grew hard and businesslike.

'Guthrum 878.'

'What do you mean?'

'Meet me there. I repeat: Guthrum 878. You're an historian. Work it out. I'll give you five minutes. And come alone.'

❖   ❖   ❖

'Don't be a fool.'

Quayle glared at Septimus from behind the empty beer glasses.

'What else do you suggest? I've got five minutes – and counting.'

Septimus knew his reckless bravado came from the beers he'd consumed. But there was also a reckless energy coursing through him. The day's discoveries had merely served to reinforce the negatives. Maybe now he had a chance to discover something more tangible.

'Don't go,' Quayle hissed, casting a sideways glance at Hargeaves. 'After what happened in Oxford yesterday, you'll be tempting fate!'

Quayle was more animated than Septimus had ever seen him,

suddenly alive to the threat the memoir posed. Hargeaves said nothing, staring dolefully into his glass as if unable to comprehend the living consequences of the documents. It was this, and something Battiscombe had said to him when he embarked on his thesis four years ago, which made up Septimus's mind: history was about people, not things. If you spent your life in the archives you tended to lose track of the fact that documents were only the records, and not the deeds, of people. Hargeaves and his sort could stick with things; Septimus was interested in people.

Dangerous or not.

'I'm not taking the memoir,' he said. 'It's safe in the vaults of the school archive, so what can they do to me? Nothing. If I'm not back in half an hour then send out a search party.'

❖   ❖   ❖

College Street was in total darkness when Septimus stepped out of the Wykeham Arms. The cathedral bell struck as he set off down the street. He walked past the alleyway that led to Quayle's house, and along past the College Porters' lodge. It was quiet, and when he glanced back over his shoulder towards the pub, he couldn't see anyone. Perhaps the stranger on the telephone hadn't come into the pub but he'd obviously seen Septimus with Quayle and Hargeaves at some point during the course of the evening.

Guthrum 878.

That was easy for any self-respecting historian in Winchester to work out. The walk would take a very brisk five minutes because the route Septimus had chosen took him down College Street, along College Walk, round Wharf Hill and Chesil Street before coming into the end of the Broadway. He was buoyed up with a greater sense of purpose than he had felt all day. It made sense that there was more. The person or persons who had broken into

Spurlings wanted to communicate, not to injure. It was a calculated gamble and it was all he could do to persuade his old friend from following him or calling out the police. Quayle would just have to be content with knowing where he was going.

At the end of Chesil Street, Septimus lit a cigarette. It was a good opportunity to pause and catch his breath. The evening was balmy but he was glad of his jacket, though his feet were sore after the day's activities in and around London.

Guthrum 878. In the centre of The Broadway, at the bottom of the hill which ran up through the town centre, was the statue of King Alfred the Great, ninth-century saviour of Wessex and progenitor of the ancient monarchy of the whole of England. Alfred had fought a guerrilla campaign against overwhelming Viking invasions led by Guthrum, finally securing a decisive victory at Wedmore in 878. Septimus approached the statue but couldn't see anyone. The street lamps cast enough light for him to ascertain that there was nobody loitering. Perhaps Quayle's instincts had been right. He was regretting rushing out of the pub.

Then a large motor car, hood down, roared through the square, swerving to avoid a group of men spilling out of a nearby pub, and braked suddenly.

'Get in.'

It was the same clipped accent he had heard on the telephone. Septimus opened the door of the car – a Rolls Royce – and sank into the seat. The car accelerated around the statue and up Magdalen Hill.

'Where you taking me?' Septimus shouted above the scream of the engine and the rush of air.

The driver shook his head. He was about Septimus's age, wearing a leather coat with the collar turned up, his gloved hands gripping the wheel with a grim determination that invited no conversation. Septimus resolved to hang on as the Rolls roared up

St Catherine's Hill now at top speed before turning abruptly into the park, where they came to a bumpy halt on the grass.

'Smoke?'

After he'd switched off the engine, the driver's voice sounded unnaturally loud. The park was in darkness, and the Cathedral below them shimmered like a ship at sea. The gas-lit street lamps flickered dimly, the occasional motor car headlamps momentarily illuminating a shopfront or a public house. Voices drifted up from the town. It was a familiar sound. Septimus had often come up here to read and to escape the tedium of school life. Then, it was a place of sanctuary, but now, with this menacing stranger sat beside him, his old refuge seemed to have trapped him.

'No thanks. I have my own.'

As Septimus lit his cigarette the driver took out a crumpled packet and knocked one into his hand.

'Before we start, I owe you an explanation. I had nothing to do with the murder in Oxford. But I did break into your friend's house this morning. I mean you no harm. Quite the opposite. I needed to ascertain whether you still had the memoir.'

'How do you know who I am and what happened in Oxford?'

'Hahn worked for us,' the young man continued, ignoring the question. 'His task was to give you the memoir and the documents. We knew he was being tailed, but his murder caught us by surprise. It was horrific, but we have to move on. War has its casualties.'

'War?' Septimus asked. 'What sort of war is this?'

'A war for the truth, Mr Oates. That is what it is. It's a war for the truth, to vindicate long-dead people. And to vanquish present untruths.'

Septimus studied the fellow more closely: dark hair oiled back across his forehead, a firm jaw and startling green eyes, white teeth gleaming in the dark. A ladies' man for sure – reminiscent of the young bloods at Oxford – but something told him that despite the polished English accent, the stranger was not British. And the steel in his voice suggested a certain ruthlessness.

'Who killed Hahn?' he asked.

'We don't know. There are many who would kill to get their hands on such documents – anarchists, Bolsheviks, royalists, secret services acting for the state, perhaps even the press – take your pick. As you are aware, this is a revelation that could shake the monarchy to its very core – or worse, much worse.'

'Why should I continue to be involved in this if my life's in danger? As you rightly say, the political consequences for a public exposure would be unthinkable.'

'*Thinkable,*' the young man corrected him. 'You will have to move beyond the theory which dominates your line of work. You left that behind the moment you agreed to meet Hahn yesterday. There are many potential consequences for such a public exposure. The fall of the Establishment, a new monarchy . . . a revolution even.'

Septimus let the words hang in the air with the cigarette smoke drifting from the car. Yes, it was thinkable. The old monarchies of Europe were not popular. Assassins and revolutionaries proliferated in London, Paris and Vienna. King Edward VII realised this and tried to link arms with republican France with the Entente Cordiale and had damned the Kaiser as Satan, but he hadn't lived long enough, and his son was a rigid martinet of the old tradition, the very image of his cousin the Tsar. George, Nicholas and Wilhelm, the triumvirate of Europe – but for how much longer?

'We have a proposal for you,' his companion broke into his thoughts. 'Something you might be willing to accept given your – how shall I put it – somewhat straitened circumstances.'

'What sort of offer? Research?' Septimus bridled at the mention of his circumstances, but let it pass.

'Oh yes. You're the expert Hahn was seeking. And there'll be money. A great deal.'

'Do you believe I can be so easily manipulated?' Septimus finished his cigarette and hastily opened the door, anger bubbling inside his chest. He'd had enough of this. Quayle was right, after all. He was being drawn inexorably into a dangerous situation and had to get out of the car before it was too late. 'Who the hell do you think you are?'

Smoke drifted across the open cab of the car. The young man smiled graciously.

'I'm Charles Rex, the great-grandson of George Rex. We need you to locate the missing section of the memoir and restore the good name of my great-grandfather. A grave dishonour has been done and you're the man to rectify it.'

Quayle listened in stony silence. When Septimus had finished, he took a long sup from his pint, put the glass down carefully on the table and declared:

'I think you're mad. Barking. This is completely and utterly insane. It puts me in mind of the Tichborne Claimant. This Rex boy is nothing more than an imposter. He says he wants you to go to Prague?'

'To meet his father, William Rex.'

'Ludicrous!'

'I think Oates should go,' Hargeaves said, immediately putting his hand to his mouth as if to catch the words.

'Do you?' asked Septimus, relieved to have found an ally, unlikely though Hargeaves seemed in such a role.

'Yes, I think you should. This is a chance in a million. It simply doesn't happen in libraries or archives . . .'

'You'll be saying next you want to go with Septimus on this . . . this . . . wild goose chase,' snapped Quayle.

'Well . . .'

Hargeaves looked into the bottom of his glass and for an awful moment – pleased though he was to have the support – Septimus wondered whether he was going to reply in the affirmative. Visions of trailing across Prague with Hargeaves popped into his mind, and this wasn't exactly what he had planned after his discussions with Charles Rex.

'I'm not up to coming to Prague with you, Oates, but if I can help you get there and get to the bottom of this little mystery, then it's the least I can do.'

Septimus pulled a folded envelope from his pocket, quelling the over enthusiastic Hargeaves, touching though his pledges of support were.

'I have here a passport and money – lots of it – to get me to Prague and back. I have instructions about where and when to go, even down to an appointment at a tailor's in Jermyn Street who will kit me out for the journey. There is no need to return to Oxford. Thank you for your kind offer, Hargeaves, but I believe I must make my own way.'

And that said, even Quayle had the grace to look down into his half-empty glass, without further comment.

The instructions were detailed down to the last minute. After the uncertainty of the previous day, Septimus was only too glad to have something to do which left nothing to chance.

The following day, after lunch with Quayle (whose last words 'You're insane, Septimus, don't do it!' continued to ring in his ears throughout the day), he caught a mid-afternoon train to Waterloo, sitting in the first-class compartment that had been reserved for him. As the journey unfolded, the lengths to which Rex had gone to ensure smooth passage soon demonstrated how confident he had been that Septimus would take him up on the offer. A taxi took him across London to a discreet and

103

exclusive tailor on Jermyn Street. Here, three tailors attended to Septimus, measuring him for suits, boots and shoes in a rapid and unobtrusive style that only tailors of that ilk can muster. Septimus chose five shirts, collars and three silk ties, and while he waited for the suits to be adjusted to his fitting, was escorted to the barber's shop for a shave, where fresh coffee and a selection of newspapers were available. On his return – there must have been half a dozen assistant tailors working on the adjustments in that hour – he found his new wardrobe was already packed for him in a large leather suitcase, and that there was nothing to pay, only a slip of paper to sign. Dressed in his new clothes he felt like a different man from the one who had been ruthlessly chased through Oxford by a callous assassin. Another taxi then took him to the East India Club, where he dined on beef Wellington washed down with a bottle of claret, all at Rex's expense.

The instructions then set out the journey to Prague. He was to remain at the club for the night and board the nine o'clock departure the next morning from Charing Cross to Calais-Maritime and from there take the through train across Germany to Prague. Tickets, seats, sleeping compartments and meals had all been arranged. It was suspiciously easy, but, for the moment, Septimus was prepared to deflect his thoughts from the payment which surely would be demanded at some point and allow himself to indulge in the moment.

After lunch on Monday, he duly changed at Calais for the through train, where he was shown to his seat and informed about the dinner arrangements and his sleeping compartment. It was a luxury Septimus was unaccustomed to, and one his parents could not have afforded. Although many of his peers at Winchester were familiar with travelling in style, routinely going to the glamorous Riviera in southern France and even to the United States, Septimus was an impoverished scholar whose fees were fully discounted.

Family holidays were normally taken in Brighton or similar south coast resorts suited to the lower middle classes. Which was why the deaths of his parents in Belgrade eleven years ago were so tragic. It was to have been a trip to remember combining a holiday, so well deserved, with business.

The memory of his parents' horrifying death in the Balkans framed in Septimus's mind something of a common purpose as he began his own journey east. He was heading into the dark past of Hanoverian royalty, and was about to expose an ancient secret with explosive implications for the present, brought into focus by the murder he had witnessed yesterday. Maybe this quest was a means of laying to rest the ghosts of his own parents, a purpose he now knew had lain dormant within him all these years at Oxford.

It was night when the train pulled into Cologne. All the dinner settings had been cleared and the dining car was quiet. Splendidly attired in his new dinner suit, Septimus remained at his table, smoking a cigar. There was, he thought, some satisfaction to be gained from his situation. Was he a hunted man or not? Nobody had pursued him to Winchester. The newspapers hadn't reported the fatal shooting in Oxford. The best he could do was to investigate the mystery of George Rex's memoir and report to the police when he had identified the killer and prove to Inspector Coppard that he hadn't invented the whole story after a long luncheon. He was convinced the identity of Hahn's murderer must lie in the Rex memoir. Going to Prague would set him on his way to solving the mystery, despite Quayle's reservations. His old friend was too cautious. It was for Septimus to seize the initiative. After all, it was he, not Quayle, who had witnessed the killing.

He finished his cigar and returned to his compartment. Outside, the rain hissed on the platform as the porters and station staff scurried back and forth preparing the train for its onward journey across Europe. Secure in his privileged sleeping berth,

Septimus prepared for bed, marvelling at the silk nightgown and elegant slippers the London tailors had provided. It had been a long day's travelling. He extinguished the lights and was asleep in seconds.

❖   ❖   ❖

He was woken on Tuesday morning by a discreet knock and the aroma of fresh coffee and pastries.

'We'll be in Leipzig soon,' the attendant informed him with impeccable English. Septimus grappled for his watch. Almost eight o'clock. He'd slept for nine hours, cushioned by the rhythm of the train, locked in his own small world far from assassins and any wretched historical documents. He slurped his coffee and drew the curtain open to reveal the German countryside flashing by. He was in the old Holy Roman Empire, once upon a time Habsburg territory; and the kingdom of Hanover too, ruled by George III, was part of this new Germany he found himself in.

Washed, shaved and breakfasted in comfort and privacy, Septimus ventured to the dining car to read the morning papers as the train continued on to Dresden. An attendant informed him they would reach Dresden in time for him to make the connection for Prague, and that the connecting train would have a restaurant car where he would be able to take luncheon. Some people travel like this all the time, Septimus thought, as he selected the schnitzel and a bottle of mosel from the menu.

The train arrived without incident at Franz Josef Station in Prague later that afternoon. Whilst his luggage was deposited at his feet by the porters, Septimus opened the next set of instructions. Trams bustled by, motor cars rumbled along, braking and hooting, filling the busy street with noise. Imperial police dressed in Habsburg uniforms strolled past, occasionally stopping people to check their identity papers, a reminder to Septimus that he was in an empire where the web of bureaucracy reached far and wide and entangled all who were exposed to it, a web spun by the ageing Emperor Franz Josef himself, incumbent for sixty-six years. Nobody, it seemed, did anything in his empire without his police knowing. Septimus had no more time to concern himself about what to do next or whether the police would eventually target him because two men, one rather large, both dressed in white suits and sporting large fedoras, approached him not long after he exited the station building.

'Mr Oates?' said the smaller of the two, a broad smile on his face. He had a pencil-thin moustache and had removed his hat to reveal black hair oiled back in sleek long lines. Septimus noted that his eyes were smiling too, and decided he could trust this man.

'That is I.'

'Mr Rex sends his compliments,' said his companion, speaking strongly accented English. He did not smile. 'I am Marek and this is Pavel. There is a car for you, to convey you to your lodgings this evening.' He indicated a white Daimler across the street.

'What about Mr Rex? Where I am to meet him?'

'It is all arranged.' This came from Pavel, the more gregarious of the two. 'You're to dine with Mr Rex tonight. But first, allow us to escort you to your hotel.'

Septimus crossed the road and got in the car. The Daimler raced away from the railway station, driven expertly by Pavel, weaving through the narrow streets, past the trams and crowds, then crossing the Vltava, before turning off the main road and entering a side street.

'*Mala Strana*,' he said, by way of explanation. '"The Little Town". We are under the shadow of the great castle and cathedral of Prague.'

The Daimler rolled up a cobbled street, lined with elegant *fin de siècle* town houses commanding stunning views across to Prague. High above them towered St Vitus' Cathedral.

The car stopped outside a small hotel – not at all a grand place but one that exuded a quiet air of quality nevertheless – bearing the name *U Zlateho Stromu*. Three porters approached and removed his luggage and, before Septimus could thank his companions, the boot had been slammed shut and the car departed at full speed. Septimus tore his gaze away from the speeding Daimler. No doubt Rex would be informed in double quick time of his guest's safe arrival in Prague now.

'Pleased to make your acquaintance,' a tall, sleek man in immaculate pinstripe was saying. 'My name is Bruno. I am the manager of The Golden Tree. If you need anything then you must ask for me direct, not anyone else. We hope your stay here will be an enjoyable one.'

Septimus allowed himself to be escorted to his room, which turned out to be an elegant suite with windows opening to the front and views across the whole of Prague from the balcony. A bottle of Veuve Clicquot nestled in a bucket of ice. He stretched out on the large bed and yawned. Despite the previous night's sleep he was exhausted. Time for a nap, perhaps, though it would be good to take a walk.

Hearing a knock at the door, Septimus rose from the bed. It was probably the chambermaid.

But it was Charles Rex who walked into the room, clothed in a linen suit and panama hat and brandishing a Malacca cane.

'News travels fast around here.'

Septimus sounded more confident than he felt; how had Charles managed to get here so soon after seeing him in Winchester? He must have left England almost immediately after their encounter, presumably catching the dawn boat train.

'I see you've made yourself at home.' Charles ignored the sarcastic tone, accepting the glass of champagne offered and taking a chair. 'To your very good health.'

'Yours, too.'

Septimus sat down too and sipped from the glass. Who was this William Rex who could arrange passports, papers and tickets across Europe at a moment's notice, open up the best tailors in London on a Sunday and provide all the trappings of luxury with it? Septimus sensed Charles was more at ease here on his home turf than he had been in Winchester, where he had been tense and brusque, perhaps even resentful at having to deliver the message from his father. Was he afraid of failure, perhaps? Now Septimus had been hooked, Charles had him where he wanted him, and he could relax.

'You had a good journey, I trust?'

Septimus nodded. 'The train from Calais to Dresden was quite wonderful, something I have not experienced before.'

'You enjoyed the oysters at dinner?' Charles chuckled at Septimus's shocked expression. 'Yes, and the steak en croûte to follow, washed down with the finest St Émilion. A 1900 Château Cheval Blanc, if I am not very much mistaken. My father is looking after you well. He must have known that an Oxford man would enjoy the finer things life has to offer.'

'So you have the receipts for my journey.'

Septimus should have guessed how closely Rex was watching him.

'Oh, more than that.'

Charles smiled a genuine smile of amusement this time, as the truth finally dawned on Septimus.

'You were on the train?'

'We had to ensure you would travel all the way to Prague,' Charles explained, almost sheepish now that his moment of triumph was revealed. 'You might have changed your mind at any number of stops – Calais, Leipzig, Dresden – en route.'

'Why didn't you join me?' Septimus fought to quell the anger rising in him. 'We could have dined together.'

'I thought you might prefer to journey alone. I took supper in my compartment. I'm reading an excellent book at the moment. *The Riddle of the Sands*. Do you know of it?'

'Yes, I know it. I read it when I was a boy. It's an impressive conspiracy story and a good many people think it's for real.'

'Yes, you English, you're obsessed with mysteries. Look at Sherlock Holmes with his silly violin and opium habit. It's all so amateurish; you don't know what it is to live in a real secret state. The Emperor's spies are everywhere.'

'Your accent is very English,' Septimus observed. 'We can't be that bad.'

He surmised that Charles had the accent of a public-school-educated foreigner. At Winchester, Septimus had met similar characters who tried just a bit too hard to fit in.

'I was at Eton,' Charles said. 'My father wanted the very best for me. You will discover, however, that there's more to my family than this. My father believed it appropriate for me to be schooled in the shadow of Windsor Castle, where George Rex himself attended. It was of course George III's favourite school. You know they still celebrate his birthday there, on the Fourth of June?'

'Yes, I know.'

Charles seemed to bear no rancour to his ancestor who had cast off his first wife and children, and none to the present occupants of Windsor Castle.

'Presumably your family has lived in Prague since your great-grandfather George Rex settled here?' asked Septimus.

Charles smiled.

'More or less. But you'll hear the full story when you meet

my father this evening.' He finished his drink and got up from the chair, brushing an imaginary speck of dust from his suit. 'He's expecting you to dine with him tonight. The chauffeur will collect you at eight o'clock.'

Septimus got up from his chair.

'I have a prior engagement at the university this evening, so I won't be with you on this occasion,' Charles said. 'I am attending a political seminar at the faculty where I study. However, I'm sure you'll find dinner with my father an illuminating experience. And I look forward to seeing the fruits of your research in due course.'

As his visitor strolled from the room without a backward glance, Septimus felt a pang of pity for him. For all the debonair appearance, Charles Rex was a young man in search of an identity. Revenge was not quite the word Septimus would have used – that would come later – no, catharsis was the word which came to mind. Septimus would soon discover how wrong he was.

After his visitor had left, Septimus took a short walk through the centre of the city. It was good to take in the air as he crossed the Charles Bridge and looked down at the Vltava River, snaking its way around the bend under the castle and cathedral. He wandered on into Old Town Square and paused to watch the crowd of tourists waiting for the six-hundred-year-old clock to strike the hour. This fascinating, antiquated event drew people in their hundreds. Septimus didn't linger, instead carrying on through the narrow cobbled streets, to the Theatre of the Estates – where Mozart had premiered *Don Giovanni* – and bought himself a beer in one of the quiet bars nearby. Sitting there with a glass of *budva* and smoking a cigarette, he felt the history of the place envelop him. Here he was, nowhere near a library and yet he felt closer to the past than ever before. Could he go back to burying himself in archives after this? To have met a descendant of George Rex, and to have discovered proof of a secret marriage, was more potent than anything he had encountered in all his years of research. It was a story greater than all the others, and one that could make him famous. Was that what he was seeking however? Fame and fortune? Didn't historians wish for a quiet life – studying events long since concluded and the deeds of people dead for many centuries? Surely as an historian he had been actively seeking solitude and seclusion from the wider world for all these years?

Septimus finished his beer. No, maybe he didn't want a quiet life after all. Perhaps he had always sought to be noticed. It was only now that he realised it.

There was a message from Bruno waiting for him at reception when he returned, inviting him to be ready for dinner at eight. The Daimler arrived on time and Septimus, dressed in his new dinner suit, stepped inside. This time the driver remained silent and Septimus, aware that his journey was nearing its final stage, did not instigate conversation. The car crossed the Vltava River and entered the Stare Mesto district before parking outside a rather nondescript restaurant – *U Modré Kachničky* – the Blue Duckling. Wordlessly, the chauffeur opened the door and ushered his passenger inside.

The interior – low ceilings, heavy furniture and candlelit alcoves – was what Septimus supposed a typical Prague restaurant to be. He was led across the restaurant by the maitre d' and waved to a corner, where William Rex was waiting to greet him.

Rex was a little taller than his son and heavier set. To Septimus's trained eye, there was a distinct likeness to George III. The same fleshy cheeks, the eyes rather too close together, the protruding jaw. His long white hair was cut to below his ears, waved and set like a wig. Septimus put him in his late sixties. He had the bearing of a prince and the dignity of a monarch – or so Septimus led himself to believe.

'I am delighted to make your acquaintance at long last.' Rex had a firm handshake, a deep resonant voice and sparkling green eyes. Septimus warmed to him at once. 'Please do be seated.'

Champagne arrived.

'Here's to prosperity,' he said, raising his glass. 'And, as we say in Prague, *na zdraví!*'

'To good health,' Septimus responded, taking a cigarette from the box on the table. More Sobranies. These *mitteleuropeans* knew how to enjoy life.

Rex sat back in his chair and cast his guest an appraising look.

'It is a pleasure to have you here,' he said, in an unmarked English accent. 'I cannot apologise enough for Hahn's brutal senseless slaying. He was a loyal and faithful servant of mine for many years. We knew how hazardous it would be for him to break cover and seek you out, but he accepted the mission without reservation. You see, our every move is watched and once we had resolved to contact you, our enemies moved in. They want what we have but thank God Charles traced you to Winchester and you are now here. I am so very grateful to you for all the trouble you have been through.'

Reassured by Rex's gratitude, Septimus relaxed.

'Who are they, these people who want the memoir?'

'Our perennial enemies,' Rex grimaced, 'the Saxe-Coburg-Gothas. That is, the present family seated on the throne of Great Britain. They need the memoir so they can destroy it otherwise there is real proof of their illegal position on the throne. As you know, the memoir records that Hannah died long after the eldest children between George and Charlotte were born. They were, therefore, illegitimate.'

Rex said the word 'illegitimate' with relish, rolling it on his tongue like a fine wine.

'Are you suggesting that the British government is acting on behalf of the Royal Family to eliminate those who might uncover their secret?'

Rex shook his head and smiled.

'No, it is not the government. The Royal Family has its own means of action.'

All his instincts told Septimus this was nonsense, but the fact of Hahn's killing was incontrovertible. And Rex was correct about the date of Hannah's Last Will and Testament, which could now be fixed to 1784, rather than 1764, and the year of the second marriage between George and Charlotte. Hannah had lived too long for George III to cover the traces of his bigamy. Both his second marriage to Charlotte and the Royal Marriages Act failed to invalidate the secret union with Hannah.

'Surely the marriage certificates are proof of the illegitimacy of the royal family? And the case of Mrs Ryves?'

'Yes, there is all that, but the establishment has waved them away as forgeries, or a marriage that was not approved by Parliament and so on. There is no evidence that George and Hannah had any children – until now. The memoir says it all. It proves without doubt the existence of George Rex. It has been in my possession all my life, handed to me by my father on his deathbed and by his father on his deathbed, together with this ring.'

Rex took a gold ring from his little finger and passed it to his guest. Septimus recognised it as the ring given to Hannah by George III. It was overwhelming evidence of the honesty of the man seated opposite him – so much so, he felt his flesh crawl. This was real, living history. Nothing like this would be found in a library.

'There is something missing,' Rex was saying.

'The rest of the memoir?'

Rex nodded.

'Indeed. There is more to be located.'

The waiter arrived with the menus, but Rex waved them away.

'Trust me,' he said expansively as he ordered. 'I know what is good here. It is the very best Czech cuisine. No fuss. Just what you will like.'

He tasted the red wine and nodded to the waiter. When both their glasses were filled, Rex continued.

'George Rex was sent to southern Africa – where he would be as far away as possible from society – and was ordered never to marry and have children. The Establishment knew that any issue would be the legitimate heirs to the throne of Great Britain. He was paid off, and warned to disappear. But he didn't. Quite the opposite. The memoir is proof of his existence and perpetual threat to the British monarchy.'

'What became of the second part of the memoir?'

'It was stolen from my grandfather's house here in Prague in 1866.'

'But that's . . .'

'. . . just after the Ryves's hearing, yes. The Saxe-Coburgs-Gothas were battening down the hatches, impounding the evidence and denying any truths whatsoever. Mind you, we have no proof that the British establishment stole the memoir. Fortunately, the personal safety of my family was secure here in Prague, granted the full protection of the Habsburg Empire. But sadly, they mislaid the second part of the memoir.'

'Do you think it has been destroyed?'

The main course arrived, a simple but delicious dish of pork medallions, dumplings and a spicy sauce. The waiter refilled their glasses and after he had taken away the empty bottle, Rex said,

'No I do not. What is interesting is that so much of the evidence – the marriage certificates, the scraps of paper at Mrs Ryves's hearing and so on – was never destroyed. It is as if the Saxe-Coburgs-Gothas could not bring it upon themselves to do such a thing.'

'And you would like me to find the second part of the memoir?'

'Yes. Hahn was to have given you all the documents we have located and explain this to you. I was not intending to meet you in such circumstances, but here we are.' Rex pushed away his half-eaten meal, and leant across the table. 'My request to you is to find that memoir and return it to me. You already have the first part. You can make your name as an historian and you will prove to the world that the Saxe-Coburg-Gothas are impostors. It is I, William George Habsburg-Rex, who is the rightful king of England. But . . .' Rex smiled warmly, '. . . I make no claim whatsoever to the throne. What is gone is gone. My son has no wish to be king of England. We are rich and secure here. We just demand acknowledgement; that is all. It is inconceivable that the complicated legal system in Britain would lead to any official titles or change in the constitution. We do not seek that. As I say, we just want recognition.'

Septimus cleared his plate and took a swallow of wine. That William Rex was determined could not be doubted. So far, the first part of the memoir and the documents relating to the marriage seemed genuine enough, although tests would have to be carried out on the paper and ink. George's duel with Meadows clearly wasn't the end of the memoir. The contents of the second part promised to be explosive.

'I will pay you for your expert services, of course,' said Rex. 'Three thousand pounds now and another three when you have located the memoir. All expenses paid. Enjoy life while you can. You can draw the funds from Coutts tomorrow morning.'

Like his son Charles, William Rex was confident Septimus would take up the offer. There was nothing to contradict the unassailable fact that six thousand pounds was more money than he would earn in fifteen years as a don at Oxford. It was a small fortune.

'I should make one thing clear, however,' he added, fixing his

117

companion with a bleak stare.

'What's that?' Septimus lowered his glass.

The look from Rex was completely at odds with his earlier gregariousness.

'It will be dangerous. Not just for you but for those close to you. Whoever murdered Hahn will not hesitate to remove you if they consider you to be an obstacle in their path.'

It was too late for warnings. Septimus didn't hesitate before saying: 'I accept.'

'You will not regret it.' Rex's eyes twinkled. 'Ah, here is dessert. A delicious honey cake which we call *medovnik*. I think we'll finish with some champagne.'

Rex had booked Septimus on the early Wednesday morning train from Franz Josef Station, thereby allowing him time for a good breakfast but little else. The expectation was that he would return to England as soon as possible and begin his search for the missing memoir. Pavel and Marek had even escorted Septimus from the hotel foyer onto the train, the former slipping a brown envelope into his jacket pocket as he boarded. So be it, thought Septimus, as the train accelerated away from Prague at a cracking pace, almost as if Rex had tipped the driver to put on the speed. It wouldn't be too much for Rex to engineer that, given his masterly control of the past forty-eight hours. Septimus steeled himself not to open Pavel's envelope until the train was well on its way out of the city. Inside was a cheque for three thousand pounds and a letter from his new benefactor which read:

My dear Septimus,

I am certain that you will not fail me in your quest to find the memoir and show the world what an injustice was served to my grandfather. You must surely know that History is not an exact science, rather a story, and there is such a remarkable tale to be published here. Indeed, with your association, you need never fear for a position in the ancient universities. There will be publishing houses who will want the rights and serialisation in the Press. The world will be your oyster and I am happy to allow you the credit for your findings.

Good luck!

Yours,

William Rex

Attached to the foot of the letter was the telephone number for the East India Club that Septimus was to use once he had located the memoir.

Publishing houses and a position in the ancient universities, Rex had written. Septimus returned to this observation on several occasions during his journey to Calais, where he arrived in time to catch the last boat train to London. That was the undeniable attraction: a chance to make his name and very possibly a considerable sum of money. But what of the dangers? Hahn had lost his life in pursuit of the memoir, proving it contained lethal information. And revealing the secrets of the established monarchy might outweigh the benefits from any appointment to an Oxford Fellowship. Could it even be construed as treason? More importantly, what would Quayle make of his implicit acceptance of Rex's offer and of the very real Coutts' cheque burning a hole in his newly tailored suit?

Quayle was deeply sceptical about the whole business.

'Ridiculous,' he sneered dismissively, over breakfast in the garden at Spurlings the Friday after Septimus's return from Prague. 'It'll be like finding a needle in a haystack.'

'We'll have to take it one step at a time,' Septimus retorted, stung by the schoolmaster's vehemence. 'Rex hasn't insisted I meet any deadlines.'

Quayle peered at him over his spectacles.

'And you believe this William Rex is genuine? He's certainly a man of means, judging by the comforts of your journey.'

'I do think he is authentic.' Septimus didn't treat Quayle's query lightly. There was no doubt in his mind but he wanted his old friend to trust him and to help him in the search for the second part of the memoir. 'And so would you if you met him. He is quite charming and, I believe, harmless.'

'But the memoir isn't harmless, is it? Quite the opposite, as we well know.'

'I've agreed to accept the task, Quayle. I'll take the risks.'

Quayle snorted and Septimus thought he might be about to launch into one of the tales from his time with Kitchener in the Sudan – tall tales which had kept them enthralled in the schoolroom – but now was not the time.

'We've established the marriage certificates have a strong claim to authenticity, haven't we?' he said. 'The memoir appears to be genuine. The missing documents at both Chancery Lane and Somerset House confirm that.'

'You'd be wise to stay away from Oxford, however,' Quayle observed, lighting a cigar.

'There are plenty of other places to start looking. I'll revisit Chancery Lane to see what else there is, but I think the search needs to go in another direction.'

'Such as?'

'On the train from Prague I drew up a list of locations George Rex mentions. They may provide some clues. There's Bruton – Rex's childhood home where Hannah lived until her death – Eton, Christ's and Middle Temple.'

Quayle chewed his lip.

'Eton's easily done. I'll cable my old chum Cornelius Pothecary, who's a science master there. We left the regiment at the same time. He'll check the attendance registers.'

'I can check the records at Christ's.'

'I don't think you should return to Oxford just yet. I'll go up and take the memoir with me so Battiscombe can examine it.'

'That's a good idea.'

Septimus was relieved to have the burden off his shoulders. Perhaps Battiscombe could find all the solutions and he could return to Oxford and carry on just as before. But just as the thought crossed his mind, he realised that life could never carry on as before.

'That leaves the Inns of Court records, but it's just a simple list,' Quayle continued. 'Bruton, on the other hand, might hold the key. Can't say I've ever heard of it before now. Doesn't the memoir say it's in Somerset? You should go there and see what you can sniff out.'

❖   ❖   ❖

Early on Saturday morning, Septimus took the train to Basingstoke, where he caught a connecting train to Bruton and there go to the heart of the mystery of the Quaker's daughter. Something had to yield from Bruton. Septimus's visit to the Middle Temple the previous afternoon confirmed the existence of a 'George Rex' in the registers for 1780–1 and Quayle had found him in the matriculation list at Christ's. Pothecary had cabled from Eton in the evening to confirm that a boy named George Rex had attended Eton from the autumn of 1772 but none of this pointed towards the concluding part of the memoir.

❖   ❖   ❖

The pleasant and quaint market town of Bruton consisted of two main streets of stone cottages divided by the river and meadows in the centre, which formed the location for the King's School, a small foundation built on the site of the former abbey in the sixteenth century. Apart from King's, whose pupils spilled out across the town in their various boarding houses, life in the town was almost in a state of genteel decay. The town had benefited from the prosperity of the wool trade, and by Septimus's reckoning Bruton in the eighteenth century must have been a well-to-do place, within a half-day's ride of the fashionable Bath and three days to London. This put Hannah and her children at a safe – but accessible – distance from the prying eyes of the court and the press. There was nothing in the memoir to suggest that George III had visited Hannah however. Had he managed to see his first love – indeed his only love – after she had been moved to Bruton?

Given that Hannah had spent the rest of her days in Bruton, Septimus assumed she was buried in the churchyard at St Mary's. It was possible that the church might have a memorial plaque in her name. It would be very satisfying to see that – a tangible piece of evidence to show she existed. Surely George Rex, if not the King himself, had paid for something?

Septimus wandered into the churchyard. It had turned out mild and breezy with no trace of rain – splendid weather for exploring. He spent a good half hour searching around the tombs, but the oldest were too weathered to read. The interior of the church was spectacular, and included a wonderfully preserved fifteenth-century roof. The abundance of tombs and memorial plaques raised Septimus's hopes. It was a well-kept church, too, smelling of polish and faint traces of perfume. On the Parish noticeboard, he spotted a boxed advert for the local museum. That would be worth a visit, after he'd had finished in the church.

Here, at last, there might be an inscription to Hannah Lightfoot. Septimus searched the church for an hour, meticulously reading every inscription on every wall and on the floor for a sign or mention of the mysterious Quaker's daughter. Every corner, every nook came under his scrutiny, the sunshine pouring through the stained glass windows and onto the mellow Somerset stone in a gentle bathe. As he searched behind some of the pews he sent flurries of dust particles spiralling into golden pillars of light. Willoughby, Keyte, Bassett, Dunning, Herkett and Kempthorne but no Lightfoot.

There was nothing. Hannah had seemingly left no trace of her life at St Mary's.

It was as if she had never existed.

❖　❖　❖

Septimus took a late luncheon in the one and only tearoom in the town and strolled down to the High Street. He poked his head into the entrance to the quadrangle that formed the Hospital founded by Hugh Sexey – a local boy made good and patron of numerous schools and almshouses in the area – and continued wandering along the street. What had the memoir said about the house Hannah and her children lived in? *Ours was the largest of all the houses on the High Street in Bruton, opposite Hugh Sexey's Hospital and School.* It was easily identifiable. The passage of time had blackened the lower walls, but the house remained a distinguished place of gentility.

And it was for sale.

There was a discreet sign in one of the front sash windows advertising this fact. Septimus couldn't believe his luck. He would be able to pose as a prospective buyer and have a look round. He noted the name of the solicitor – Clubb & Nisbet, a Bruton establishment – and wandered off along the High Street to find their office.

Clubb & Nisbet were situated at the very end of the street, the main door set three steps down from the street level and designed to accommodate very short people, judging by the unfeasibly low doorway. A bell on the door jangled, shattering the stuffy interior. Very little sunlight penetrated the room from the High Street, and it was dark enough for Septimus to have to wait a moment or two before his eyes adjusted to the gloom.

'Mr Clubb?' he enquired, noticing an elderly, diminutive figure seated at a desk.

Septimus's query met with a wry smile from the clerk.

'Only if he were to rise from his grave where he's been these past fifteen years.'

The clerk stepped out from the desk and Septimus noticed that he was not at all diminutive; indeed he was almost the same height as Septimus. He had been folded under the desk on a very low stool.

'Mr Obediah Nisbet, at your service, sir. Clearly you are not from these parts, for you would know of the demise of the late-lamented Archibald Clubb. And your accent is not local. How may I help you, sir?'

Septimus shook Nisbet's dry, wrinkled hand.

'My name is Septimus Oates and I would like to view the property on the High Street, please.'

'Allow me to fetch the keys. It is empty, you know.' Nisbet turned to his desk he said something which made Septimus' spine tingle. 'Hannah's house,' he muttered, opening the desk drawer and grasping a handful of keys that jangled so loudly Septimus was sure he had imagined those words.

'I beg your pardon? Did you say "Hannah's house"?'

Nisbet looked up sharply. 'No young man, I said nothing of

the sort.' Taking his hat from the peg, he added, 'If you would like to follow me, I think we can manage a viewing before I take my afternoon tea.'

❖   ❖   ❖

Obediah Nisbet set a swift pace along the High Street. Unperturbed by the June sunshine, he was dressed in a severe tail-coat fastened up to a black cravat. He could have been an undertaker. He paused only to acknowledge the many greetings he received as he and Septimus made their way along the street. Evidently Nisbet was well respected in the town. He would know the house well, then, who had lived there and maybe even before that. 'Hannah's house,' he had said, clear as a bell, before the rattle of the keys had obscured his musings.

'Has there been much interest?' Septimus asked breathlessly as they reached the front door after the brief but intensive march.

'One or two.'

Nisbet fished the keys out with a flourish and set to finding the front-door key.

'How long has the house been on the market?'

'A matter of months. It comes and it goes.'

Nisbet swung the door open forcefully. Septimus followed the solicitor into the house. Hannah's house. Nisbet took him on a perfunctory tour through the hallway, drawing room, dining room and kitchens. Septimus faced Nisbet at the foot of the sweeping stairway.

'You said it comes and goes. What do you mean by that? Presumably not many tenants remain here for any length of time?'

Nisbet shrugged, the lawyer's crisp certainties momentarily faltering.

'Who is the owner?' Septimus pressed.

126

'That I cannot tell you,' Nisbet snapped. 'Suffice to say the property has been in the same family for many, many years.'

Since the 1760s Septimus was tempted to say, but decided against forcing the matter, instead asking gently,

'Do you mind if I look round for a few moments?'

It was essential that he did so, for this was his reason for gaining access to the house – to see for himself whether the second part of the memoir had been hidden somewhere in the building.

'Yes, of course. I'll be down here if you need me.'

The absence of furniture and clutter made it easier to imagine how it might have looked when Hannah and her family lived here. It was Hannah's house. Of that, Septimus grew more certain as he walked through the rooms. There were graceful sash windows and high ceilings. Period fireplaces and features had all been preserved, or restored. There was the wide sweeping staircase from the top of which George had listened to his mother and Chatham as they discussed his future on that fateful visit in 1772 which had changed his life.

He is the King's eldest son and he will do what the King desires.

It was here, on this landing, where the young George had heard those fateful words uttered. Septimus tried to imagine it, how the boy had reacted; his world turned on its axis, giddy with shock. And Hannah? She was the unfortunate person at the centre of this tragic tale. Loved by the monarch but forgotten by history. Forced to live a life founded on deceit in a far-off market town well away from court gossip and the London scandal sheets. Given the rabid, relentless press which circulated around the doings of upper-class society the truth about George III and Hannah Lightfoot would have shattered the very foundations of the monarchy. But down here, disguised as a respectable widow of means, and unable to return the affections of local gentry or merchants, Hannah had been left to rot. Her love for the King had never faded; her ring and their marriage certificates had passed intact to George Rex and she had died in Bruton, perhaps still waiting for the King to come and present her to the world.

Leaving Nisbet in the hallway, Septimus climbed the stairs and peered into the bedrooms. Light flooded through the sash windows, illuminating the dust floating up from the wooden floors. He walked over to the window and looked onto the main street below. The view stretched right across the cottage rooftops to Hugh Sexey's Hospital, to King's and to the dovecote on the furthest hill on the other side of the town. There were so few cars in Bruton that he could almost imagine the rattle of coach wheels on the cobbles, and the shouts of ostlers. Was it here where Hannah had sat for so many days and years, waiting for the King to visit her, condemned to a lifetime of comfortable imprisonment, in this gilded cage?

An express train whistled loudly beyond the King's School cricket ground and the twentieth century careered back into the room. Septimus returned to the landing and was about to walk down the stairs when he caught sight of a small door in the corner. It was closed, unlike all the other doors, which were wide open. A narrow stairwell led up to another floor. He ducked through the doorway and climbed the stairs. There was no evidence of any cleaning or decoration here; the stairs were filthy with dust and grime and some of the steps were rotten. Septimus held the banister gingerly and kept going. At the top of the stairs he reached an attic room. Light filtered dimly through a small window, which was covered in cobwebs. The floor was strewn with debris: old toys, newspapers, broken furniture, all covered in dust. But as Septimus's eyes grew accustomed to the light, he realised the mess on the floor wasn't the result of decades of negligence. Scuff marks in the dust on the floor suggested the contents of the attic had been thoroughly searched, and quite recently, given the absence of dust on some of the objects. Septimus crouched and inspected the mess. There was nothing. No memoir.

But somebody had been here recently, searching through the attic. Had they found anything?

'Mr Oates?'

Nisbet's call from the lower depths of the house roused him from his reverie. Resisting the urge to wipe his hands on his trousers, Septimus took a last look at the dusty shadows in the room. He walked down the little stairwell carefully, and, closing the door behind him, returned to the landing. Nisbet was still standing in the hallway below. Septimus wondered how much longer the man's patience would last. He snatched a last glance at the bedrooms. The emptiness that had earlier conjured up images of Hannah and her children now seemed to mock him. Frustration seeped through him as he reached the foot of the stairs. Already the mystery of the attic room – and the disturbance on the floor – was fading fast in his mind.

There was nothing in this house but shadows from the past.

And only he could see them.

The town museum lay down one of the many side alleys off the High Street. Septimus picked his way along the cobbles along the alley and into a small yard. The door to the Museum was open but there was little sign of life.

'Hello?'

He stepped into the museum, which was in truth a one-room exhibition. It was a gloomy little place but he decided to have a look round. There was a large-scale papier mâché model of modern-day Bruton in a glass case and several smaller versions charting its development from the eleventh to the nineteenth centuries. There were posters and informative wall displays about the Domesday village, the wool trade and the coming of the railway. The King's School, Hugh Sexey's Hospital, the Dovecote and St Mary's Church – described in great detail – were illustrated with old prints and maps.

But there was nothing to say that the eldest legitimate son of King George III lived here with his mother, Queen Hannah, and his brother and sister. Septimus smiled at his own thought. Imagine that! It would put this sleepy town on the map. As would his research, if he ever found the rest of the memoir.

'Entry fees are thruppence. A penny if you join the Bruton Local History Society.' The prim voice sounded almost shrill in the narrow confines of the room.

'Do forgive me. I didn't see anyone when I came in.'

Septimus handed the money to the elderly lady standing behind her desk. Deciding not to remain longer, Septimus walked to the door. There was nothing in this room which would reveal anything about George Rex and his memoir. In the doorway, he turned back, unable to resist the temptation.

'Do you know anything about the connection between George III and Bruton, Miss . . . Miss Buckle?' he asked, noticing the nameplate on the desk.

Expecting at the very least a stout denial, Septimus was astonished to see the woman go as white as a sheet and take a faltering step backwards.

'I'm sorry. Did I say something I shouldn't have?'

Concerned, Septimus stepped towards the desk but Miss Buckle waved him away.

'No, there's nothing wrong. It's just a very odd question to ask. Another young man came in recently and was asking the same question.'

So others had been here before him. Had they been seeking

the memoir? Had they visited Hannah's house and discovered the attic? Who was it? Charles Rex? Or someone else? Perhaps it was the same person who had murdered Hahn?

'When was that? What was he looking for?' he asked, impatiently, sensing Miss Buckle was about to tell him.

'That's none of your business!'

Septimus spun on his heel to see who had spoken with such vehemence. In the doorway stood an elderly gentleman of military bearing. A Jack Russell sat at his feet. He was leaning on a stick and breathing heavily, looking belligerently at Septimus through narrowed eyes. He was clothed immaculately in a tweed suit, regimental tie and brilliantly polished shoes. Septimus was aware he had an inner strength that belied the need for a stick.

'Colonel Fitzgerald, please leave us. I can deal with this,' Miss Buckle snapped, having recovered her composure. Turning to Septimus, she said, 'He came last week. He was looking for . . .'

'Enough, Miss Buckle, I implore you. Kindly keep your counsel! These questions bring nothing but trouble.'

Colonel Fitzgerald flicked his stick upwards and jabbed it at Septimus.

'Now listen here, young fellah-me-lad. It doesn't pay to ask such questions here. Miss Buckle has a weak constitution and must not be placed under pressure of any sort. I will summon help if you persist.' The Jack Russell growled.

Miss Buckle didn't look as if she was ailing but Septimus realised it was no use asking further questions and so, reluctantly, he left the museum.

❖ ❖ ❖

Septimus walked down from the museum and turned off the High Street in the direction of the railway station, pausing to light a

131

cigarette on the hump-backed bridge which crossed the river Brue. Ancient stone cottages backed the water and a horse-drawn cart rattled past, the drover tipping his hat at Septimus. It was an idyllic scene that would not been out of place in Hannah's time. In fact, Septimus didn't think he had seen a single motor car while he had been in the town. The church bell chimed four o'clock and just then grey clouds obscured the sun, the wind lifting a little. It might rain after all. Septimus finished his cigarette and decided it was time to return to Winchester. There was nothing to be found in Bruton.

As he sat on the train, Miss Buckle's words came unbidden to his mind. Somebody had been asking questions about George III and his connections with Bruton only last week; Hannah's house had been viewed by a potential 'buyer'; the attic floor had been disturbed. In the museum, Miss Buckle had been shocked by his question. Colonel Fitzgerald had been angry. No, it was more than that: defensive and scared. Each of them had certainly known something, but fear prevented them from revealing anything.

Why? What – or who – were they afraid of?

Spurlings was silent the next morning. It was Sunday, and Quayle had gone to Mass. Septimus went to the water pump at the back of the kitchen, washed and shaved in the chilly water then made himself some breakfast, or at least as much of a breakfast as he could rustle together from the contents of the larder. Afterwards, he went for a walk across the water meadows in the sunshine.

When Septimus returned he found Quayle reading a newspaper in the garden.

'Telegram from Battiscombe,' he said, looking up and waving a piece of paper. 'The boy came just half an hour ago.'

'What does it say about the memoir? Is it genuine or not?'

Septimus took the telegram from Quayle and scanned it quickly.

RING BATTISCOMBE IMMEDIATELY. TELEPHONE COLLEGE LODGE. AWAIT YOUR CALL.

'That's it?' Septimus turned the telegram over.

'That's it,' said Quayle shrugged impatiently. 'You can put a call through from the Swan Hotel. Get to it!'

Sensing the urgency in his friend's voice – and Quayle was rarely urgent about anything – Septimus took the telegram and set off down College Street, turning into the Cathedral Close

133

and then into the Butter Market. The porter at the Swan Hotel ushered him to a telephone booth and a connection to Christ's College was made. Over the crackling line, he asked for the Professor and a few minutes later, Battiscombe came on the line. Septimus imagined him scurrying across the quadrangle, head bowed in concentration, gown flying behind him.

The elderly don's voice was as clear as a bell.

'How good to hear from you. It was most unfortunate you were not able to deliver your lecture but I am sure there will be other opportunities.'

Septimus had completely forgotten about the lecture and his dissertation. Hahn's death and the memoir had dominated his every waking moment. His absence from the lecture was extremely discourteous and certainly hadn't helped his chances of gaining the Fellowship but now he had evidence of a secret marriage and George Rex's memoir, his dissertation would be rewritten. No, *history* would be rewritten. It would depend upon what Battiscombe would tell him now.

'What do you make of the document? Is it genuine?'

There was a pause on the line before Battiscombe answered.

'Genuine? I can't answer for the memoir but you do realise that the whole story of Hannah Lightfoot is pure nonsense? It's all gossip, much of it printed in a book called *Anonymous Records of the Court of England*. It was full of scandal and so-called revelations. "Exclusives", I suppose we would call them today,' Battiscombe sniffed. 'In fact, the gutter press have been operating in England for over one hundred and fifty years.'

Septimus had to restrain himself from asking Battiscombe to get to the point.

'And before you tell me to get to the point,' said Battiscombe, 'let me first tell you about George Rex of Knysna. He was born in Whitechapel in 1765. He became the Marshal of the Vice

Admiralty Court at the Cape of Good Hope and established himself and his fortunes in the area of Knysna, west of Plattenberg Bay. He was rumoured at the time to be the illegitimate son of George III. He died in 1839, the same year as the George Rex in your memoir. The likeness of the Knysna George Rex to George III was widely believed at the time.'

Septimus shifted his weight from one foot to another. Battiscombe was now in full flow and wouldn't be diverted until he had finished his piece. Over his shoulder, Septimus could see a short queue had formed, with one or two guests milling around the reception desk clearly asking when the telephone would be available, but he wasn't going to be put off now.

'We've got to start with the will of George Rex's sister, Sarah. She died in Bath in 1842, leaving a freehold estate in Essex Street, Whitechapel, as well as one thousand pounds to her nephews and nieces, the children of her late brother George Rex of the Cape of Good Hope. But the copyhold lands in Whitechapel are the key. The records of the manor show that a John Rex of Goodman's Fields, Whitechapel, distiller, claimed the copyhold property under the will of Thomas Hopkins, his maternal grandfather. Hopkins's daughter, Theodorus, married a Thomas Rex, distiller, and so it was John Rex who claimed the land. Are you with me, Septimus?'

'Yes, of course. Carry on.'

'Good. John Rex, distiller, appears in the London merchant directories. When he died he left his eldest son, George Rex, nothing because he had already advanced him a great deal of money – presumably so he could travel to southern Africa – and Sarah was bequeathed the land in Whitechapel. So that's it. George Rex was the son of a London distiller who made good in his adventures abroad, so much so that his father didn't need to leave him any money. There is no connection between George Rex and George III at all.'

'But so what? There was clearly another George Rex who died in 1839 in Prague, and who was the son of George III.' Septimus tried not to betray the panic in his voice. 'The answer lies with the memoir, doesn't it, Professor?'

'It does. Because my point about George Rex is that he was the son of John Rex, a distiller from Whitechapel, and nothing more. You'll have to hope that the memoir proves your George Rex is genuine, because the main candidate in all the stories has no relationship with the Royal Family. You do understand, though, that you need to find the remainder of the memoir to discover whether this George Rex had children?'

'I have been looking.' Anticlimax was not the word after Battiscombe's long-winded story about George Rex of Knysna.

'Where? Where have you searched?'

Septimus related the places he and Quayle had checked.

'What about Carmarthen?' asked Battiscombe, his voice as sharp as a knife. 'Have you been there? It's in the memoir.'

Septimus racked his brains for a reference to Carmarthen in the memoir.

'Where is it mentioned?'

'Rex tells us that's where his sister settles after marrying James Dalton. He was a doctor.'

Then Septimus remembered. He and Quayle had completely missed the town off their list. Battiscombe had spotted the detail – they hadn't.

'Go there as soon as possible,' Battiscombe urged him. 'See what you can find.'

'I'll catch the next train,' said Septimus. 'I doubt I'll . . .'

But before he could express his doubts about the journey to south west Wales and before he could even ask the Professor where he was supposed to look when he got there, Battiscombe had already put the telephone down and cut off the connection.

❖ ❖ ❖

The old market town of Carmarthen was basking in the afternoon sunshine when the train from Cardiff pulled into the station. As the train departed with a loud whistle and a smart beat of acceleration, the smoke and steam cleared to present them with a very handy map of the town on one of the platform billboards.

'Let's find the church to start with,' Septimus suggested. 'Churches are always a rich source of local information. Plaques, memorials and family tombs often provide clues.'

Carmarthen had three churches: St Peter's, St Michael's and St David's.

'We'll try St Peter's first,' said Septimus. 'That seems to be the main one. It's on the High Street.'

'Decent folks, the Welsh,' Quayle announced. 'Had a Regimental Sergeant-Major once. Name of Price. He hailed from Brecon and had a voice like an angel. Took a bullet in the lung on the Mashonaland expedition and that was the end of that.'

They dashed away from the station, weaving between the mostly horse-drawn traffic. Three hundred yards ahead, at the far end of the High Street stood St Peter's. They walked through the lych-gate, churchyard and up to the main door which was locked. Septimus wandered all round the church but every door was bolted. He returned to the porch and spotted that the Parish Council meeting was due to begin in half an hour's time. The rector was Thomas Dunham.

'What shall we do now?' said Quayle.

'Let's wait here and see who turns up for the meeting. We can have a quick look around. Then we can try the other churches.'

'And if we find nothing in those?'

'Then we'll book a hotel and try the local museum and library tomorrow.'

The bench was in a sunny spot. Septimus enjoyed the warmth on his face and closed his eyes. What had Charles Rex said? A war for the truth. To vindicate long-dead people and to vanquish present untruths. Yes, certainly present and unpalatable untruths, deadly enough for a murder to occur. Powerful enough to summon him to Prague and to despatch him to this quiet corner of Wales on a June afternoon.

Septimus appreciated the stillness of the moment. They'd caught the first train from Winchester that Monday morning, since the connections didn't run on a Sunday. The enforced wait had given Septimus an opportunity to read the memoir again and reflect on its contents. It had been an arduous journey, with changes at Newbury, Reading and Cardiff and Quayle chivvying and cajoling all the way. Septimus was not convinced that having his old schoolmaster with him was the best idea, but Quayle had insisted on coming, acting like the old military hound he was, unleashed after a long spell in kennels. Septimus had already been to London twice, as well as all the way to Prague, and his backside was sore from all the travelling.

'Oates!'

Septimus opened his eyes. Quayle poked him sharply in the ribs and pointed to a bespectacled, clean-shaven man not yet thirty wearing a cope and dog-collar, striding across the churchyard. Just as he was about to pass them, Quayle leapt to his feet and all but barred his way.

'Reverend Dunham?'

To his credit, the young cleric showed no sign of concern at Quayle's towering presence and answered mildly,

'No, I'm the curate. Thaddeus Unsworth. Can I help?'

'We're sorry to interrupt your business,' Septimus said, getting to his feet. 'We know you have a parish meeting to prepare for, but we would like to have a look at the church beforehand if that is possible. We are looking up a distant ancestor of mine and we found the church was closed. The name is Oates, by the way, and this is my good friend, Mr Quayle.'

Unsworth smiled.

'I wish you a warm welcome. Be my guests. I only apologise that the church is locked. There are some repair works going on inside and we were concerned about people coming to harm. Come this way.'

Unsworth led them to the church and showed them in. It was a chilly, dark place. Septimus couldn't quite shake off a sense of foreboding as he walked in behind the curate. Unlike St Mary's in Bruton there was little sense of a welcome or of any warmth. Scant light glinted through narrow windows and high pews filled the nave. It was an impressive building though. Immediately Septimus could see that there were numerous memorial plaques and tombs. Near the high altar was a well-preserved medieval tomb.

'Is there anything particular you're searching for?' asked Unsworth.

Septimus sized up the curate. He seemed an honest, decent sort. There was nothing he would say that might endanger the man or arouse his suspicions.

'Yes, we're looking for a reference to the name of Dalton. Have you ever come across the name?'

To Septimus's surprise, Unsworth nodded.

'Yes, there's something over here. You'll realise why I know exactly who you mean when you see the location.'

Unsworth escorted Septimus up to the end of the nave between the choir stalls and pointed to the ground, where there was a large stone slab with a lengthy inscription that was impossible to miss:

In this vault
Are deposited the remains of
Charlotte Augusta Catherine Dalton,
eldest daughter of James Dalton
Esquire, formerly of this town and
of Bangalore in the East Indies, she
died on the 2nd day of August 1832
Aged 27 years.
Also the remains of Margaret Augusta
Dalton, second daughter of
Daniel Prytherch, Esqr. Of this town
and of Abergole, in this county,
by Caroline his wife, youngest
daughter of the above James Dalton
she died on the 24th day of January
1839 in the Ninth year of her age.

'The chancel was restored in 1876 and they discovered a brick vault with a domed roof,' Unsworth explained. 'The bodies are interred down there. There is a strange theory that Charlotte was the granddaughter of George III by a secret marriage.'

'Whose theory is that?' Septimus asked, trying to keep the panic out of his voice.

'Oh, just some of the local scholars. You see, also unexplained is the church organ.' Unsworth pointed to the large and very ornate organ. 'Apparently it was destined for Windsor but for some reason it was installed here. George III commissioned it. We're very grateful for it, I'm sure. It's thought it was donated to the church because of the connection with Charlotte Dalton. The funny thing is . . .'

'What?'

The curate cleared his throat.

'The funny thing, Mr Oates, is that others have been here searching for the Daltons.'

Septimus suppressed a shiver. Others had been here, too. The same people who had been to Bruton?

'Where are the tombs now?' he asked, trying to keep his voice level.

'They're still down there, in the crypt, but it's all sealed up at this end.'

'At this end?'

'Yes. There's an entrance through the vestry.'

'Can we get in?'

Unsworth gave an apologetic look.

'Not allowed, really. I'm sorry.'

They needed access to the crypt. In desperation, he pulled out his wallet.

'Look. I need to get down there. I have money here to donate to the fabric fund or whatever fund you need.'

Septimus pulled out a ten-pound note. The curate looked around. Septimus felt him wavering, and pulled out another ten. It was a small fortune, more than Unsworth could hope to raise in six months.

'Come with me,' he said, diffidently, taking the money.

Septimus looked for Quayle, who was busy reading the plaques at the far south end of the church. He decided to leave him to it. After Unsworth had locked the church from the inside, he led his visitor into the vestry, taking a large key from behind the door and a lantern from the shelf. He drew aside a small curtain in the corner to reveal a spiral stone staircase. At the bottom of the steps, he fiddled with the key and pushed hard on the iron-bound oak door which opened grudgingly. Septimus followed him in. It was dark until Unsworth lit a match and put it to the wick of the lantern, saying,

'Reverend Dunham wouldn't be at all pleased if he knew we were here. He's such a stickler for the rules.'

Septimus surveyed the crypt in the flickering light. It was small with a low ceiling, so they had to stoop slightly. A cloying, musky smell filled the freezing black air.

'These are the Dalton tombs.'

Unsworth led the way across the crypt, swinging the lantern so that light fell onto two rather plain slabs. Septimus leaned over them and identified Charlotte's tomb from the inscription. Was this the resting place of a granddaughter to Hannah and George? Was this George Rex's niece? He noticed the corner of the slab was chipped, so that a gap opened up.

'There isn't a lot to see, really, is there?' Unsworth whispered in the dark.

Not much to see, Septimus thought, but plenty to feel.

Unsworth's lantern cast great shadows across the tombs and for a moment the two men stood in silence, Septimus vainly searching the crypt for any clues or any sign of the memoir. If only the curate would leave him alone, then he could have a proper look, perhaps even open up Charlotte's tomb . . .

Unsworth turned the light back to the entrance.

'We'd better be getting back.'

Unsworth led the way up the steps to the vestry, closing the door behind them, extinguishing the lantern and replacing it and the key. Septimus was disappointed. He felt he had come so close but so far at the same time. He wasn't sure what he had expected to find, but once the curate had agreed to open the crypt, his expectations had soared. But nothing down there had answered his prayers.

'Were the tombs not disturbed in any way at all?'

Unsworth shrugged.

'As I say, it was before my time.' He turned to leave the vestry, adding, 'There were some bits and pieces brought out during the 1876 restoration. Old books and things, stacked up there. We haven't been through them for years.'

Septimus took a step forward. Unaccountably, his heart was thumping.

'Have a look if you want to while I prepare for our meeting.'

Septimus didn't hear Unsworth leave the vestry. He moved to the shelf of books. His mouth was dry. All his instincts told him that what he was looking for was there on that shelf. He reached into the centre of the pile and pulled out a leather-bound volume. It looked exactly like the first part of the memoir, but much thicker. He opened the first page and he knew this was what they had been searching for.

1788

They took me away in the carriage, my hands bound, flanked by hatchet-faced thugs from Bow Street. My last sight of the darkening scene of the tragic duel with Meadows was of Pitt staring open-mouthed at me in the snow. For once, it occurred to me even at that moment of indescribable horror, the great orator Pitt was silenced.

I was taken to Newgate Prison. I was not, however, placed in a cell with others. Instead, I was thrown, hands still bound, into a stinking wet cell in an old, unrestored part of the prison. The walls were covered in slime and the only light came from a tiny grille high up near the ceiling. The floor was sticky with human excrement and urine. There was no bed or seat of any kind. I huddled in the corner, not caring that the excrement soaked slowly into my breeches. Hours later, in the pitch dark, a bowl of cold gruel was shoved through the door. I took one mouthful and retched, more from the awfulness of my plight than the disgusting taste of the food.

I slept fitfully, driven to it by exhaustion and despair. When I awoke, the grey light of day illumined my dreadful cell. My throat was dry, my hair matted with sweat and excrement, my wrists raw from the rope. Somehow I managed to manoeuvre my breeches down so I could empty my bowels in the corner of the cell. The sharp stench of my own effluence filled the cell and at each intake of breath I fought the urge to vomit. I retreated to the corner. Surely, I reasoned, I would be taken before the magistrate and committed for trial. But it was Christmas, and the members of the legal community would not be hurrying from their warm fires and plates of roast beef to sit in judgement on murderers. Scum like me could languish in the cells for weeks, maybe months, before the wheels of the law turned. I knew this well; as a lawyer I had seen it happen many times before.

The thin glimmer of light coming through the grill faded early in the day and I was faced again with the darkness and my own company. Who would come for me? My mother was dead, my brother in another country and my sister Sarah in Carmarthen, four days' journey from London. I had killed a man in a duel. There were witnesses. Pitt would never save me – the reputation of his name could never be jeopardised. It was an open and shut case. And what of Catherine? What had I done which had caused so grievous an offence? I was none the wiser. Her brother had challenged me to a duel because I had, in some way, impugned his sister's honour. And now Lionel Meadows was dead. There was no going back into her heart and I would never know the reason why.

I had one weapon at my disposal however which I could use to devastating effect. It was my royal blood. I would speak out at my trial, and let the world know who I was. The press would go mad. There would be riots like the Gordon Riots eight years ago. John Wilkes and Charles Fox would champion my cause. Questions would be asked in the Commons. I would ruin Pitt and bring down his government. I would also ruin my father's name, only months after the illness and temporary madness that had almost destroyed the monarchy. This would have to be an inevitable consequence of my claims. Otherwise, I would hang.

I may have remained incarcerated for three weeks or three months. My senses were dulled in that noisome rat-trap, and time had no meaning. At some point I was taken before the magistrates and committed for trial, but was not permitted to speak, before being returned to the cell. Only the slow fading of the light indicated that another day had passed, but I slept heavily and feverishly through day and night. I ate some of the morsels which were pushed under my door and closed my ears to the frequent screams and shouts of other inmates in the darkness. The women were the worst. I knew that some of them offered their bodies in return for more food and water, but these voluntary services were cruelly exploited as the gaolers took their pleasure, often bringing friends to join in, and never gave the women extra food as part of their bargain. Men were beaten and tormented and I knew too that some gaolers were not averse to forcing themselves upon male inmates in an abomination of nature.

Mercifully, I remained untouched, save the occasional curse and spittle on my food. Why, I do not know, but I cared even less. I lay in silence, conserving my energy for the trial I knew would come, and my opportunity to speak out, regain my freedom and destroy the very fabric of the state.

When they came for me, I was ready. The footsteps outside the door of the cell were heavier than usual, and imbued with a graver sense of purpose than merely shoving a plate of rotting potato under the door.

When the door opened, the light nearly blinded me. Dazed,

149

I felt rough hands grasp my tattered and foul tunic, and drag me from the cell. I was taken up the stairs to where the ropes were cut from my wrists and the clothes stripped from me. I stumbled into another cell but instead of the door slamming behind me, men hurled buckets of icy water over me.

'Clean yourself!'

I took the cloth from the floor and wiped myself down, using the remnants of the water in one bucket to clean my private parts and to soothe the weals on my wrist. I was handed some clothes to put on: an ill-fitting pair of breeches and blouse, which I knew from my legal experience had come from the corpse of a recently hanged man – one of many such fine traditions of the English justice system. The boots pinched, but I knew better than to complain.

'Come with us,' said one of the gaolers, placing handcuffs on me.

I stifled a cry at the pain inflicted on my bleeding wrists.

'Where are we going?'

'To your trial.'

I was led down the long stone passageway to the Sessions House, where the courts sat. I half-walked, half-staggered – my time crouched on the floor of the cell had caused the most awful cramp in my legs – but I felt exhilaration. Now I would be able to shout my innocence to the courts and make my claim as the true heir to the throne. Nothing would stop me. The cause of Meadows's outrage would be made clear. I would be released, and poor Captain Lionel's death recognised for what it truly was: a ghastly mistake.

We climbed the steps up to the dock at a shuffle. I wondered who would recognise me in the courtroom – I had been there many times, when the law was on my side – but the vast courtroom was almost empty. Three lawyers sat on the bench below me, scratching ink onto papers without looking up. The public gallery was empty. To my right, the jury box was also empty. They had not yet been sworn in. Members of the public would come in at any moment. I would be able to shout my story to them, and tell the world.

We waited. I could not tell what time it was, though the light in the high windows indicated early afternoon.

The jury came in. Twelve rather sullen, shifty-looking types who took their seats uneasily. I looked around, wondering why the public gallery remained empty. I was standing when the judge entered and the others took to their feet, but my gaoler gripped my arm forcefully, twisting me around to face the judge.

He was not a judge I knew by sight. When he sat down, the jury sat but my gaoler maintained his grip on my arm. One of the lawyers below us approached the bench and handed the judge a piece of paper. The judge read it and glanced at me sharply. He whispered something to the lawyer, who nodded and sat down. Then he spoke to the jury.

'Members of the jury, you are dismissed. Thank you for attending. Your services are no longer required. This court will proceed in closed session. There will be no jury or members of the public or members of the press present.'

I watched the jury file out. I was in total confusion. The lack of food and the feverish nights in the dung-smeared cell had befuddled my wits. Was this a trial or was it a hearing? Was the judge about to throw the case out? Had someone intervened on my behalf and saved me? The judge's next words communicated to me that no such thing had happened. It was the very worst I could have dreamt in my filthy cell.

151

'Prisoner at the bar,' he said, across the deathly silent and suddenly very empty court.

'This case is of the utmost severity. Information here has come to me of your heinous crime. A crime so severe that I have dispensed with the jury.'

What crime? I wanted to cry out. Deaths in duels were not uncommon. What of my right to defend myself? I may have moved to voice my confusion, for I felt in my back the point of a knife prick my skin.

'Don't move a muscle or say a word or I'll gut you like a fish.'

My gaoler's words went unheard by everyone else in the courtroom and even I had to pause to convince myself that he had uttered such a threat. I stood rigidly, the blade not quite breaking the surface of my skin, his grip on my arm tighter than ever.

'You stand accused of High Treason,' the judge continued. 'These papers attest to your incontrovertible guilt. You are a hideous and despicable human being to plan such deeds against our King, his Majesty King George the Third.'

As he spoke this last sentence, the judge rose from his chair, followed rapidly by the three lawyers who ceased their scratching. Then, reaching for a black cap on the bench, the judge intoned words I had heard many times before, but this time I listened transfixed because they were addressed to me.

'The sentence of this Court is that you be taken hence to the place whence you came, and thence to a place of execution, and that you be there hanged by the neck until you are dead; and that afterwards your head shall be severed from your body, and your body divided into four quarters, to be disposed of as his Majesty shall think fit. And may God in His infinite goodness have mercy upon your soul.'

Before my gaoler could drag me down the steps back to my cell I turned my agonised gaze from the judge across the courtroom and saw someone slip from the corner of the room. In the depths of my despair and shock I recognised him.

It was Pitt.

I was led back along the passageway, but not to the cell where I had resided since my arrival at Newgate. I was taken to the condemned cell, whence I would be taken into the outdoor courtyard for my public execution. Mercifully, the cuffs were taken off me before I was pushed into the cell. The door banged shut behind me, and the realisation dawned upon me that I was to die. And it would be soon. Judging it to be late afternoon, I thought they might leave it until the dawn. After all, I was entitled to a priest, if not a fair trial.

Curse Pitt. He had engineered all this. I had seen him slink away from the court, satisfied I had been stitched up like a tailor's dummy. Pitt had ensured I was removed from the public eye and that some charge of treason had been placed in front of the judge, who would no doubt receive a landed estate or an heiress for his silence. The law is an ass, blindfolded and prodded by its masters. Pitt's plan for the duel had gone horribly wrong and he would stop at nothing to cover his tracks. I was an inconvenient slur on his otherwise brilliant career. His ruthlessness was well known to me. I was not surprised at the man's determination to stop at nothing to secure his ends. And the ends justified the means. Total victory: the murderer at the duel and the first born legitimate son of the King could be dispensed with in one stroke. And nobody would know anything different.

I lay in the condemned cell utterly bereft of hope. I was so numb to the world that I barely registered the door opening and the gaoler's foul breath in my face as he wrenched me upright. This was my time. I was going to die. I did not care. I was ready.

'You have a visitor,' said my gaoler.

Who was this? Was it Pitt, come to gloat, in his hour of triumph? It would not be unlike him to do so.

A shadow fell across the doorway. My visitor was certainly not Pitt but a woman wearing a hooded gown. The gaoler nodded briefly to her and shut the door to the cell behind him as he walked out. As I strained to see who it was, the woman stepped into the cell and revealed her face. Even then, in my despair and distress, I was gripped with shock.

It was Catherine.

We looked at one another for what must have been several minutes. When she spoke, it was in a whisper I barely heard, and just the one word:

'Why?'

'Why did I kill Lionel? I had no intention of doing so. He was the expert marksman, not I.'

'No, not that.' Her tone was surprisingly gentle, and my heart ached for her. How had it come to this? 'Why didn't you tell me?'

'Tell you what? Do not play games with me, Catherine. I do not know of what you speak.'

Her expression hardened.

'I? Play games with you? I think you toy with me to the end. You know very well of what I speak and still you cannot admit to it, even now, as you await execution.'

I hesitated, wondering what to say. There was nothing I could think of. And yet she truly believed I had wronged her. Catherine pulled from her gown a slip of paper and brandished it in my face. In my confusion, I managed to read it, stifling a cry of horror at the contents. What she had shown me was a marriage certificate.

It declared, with an expert forgery of my signature, that I had married a certain Anne Jones in the parish of St Nicholas, Pimlico.

❖   ❖   ❖

They came for me that evening.

When the door clanged open and the black-robed priest stood before me, the line from Homer's *Odyssey* – one of the few things I had enjoyed at Eton – came to me: 'bear, O my heart; thou hast borne a yet harder thing'. I received his blessing without a word and he left me still kneeling on the floor. My gaolers pitilessly grasped my arms and took me along the passage and up into the courtyard.

My protestations to Catherine had not convinced her of my innocence. I had begged and pleaded that she was the only love of my life, but the proof was in her hand. I had married another woman, perhaps got her with child, and kept her secretly, whilst all the while plotting to make a respectable union with Catherine. It was no use attempting to persuade Catherine otherwise. I was the victim of a hideous conspiracy. I would go to the gallows a murderer and a dishonourable lover. Catherine's eyes poured equal measures of pity and hatred into me as I begged. She said nothing when the gaoler came, not even when I was hurled to the floor and brutally kicked in the ribs. There were no parting words of regret or sorrow – just a dreadful emptiness as she walked away from the bruised and bloodied creature on the floor of the cell.

It became apparent to me very quickly on leaving my cell that I was not being taken to Tyburn, where traitors traditionally met their end. There was no hurdle for me to be drawn on through the streets. It was almost dark. There was nobody in the courtyard. A small gallows had been erected. I was to be despatched without the chance to shout my innocence and my true identity to the crowds. Even at the point of my death I was to be denied rudimentary justice.

Still held by my captors, I mounted the gallows. I felt quite calm. The time since the shambles of my mock trial and the present had been so short that I was in shock and unable to make the slightest protest.

The hood was slipped over my head. My hands were cuffed behind my back, my feet bound also. I had witnessed several executions and I knew that I would swing for several minutes until the life was squeezed out of me, leaving me jerking and pulsing at the end of the rope. Then, with a punishment reserved for my so-called crime of High Treason, my head would be cut from my shoulders and my body hacked into four parts on the butcher's slab. The priest had reappeared and in the darkness I heard his muffled voice ask God to have mercy on my soul. The end of my life was seconds away.

The executioner put the noose around my neck and placed his boot to the small of my back and shoved hard. I dropped through the gap in the boards and felt the noose tighten. I gasped – my last breath. There was a flash of light and I saw my mother, my brother and sister and the streets of Bruton, my childhood home. Then I hit the floor. Hands grabbed me and lifted me bodily into a coffin. A voice whispered in my ear:

'Keep quiet or you're a dead man.'

I thought I was already dead. But I recognised the voice of Dickon, my gaoler, who had pricked me with his blade in the courtroom. Still bound and hooded, I heard the coffin lid nailed on inches from my face. The coffin was lifted and shoved roughly on a cart. Inside, I was breathing fast. The cart jolted out of the courtyard. I lay there, rigid, curtailing my every instinct to scream and vomit my distress.

The cart proceeded down several streets. My breathing

gradually slowed. I realised I was alive. For what purpose and by whose manipulation I knew not. Elation bubbled within me. Fear still gripped me like a vice. I was in the hands of fate. The cart halted. Voices muttered in the darkness. The coffin was lifted from the cart and placed on the ground. Somebody swore, and the lid next to my face was forced open. Hands seized me again and lifted me from the coffin. I was placed on the ground. My cuffs were released and the rope between my legs quickly cut. I removed the hood from my face. As my eyes adjusted to the darkness, I could see we were in a cemetery. The ground was hard with frost and our breath clouded the air.

'He's coming,' muttered my gaoler, standing back from me.

I strained my eyes in the darkness and there before me was a cloaked and hatted figure I recognised, but I failed – understandably at that moment – to put a name to the face.

'Dr Wilmot,' the man said, 'at your service.'

My reaction was one of enormous relief. Here was the man who had conducted my parents' marriage. He was the nearest I had to family at that moment. I grasped his hand and shook it repeatedly, afraid he would vanish into the night as silently and as suddenly as he had come.

'You are in shock, of course,' Wilmot was saying, placing my hands by my sides. 'This is no surprise. Let me reassure you: you are alive. This is indeed real.'

I glanced around the cemetery. My gaolers had vanished. It was just the two of us in the graveyard.

'You have come from the King?' I asked him. 'He has arranged all this.'

'No, not the King, George. Not the King.'

'Then who?'

Wilmot placed a finger to his lips and whispered: 'Pitt.'

So convinced was I that my father had intervened to save me that the mention of Pitt rendered me speechless. Pitt? I had seen him slink away from court. He had come to secure my condemnation and my death sentence. To remove me from his path so that he might continue as First Lord without the inconvenience of the true son and heir to the throne getting in his way. Wilmot saw the confusion in my eyes.

'Pitt saw to it that your execution would be tonight, in darkness and out of the public eye. He bribed the guards and arranged for the rope to be too long so you would drop all the way to the floor. The priest knew nothing. Neither did the jury.'

'But the judge,' I asked. 'What about keeping the judge quiet?'

Wilmot gave a rare smile and rubbed his fingers and thumb together quickly.

'A baronetcy and a small estate of say, three thousand acres in Hertfordshire was enough to convince His Honour Justice Waynfleet. Every man has his price.'

And what, I wondered, was Wilmot's price, for keeping quiet all those years ago after performing a secret marriage?

'I had thought the King may have intervened on my behalf.'

Wilmot cast me a glance of sympathy.

'There is much you should know about your father the King but I cannot tell you here. We are waiting for a coach which Pitt said he would send.'

So we sat in the graveyard on that blackest of nights. Not a sound was uttered in that place of the dead. I wondered whether Pitt would come in the coach to greet me. The paths of our fates, from his father's presence at my parents' wedding, to our first meeting at Eton and to my trial for High Treason, were inextricably intertwined. His life of brilliant success and public approbation very much mirrored mine in reverse – a lifetime of secrets, public disgrace and private torment. I was borne along by events at this stage, not knowing whether the coach would ever arrive, for the past hours had been so fantastical. When it did, I climbed aboard. It was empty.

'Your father did not intervene on your behalf, George,' Wilmot said when the coach was moving through the streets. 'He did not help at all.' His voice was harsh. I could hardly see him even though he was three feet opposite me. 'I have to tell you that your father has done far worse than refuse to help you. He wants you dead, George. The King wants you dead.'

The coach rattled on. I said nothing. The last hours had shocked me into numb acquiescence.

'The King has recovered from his madness. He remembers meeting you. You are his very image. He is terrified of your existence. He feels his position on the throne is very weak. After all, the Americans rebelled and threw him out, so why not the people of Britain? His family is only on the throne at the behest of Parliament because of the Act of Settlement. And Parliament is made up of many radicals and troublemakers – Wilkes and Fox, to name the two most prominent. Your visit to the King during his madness was not kept secret enough, and in a moment of lucidity, the King hatched a plot to bring about your downfall. Messages were sent to the Meadows family, informing them that you had already contracted a marriage. Certificates were forged. This prevented the marriage and thus any likelihood of children but no one foresaw the duel or its outcome. Pitt tried to rescue you by acting as your second in the hope of discouraging Meadows, but you ruined it by killing him. When the King recovered in January, he ordered that . . .' here Wilmot faltered.

'What? He ordered what?' I leant forward in the coach and grasped Wilmot's wrist.

'That you be arraigned on a charge of High Treason. The sentence would be death. You might have stood a chance on a charge of death by misadventure because of the duel. Pitt discovered this and bribed the judge to get rid of the jury. His conscience would not allow you to go to your death.'

Wilmot pulled clear of my grip and sank back into his seat. In the darkness my mind was racing, injected with a new energy which was infused with hate. Pitt had not condemned me. He had done everything in his power to save me. And he had succeeded. I had cursed him at my trial. He had been the focus of my hatred. It had seemed so obvious that he had used his powers to silence me forever. But those powers had come from a far greater source. They had come from the King of Great Britain.

My father.

My father the King had recovered from his madness and the consequence of meeting me had spurred him to destroy the love of my life and then to destroy my life altogether. And the irony of making me a bigamist! My God, if the world knew his sordid secret. It seemed his illness had turned his mind against me, even though he was now recovered in all other ways.

'You said the King regained his health in January. What month is it now?'

'February. The eighth.'

So I had been imprisoned for over one month. Weeks on end in that infested pit of a cell and then execution: all at the behest of my father.

'The King faced the Regency Bill in Parliament. There were plans afoot to install the Prince of Wales as Regent, who would have immediately replaced Pitt with Charles Fox. The monarchy would have suffered permanent damage. So, you had to die. The King was convinced he had to act to save his crown and secure his family.'

'Which family?' I spat, bitterly. 'Only his German kin.'

'Pitt was advised to let you hang. It was in his best interests, too. But he could not accept that. His conscience would not allow it. However, your execution had to be convincing. George Rex is now dead. The judge, priest and prison guards believe that.'

'Where are we?' I asked as the coach rolled to a halt. It was too dark to make out anything.

'We're at the docks, George. This is where we must part company.' Wilmot reached for his leather bag and snapped it open, pulling out a sheaf of documents and a large wallet. 'George Rex is dead. He must never be seen in London – or in England – again. But John Boyce is alive and well.'

'John Boyce?'

'That is you, George. John, I should say.' Wilmot handed me the papers. 'These are your passports for your new identity. And this is your money.'

The wallet was bulging with coins and notes. I took it, with the papers.

'There are five thousand guineas in there. That's the price of your exile: a new life for a new man. At dawn a boat will take you from here to southern Africa. The journey will take weeks. You will arrive at the Cape of Good Hope and begin your new life. This money is more than sufficient to buy some land and a house. You could start a business or buy a farm.'

'This is a fortune,' I said. 'Where . . .?'

'Do not ask where it is from. Just be grateful. And do not ever return to England. The past is dead. Only the future is alive for you. Never communicate with Pitt or myself again. You would endanger our lives.' He paused. 'There is one other thing.'

'What?'

'You must never marry and you must never have children. Your life and theirs would be imperilled by such an act.'

And with that, Wilmot opened the door of the coach and ushered me out. The door slammed and I heard his sharp word of command. The coach rolled away and left me alone in the dark.

❖ ❖ ❖

And so it was that I was left standing at the dockside in that black February night, clutching a fortune, a new identity and my life. It was as if I had been born again and had an opportunity to begin afresh. I would never return to England. But in that moment of realisation, the moment of my rebirth, I knew that I had brought with me to my new life an old hatred and a thirst for revenge upon those who had destroyed my old life.

And on one person in particular: the King of England.

Moments after Wilmot had departed, figures emerged from the darkness and took me to my boat. One of them was my gaoler, Dickon, We boarded the forty-foot fishing craft, and I was told the plan was to convey me to France, where I would join a ship bound for the Cape. But as I settled into my bunk to sleep the final hours of the night, Dickon bolted the hatches down and I was left in no doubt that he was as much my guard as my companion. At that time I supposed it only reasonable that Pitt and Wilmot needed to be sure that I was out of the country.

We set sail at dawn, and I remained below deck until we were far out to sea. When I emerged, the coast of England was a distant blur in the cloud and fog. The old boat pitched and heaved, but the crossing was relatively smooth for the middle of winter.

Despite this good start, I knew something was wrong as soon as I set foot on deck. There were two other crewmen, Benjamin and Joseph, who had been surly and silent throughout the night. When I came out on deck, I interrupted a hushed conversation between the three men. Instantly they drew apart, and busied themselves with ropes and sails, as if we needed to alter our course. Dickon nodded at me, but I felt uneasy. I was in possession of a fortune and nobody would ever know if I was murdered and thrown overboard. I reassured myself that Pitt and Wilmot would not have gone to all this trouble – and vast expense – to leave me to such a fate. They would surely pay these men good money and no doubt bring down the full force of the law on them if they broke their part in the agreement.

I retired below deck, resigned to whatever might come from the crossing. Land was sighted in the early afternoon and as it grew dark, we approached the port of Dunkerque.

We ate aboard the boat in the harbour that night. There was a merchant ship sailing for the Cape in three days and I would be on it. Dickon would stay with me until that point, while his companions would return to London in the morning.

My heightened senses left me watchful and barely able to sleep. Late into the night I was awake again, and this time heard whispering voices outside my cabin. Benjamin and Joseph had gone ashore after our meal, probably to spend some of their earnings on drink and whores, but I heard them return hours ago. There were only two cabins, and the two crewmen slept on the deck. Dickon had remained below with me, sleeping in the next cabin.

I was wide awake and fully dressed, my money in the leather bag wrapped in my jacket. Slowly I eased off the bunk. The whispering had ceased and the boat was silent. I tiptoed to the door which joined my cabin to Dickon's and opened it very slowly. A tiny chink of dawn light filtered through the side hatch. Dickon was asleep on his bunk. I breathed a sigh of relief: my imagination had got the better of me. But as I moved to return to my bunk, the whispering began again, more urgently. The deck above creaked.

I whispered as loudly as I dared.

'Dickon?'

I walked slowly towards Dickon's sleeping form and touched his shoulder, shaking him gently. He did not move. I shook him again and when I removed my hand I realised it was wet with blood.

He was dead.

Suddenly, the hatch above my cabin opened and a figure jumped inside, followed by another. I stepped back, in an involuntary movement, into Dickon's cabin. It was dark enough for me to remain unseen as Benjamin and Joseph launched themselves at my bunk, stabbing and hacking at the bedding in a drunken fury.

I stepped out of the door of Dickon's cabin and ran up the steps to the deck. Behind me, I heard curses and loud footsteps. Pausing at the top of the steps, I smashed the heel of my boot into Joseph's face, satisfied at the sound of crunching bones and the resultant scream. Leaping nimbly off the boat and onto the quay, I almost twisted my ankle on the ropes, before running with all my might away from the boat.

Breathing hard, I dashed round a corner and into a street. I paused. It was dark, but the dawn light, faint though it was, began to illumine my surroundings. I walked up the street as fast as I could but without breaking into a run. I needed to conserve energy. I had with me my papers and my fortune. Soon I heard footsteps behind me. Ducking into a doorway, I held my breath and peered back down the street.

Benjamin stood at the harbour end of the street, wondering whether to press on or turn into the street. In that second I willed him to go on, but he turned and began running towards me. If I ran, he would see me and give chase. If I stayed where I was, he would run past me and I would be finished. As he approached, I found inspiration. I raised my leather bag, heavy with coins, and, as he was almost upon me, brought it down with all my might on his skull.

The blow stunned him. He was built like an ox and now enraged like a wounded beast. Horrified, I kicked him as hard as I could in his ribs and he doubled up. As I made to escape, he grasped my jacket and pulled me back. I felt his ale-sodden breath on my neck, and twisted like a snake away from him. His knife slashed past me and I jabbed my elbow hard into his face, by a stroke of luck finding his eye. He roared with pain and dropped the knife. I could have picked up the blade and killed him, but I chose to run. It was the right choice. The sound of our struggle had aroused people and as I left him nursing his eye, several doors opened and people demanded to know what was going on. I kept running, on the lookout for harbour watchmen, and eventually found my way into the centre of the town.

It was dawn when I arrived in the town square. Hungry and exhausted though I was, I needed to put as much distance as I could between myself and my assailants. It would not be safe to remain in Dunkerque for any longer than was necessary. My enquiries at the largest inn in the square led me to the staging post, where I selected the nearest coach and climbed aboard, not caring where it was going. Within minutes, we were off, and I was seated between a woman whose jowls wobbled like an old turkey's and a sickly, grey-faced priest who looked likely to meet his Maker at any moment. As we rattled away from Dunkerque, I tried to hide my relief. My curiosity grew, and I sheepishly asked where we were going.

'Where do you think?' The fat woman looked at me as if I was an idiot. 'You get on the coach and you do not know where we are going? Why, we are going to Paris!'

It took us the better part of three days to reach Paris. During that time I reflected on my life. I had escaped my captors and was free to begin again. Even though I was away from England and the murderous clutches of my father, I could not sever all my links. I wanted revenge. I thirsted for it. It would not come quickly, though. I might have to wait years. I could not afford to arouse the wrath of the King, so I would have to retain my new identity.

When I arrived in Paris, I took my money to one of the banking houses of the Marquis de Marigny, where my papers were scrutinised by the clerks and accepted. Pitt and Wilmot had at least served me well there. I could not live off my money, wealthy though it made me. That would bring me unwanted attention. I wished to remain anonymous, and to settle into the life of the city before building on my wealth. I took work in one of the many coffee houses on the Île de St Louis. It was owned by Lucien Lefèvre, a kindly man who treated me well and provided me a modest room in the attic of the house. Within a few months of my arrival, I learnt he was seriously in debt and that the coffee house was in danger of going bankrupt. He would lose his employment and his home. Poor man – he had no sons, only daughters, and they had moved away to be near their husbands' families.

'How much do you need?' I asked him late one evening when we were closing up for the night.

Lucien gave me a piteous glance.

'More than you could ever dream of, my boy. Twenty thousand francs.'

It was half my fortune. I could lend him the cash, and buy him out. The potential to make far more money was there. But how could I make such an offer without arousing his suspicions?

In the end, my dilemma was solved not by any lies or half-truths but by an event which none of us could have thought possible: revolution.

Ever since beginning work in the coffee house I had picked up the gossip and the discontent in the streets of Paris from all the customers. When the Estates-General met at Versailles in May, the talk was of a new constitution and the right of the common man. After all, the new country of the United States of America had overthrown the shackles of the tyrannous King George of Britain, so why could not the French do the same? Even in Britain, there was a parliament, where the non-nobles decided matters of state. It was time the ordinary people in France had their say. In June 1789 the Estates-General declared themselves to be a National Assembly and in July became the National Constituent Assembly. The King, Louis XVI, refused to accept measures of reform, and despatched his soldiers. All of Paris was alive with talk of rebellion and Lucien seized upon the possibility that if there was a civil war then his debts might be wiped away. He encouraged the Jacobins, the most fervent Revolutionaries, to use the coffee house for their meetings.

'My debts are to the Marquis de Montmorillon,' he hissed at me one evening, drunk on the talk of revolution. 'He can rot in hell.'

I was dismayed by Lucien's transformation into vengeful miser. He had prospered under the Jacobins, putting on weight and dressing in fancy ways. Gone were my chances of buying the coffee house while Lucien entertained the Jacobins and spat hatred at his creditor. I was secretly enthralled by the Jacobins; their aim was nothing less than the complete destruction of King Louis and his family. Much of their hatred was reserved for Marie-Antoinette, the Queen, and there was plenty of talk of the unspeakable things they would do to her if they had her imprisoned. My interest was directed at a wider goal: if there could be revolution in France, why not in England, where Fox and his associates had already declared the King unfit to govern? That – together with a triumphant return to the country of my birth, where I would be free and unfettered by my royal connection – was my ambition.

It was after lunch on a hot fourteenth day of July when Stephan, our excitable stable kitchen boy, ran into the coffee house shouting that 'they' had seized control of the Bastille. It was a day none of us would forget, for it inaugurated a new age, an age of revolution which witnessed the rise and fall of mighty France.

'Who? Who has taken the Bastille?' demanded Lucien. 'The Jacobins?'

'No – just ordinary people. The people have seized the Bastille.' Stephan's eyes were shining with pleasure. 'The crowd stormed it and freed the prisoners. There is talk the mayor has been stabbed.'

'Where is the King?' Lucien asked. 'Has he ordered more troops into the city?'

'Nobody knows.' Stephan was hopping from one foot to the other with excitement. 'Can I go and find out what is happening?'

'Yes, boy, go onto the streets. Tell the Jacobins to come here. They will be assured the best coffee in Paris.' Lucien turned to me. 'Now we'll see what de Montmorrillon does with his debtors!'

All Paris was ablaze with revolution. The King eventually came to the city and accepted the tricolour, but nobody was satisfied. Jacques Necker was restored to power but without success; riots continued across Paris and spread into the countryside. Nobles started to abandon their châteaux, escaping to Britain, among them de Montmorillon: Lucien's debt was now wiped clean. A once mild-mannered man was now consumed with a passionate desire to destroy anyone of wealth or means. Afraid for my investment, I returned to the banking house of de Marigny and withdrew my fortune. I feared for my life if the money was found, but leaving it in the bank risked the possibility of losing it all. I hid my money under the floorboards in my little room. There was now little hope of buying Lucien out, and I would have to wait longer to enlarge my fortune.

In August, the Assembly published the Declaration of the Rights of Man and of the Citizen, and, in October, King Louis XVI returned to Paris from Versailles, forced to do so by food riots and disgust at the way in which he continued to flaunt his wealth while the common people starved. Although the ancient regions of France were abolished and replaced by départements, and many powers were wrested from the Church, there were those in the Assembly who sought to take the Revolution much further. One of the most prominent among them was Maximilian Robespierre, an Arras lawyer who frequently came to our coffee house. Whilst the Royalist democrats and the National Party in the Assembly discussed whether France should model its constitution upon the British monarchy, Robespierre argued forcefully in the Assembly for radical change. He would often sit in the coffee house, immaculately dressed, and talk captivatingly in his high-pitched voice, attracting a considerable audience and ensuring that Lucien Lefèvre's business flourished as it had never done before.

We lived in uncertain times. Winter passed. The King was in permanent residence in the palace of the Tuileries, surrounded by his National Guards. People continued to live in abject poverty in the city, begging in the gutters, and the Assembly debated how to share the wealth of the nation, abolishing the Nobles' titles and trappings of power, forcing more to flee the country. I revelled in the events. I saw myself as a citizen, and not a subject. I increasingly began to doubt ever returning to England, with its backward beliefs in the power of the monarch and the aristocracy. The stain from my royal blood was wiped clean. I was a citizen of France, now fluent in the language and one of them. For the first time in my life I felt settled. I could, I felt sure, be happy.

The Assembly continued to make laws for the benefit of the citizens. Jury trials started; the law evolved and became independent of the monarchy; hereditary offices were abolished and promotion within the army was based on merit rather than rank. The citizens of Paris greeted each new piece of legislation with enthusiasm, but it was not enough for the Jacobins and for Robespierre. A decisive event occurred in June, 1791, when the King fled Paris with his family. They were caught at Varennes, dressed in servants' clothing but in the royal carriage bearing the royal coat of arms. How we laughed at their arrogance and stupidity! The King was brought back to Paris in his rags and forced to swear loyalty to the new constitution. From Robespierre, however, we heard the details of how the Legislative Assembly failed time and time again to agree; there were too many monarchists and liberal republicans, he said, to effect a proper government. In August of the following year, 1792, the Paris Commune and rebels, led by Georges Danton, stormed the Tuileries, determined to end the rule of Louis XVI once and for all. Robespierre held back, but when the imperial powers of Austria and Prussia demanded that the King be freed, action was taken against the King and he was put on trial for his life. Here Robespierre came to the fore, telling us all eloquently that 'the King must die so that the country may live' and in January 1793 Louis was publicly executed to the great joy of us all. As far as I was concerned, if the King of France could be executed, then surely such a thing might follow in England?

I remained at Lucien's coffee house, which was often a centre of much talk. Robespierre came less frequently after the execution of the King and the next summer witnessed a wave of rioting and unrest. There were food shortages, the war with Austria was going badly and prices rose. Those who had been friends now viewed one another with suspicion; our sense of elation at the common cause of the republic was rapidly becoming soured. Then the Jacobins seized power and after Jean-Paul Marat's assassination, Robespierre, our hero, replaced Georges Danton and took charge of the Committee of Public Safety. In the Terror which ensued nobody was safe any more. Thousands of ordinary people were denounced by their neighbours as enemies of the Republic when the reason was often a long-held grudge that bore no relation to the political situation. Anyone who whispered against the Revolution, or who even murmured for restraint, was denounced and sent to the guillotine. Hundreds were beaten to death, or thrown into cells and starved for crimes against the Republic, which were rarely made clear. I stood many times in the square and watched the victims brought in by the tumbrel, beaten and mocked by the starving and hysterical mob. The violence was so sickening that I resolved to leave Paris. It was after one of these spectacles that I returned to the coffee house one afternoon to find Lucien alone, clearly drunk and in an evil mood.

'Ah, *le p'tit Anglais*,' he said, draining his glass. 'Where have you been?'

He had not called me an Englishman for a long time, and I was so accustomed to being in France that it came as a shock. The monarchy of England was outraged by the execution of Louis, and England had been at war with France. If my identity as an Englishman were known, my life would be endangered for certain. I pushed past him, eager to avoid his wrath, but he grasped my arm and gripped it tight enough to hurt.

'I know what you have upstairs, Englishman.' Wine-sodden breath washed over me. My blood froze. 'I could have you denounced as a monarchist without hesitation. You would be arrested and guillotined tomorrow, without trial.' His grip relented. 'That said, there are other ways of resolving this.'

I looked into his bloodshot eyes, hating him but willing him to go on. He held my life in his hands.

'Get the money. We will discuss the matter.'

I went to my room, pulled across the floorboard and lifted out the bag of money. Carrying it carefully downstairs, I placed it on the table between us. Lucien's eyes were alive with greed. His hands shook as he opened the bag and surveyed the coins.

'So much money,' he breathed. 'Enough to feed the whole of Paris.' Looking up at me, he snapped: 'Where did you get this? Are you an English spy?'

'No: quite the opposite. I left England and never wish to return. I rejoice at the Revolution and desire to see King George III and his family meet the same fate as Louis and his wretched offspring.'

'You are a thief, then.' Lucien licked his lips. 'I could have you denounced as an Englishman, a monarchist, a thief. Any one of them is enough to see you executed.'

'Take half,' I uttered. 'If you take it all, I'll denounce you. You'll never be able to keep all of that without arousing suspicion.'

'Perhaps, perhaps.'

As he spoke, hope fluttered in my heart. We could keep the secret safe between us. I would leave Paris, maybe even leave France. He could have his pot of gold.

'It is a lot of money.' Lucien added.

In that second, I saw what would happen. The money was too much for him: he wanted it all. Even if we divided it equally, or if he kept most of it, I could see that he would denounce me in any case, and have me executed. It would be easy, and I was too risky alive, sharing his guilty secret.

'Too much for you, Englishman, but just right for me.'

I brought a pewter jug down hard on his head, the blow landing behind his right ear. Without a sound, Lucien slumped to the table, his arm outstretched and several fingers twitching at the bag, before he slumped to the ground. A trickle of blood ran down his neck and the vacant stare in his eyes was enough to tell me he was dead.

Surprised at my own callousness, I dragged Lucien's heavy corpse into the cellar and bolted the door. Taking the money, I ran upstairs, but when I got to my room I hesitated. I could not take all the money with me. If I were caught with it, I would be a dead man. My wealth was my death sentence. The decision was simple: I put the bag back under the floorboards, taking a few handfuls of coins to keep me in food for a few days, and ran back down the stairs.

The whole episode could only have taken a few minutes. The memory of my dreadful act made me shudder as I stepped into the street outside, but my face bore no sign of emotion. My only thought was to get out of Paris, my home of more than four years.

❖　❖　❖

I took a coach out of the city, heading first south, then east, towards the Rhineland. Dressed in my workaday clothes, and carrying no belongings but the few coins I had kept, I attracted no attention. I ate once a day, and grew a beard. Of all the refugees fleeing the Terror, I was not likely to be stopped or questioned.

❖   ❖   ❖

I arrived at the border with the Palatinate well past sunset, tired and hungry. My funds were almost exhausted, but I had enough to pay for one meal and a night at a tavern. My plan then was to throw myself upon the mercy of the Germans, pleading asylum from the Terror in Paris, which, I persuaded myself, was very nearly the truth.

The hostel was rough and busy with hard-drinking travellers. The talk was all of the Terror, and by the way people spoke – their eyes constantly shifting around the crowded tap-room on the lookout for government spies – they shared a common purpose: each to ensure his own survival. I took my food and sat close to the fire, scooping greedily the few scraps of nourishment in the mass of watery soup.

'Have you come far?'

I hesitated before answering, reluctant to be drawn into a conversation which might let slip something about my purpose and identity. But to ignore the question might invite unwanted attention, so I turned reluctantly to my companion, who looked even more emaciated than me.

'From Paris. And you?'

'Paris also. It is not healthy there.'

I watched him slurp his soup. Although he was hungry and clearly destitute, his teeth were good and on the smallest finger of his left hand he wore a small gold signet ring. A casual glance down at his well-made boots suggested this person was wealthy, possibly even nobly born. There were plenty of people in the tavern who might denounce him, not for the good of France, but for the greatest motivation of all: money.

I finished my soup and took my leave of him. If he was a nobleman, I did not want to be near him should he be denounced. As I stood up to go, he grasped my arm.

'Are you lodging here tonight?'

I nodded.

'Do you wish to earn some money?' His voice dropped to a whisper, which I could barely hear over the hubbub of the tavern crowd. 'I have gold coins here,' he added, patting his pocket. 'What say you?'

He looked into my eyes. The past weeks had taught me that nobody was to be trusted, but I had no money left. In fact, I had nothing at all. Every instinct told me to walk away – but to what?

I sat down.

'What is it you require of me?'

He smiled, and I saw that his was a kindly face. There was a warm light about his eyes.

'Meet me in the yard at midnight. Come alone.'

I lay on the filthy bed in the room I shared with five others, unable to sleep, or even to rest. The sweat-soaked mattress was alive with bugs, and the foul breath of one of my fellow-sleepers wafted into my face with sickening regularity. So, rather than lie there considering my dilemma over the meeting with the mysterious traveller, I got up from the bed and left the room, fully dressed, carrying my boots. In the hallway I could see the yard from the window. It was a moonlit night, and the clock had struck eleven some time ago. I pulled on my boots and considered my options.

It could be a trap. It probably was. But why? I had no money. There was nothing about me to suggest I had any wealth. Perhaps he wanted to take me by force and use me for a labouring purpose, but I hardly had the physique for that – and he had plenty of money to hire proper labour. It could only, I concluded, be genuine. The earth had spun on its axis since the execution of King Louis. France was at war with the world. Opportunities abounded in every corner of life. People – the common people, the mass of the population – were changing the way they lived.

As I stared into the courtyard wondering what to do, a coach entered, drawn at a slow pace by two horses. The ostler took the bridle of the lead horse and, as I watched, three men walked quickly to the carriage, the first with a rapier in his hand, and opened the door. Nothing happened for a moment, until the stillness was rent by a piercing scream. A musket cracked and a fourth figure ran out of the shadows. The man at the carriage door slumped back to the ground, his rapier clattering to the ground.

I moved unthinkingly, running down the stairs and into the courtyard. There I beheld two men duelling, while another was clambering over the body of his companion, into the carriage. The ostler had vanished. I ran towards the carriage door, cursing my own stupidity. A second scream ripped through the air. I lunged into the carriage and grasped the intruder by the shoulders, wrenching him backwards. But I had underestimated his strength for a second later a fat fist smashed into my nose, sending me spinning back onto the cobbles. A light flashed before me. I heard an animal cry of pain – I did not realise then that it was my own. Above me, my opponent's great bulk loomed, and a blade hissed down, slicing into the edge of my thigh. The blade lifted and I twisted to the left, only to find myself up against the corpse by the carriage. There was nowhere else to turn. I spread my arms, waiting for the blade to finish me, and as I did so, my fingers fumbled for the dead man's rapier. In one movement, I grasped it, flicked it upright and thrust it inexpertly into the stomach of my over-confident assailant.

It held there for a moment, before I withdrew it, rolling to the right and staggering to my feet. My opponent slumped forwards and fell to his knees, both hands clutching his gut, emitting a low wail of agony.

Not having the nerve to finish him off, or watch his death throes, I turned to the duel, which seemed to be reaching its climax. The blades flashed in the moonlight, and the man who had used the musket – who looked vaguely familiar – had the advantage. His opponent was weary and after a dazzling bout of swordsmanship, lost his rapier and received a lunge to his neck.

It was over. My own opponent lay dying in a pool of his own blood, which spread without pause across the cobbles. The two other corpses lay inert. My wound was beginning to hurt, sending searing pains up my leg. There was not much blood, however, and I judged it not to be serious. The victor of the duel walked across to me, wiping the blade of his rapier on a handkerchief. As he came closer I recognised him.

'You came after all, then.' My supper companion squeezed my arm. 'Our thanks to you will have to wait. But before we change horses and move on, let me introduce you to the lady you have helped rescue.' He led me to the carriage, and in the light of the moon, I could see two cloaked ladies inside. The nearest, a beautiful young woman of less than twenty years, peered out at us. It was to her that my supper companion gestured.

'Let me introduce the Princess Augusta of Austria, second cousin to the late Queen of France, Marie-Antoinette. And, for myself, I am ReichsGraf Klemens von Starhemberg, at your service.'

❖ ❖ ❖

The planned change of horses was abandoned in the rush to leave the corpse-strewn yard. I was lifted into the coach, and the exhausted horses whipped into a gallop. The wound in my leg was worse than I had anticipated and each jolt and rattle created a hellish agony, but, for the sake of my companions, I ground my teeth and held my tongue. Within the hour I was losing my senses. In the dead of night we passed the border into the Palatinate, at last free from France, and when we halted to change horses and take on provisions, my companions saw my distress and had the wound properly dressed. It was too late; I was quickly developing a fever and was barely capable of realising that the dawn was upon us. By our next stop, I was delirious and utterly unaware of my surroundings. My last conscious act was hearing the Princess cry to her companions.

'Save him. You must save him! He saved us. He cannot be allowed to die!'

❖ ❖ ❖

The services of a doctor were solicited, and my wound was cleaned again. There was little he could do but to prescribe rest and solitude, both of which were not possible. We continued on our journey, and my fever reached its high point. It was not until the fourth day, something I was told much later, that the fever broke, and I awoke to find my head resting in the lap of the Princess, who was asleep. I made an effort to rise, which woke the Princess. She gave a little cry of delight at my bewildered struggle, and shouted for the coach to halt.

The door swung open and von Starhemberg climbed in, giving me a grin.

'How is our friend today?' he asked, helping me sit upright.

'I am better, thank you.' I took a tankard of ale from him and drank gratefully, accepting a hunk of bread eagerly.

'That is good,' he nodded. 'You have not eaten for days.'

'We thought we had lost you.'

The Princess blushed as she spoke, and put her hand to her mouth as if to take back the words.

'We were worried, yes,' added von Starhemberg. 'The Princess here has spent the past few days nursing you back to health. It is to her that you owe your recovery.'

'But it is to him that we owe our lives,' said the Princess, not blushing this time. 'He saved us.'

The Count inclined his head.

'That is true. We have a great debt of thanks to you, my friend.'

I looked out of the carriage window. Under the blazing summer sun there were stunning mountains, a dramatic and exciting landscape the like of which I had never seen.

'Where are we?' I asked.

The Count smiled.

'You are in the realm of his Imperial Majesty Francis II, the Holy Roman Emperor. We are in Austria and will reach Vienna in three days' time.'

I could not know then that my life had changed course and would follow a path more fulfilling and more enriching than I had experienced previously. Fate, chance, or God's will – whatever you want to call it – had decisively intervened and plucked me from my desperate and miserable circumstances. I was to rise to the very highest in society and receive riches and rewards; but even in amongst all those glittering baubles, I never forgot the pact I had made with myself over the way my father King George III had manipulated and ill-treated me. Revenge is a dish best eaten cold, they say, and I was prepared to wait decades for it; and now I am assured such revenge will occur even after my lifetime. But it will occur.

❖   ❖   ❖

I was installed in lodgings in a palace in the area they called Grinzing. The palace was high on the Hermannskogel, overlooking the Vienna Woods and the city itself. The palace belonged to von Starhemberg, and he made available to me the best medical care he could provide. I was served by an army of liveried servants and I ate like a fighting cock. Within a week, my leg was on the mend. No infection had set in and the blade had missed the bone and any vital arteries.

'Otherwise,' von Starhemberg's kindly doctor explained to me in a guttural French accent, 'you would have perished.'

Late in the afternoon at the start of the second week, von Starhemberg came to see me. He was not alone. With him were two noblemen introduced to me as the Counts Anton von Kaunitz-Rietberg and Klemens von Schoenborn. After dispensing with their riding coats and taking some wine, von Starhemberg ushered me into his private drawing room, a room I had not had occasion to enter until now. The summer evenings were cool and a fire was burning brightly. I surmised that word of his visit had been sent on ahead.

'You are walking well, now,' von Starhemberg observed.

'Yes, it is almost healed.'

'We must discuss what is to become of you.'

Von Starhemberg's eyes had hardened. His guests had not said a word. I gathered this was not to be a simple social visit. I swallowed some wine. Von Starhemberg had done more than the call of duty had demanded. Now it was time to set me on my way. Would I ever see the Princess again? She was such a lovely thing and had doted on me during those few days in the carriage. By now though, she would have forgotten me, a mere traveller whose path had crossed hers so briefly. Even so, I thought it odd she had sent no word, given the passion in her voice when she thought I was going to die that night. Such are the whims of women: all men are mere playthings to them. And I was now to be cast aside.

'We'll come to the point,' von Starhemberg set his glass on the mantelpiece with a firm click. 'You were delirious in the coach. You had a high fever and were rambling.'

'I was indeed.' The back of my brain stirred; something uncomfortable was about to be revealed.

'You were talking about your father.'

'My father?'

I had it now. But so did von Starhemberg.

'Yes, your father: His Majesty King George of Great Britain. You spoke of a George Rex. You said you were George Rex, not John Boyce. You claimed that you are the son of the king of England. What did you mean by that?'

'Well, I . . .'

'Speak the truth,' von Schoenborn snapped. 'The British government is an ally of the Empire. We will not tolerate treasonous slander against our ally.'

Von Starhemberg took a step towards me. I remembered the flickering rapier dancing expertly in the moonlight in the tavern yard. What I had mistaken as a wasted appearance caused by malnutrition was in fact the hard exterior of a physically powerful man. True, he had gained more colour and a little flesh after returning to Vienna, but the ruthlessness was plain to see.

'It is the truth.'

I spoke in English for the first time in three years. My native tongue sounded strange to me. I had spoken nothing but French, and French had been our common language since I had first spoken to von Starhemberg in the tavern. It was the language of all the royal courts of Europe.

'*Mein Gott*,' uttered von Kaunitz-Rietberg, an ugly and grossly fat individual.

'How do we know you are speaking the truth?'

Von Starhemberg remained with one foot slightly forward, balanced and poised to strike. My answer would determine whether or not I remained alive. I had nothing, no documents or papers or witnesses. Nothing except myself.

And my ring.

I lifted my left hand and held it out to von Starhemberg.

'The ring was given by the King to my mother. The inscription – 'Hannah – *À mon soul désir* – George R.' – on the inside is the proof you need. My father the King married a woman named Hannah Lightfoot in secret. He had three children with her before marrying Princess Charlotte of Mecklenberg. That marriage is illegal. His children, including the Prince of Wales, are illegitimate.'

'*Das ist ein Haufen Unsinn!*'

Enraged by what he considered to be nonsense, von Kaunitz-Rietberg grasped at the sword in its scabbard at his waist. But von Starhemberg placed a restraining hand on his arm. Turning to me, he asked to see the ring. Von Starhemberg inspected it closely for what seemed an age, and we all waited, holding our breath, listening to the ticking of the clock on the mantel.

'Interesting,' he said finally, passing it back to me. 'But "George R" could be anybody. Not necessarily George Rex, King George.'

He spoke these last words in fluent English. I replied in kind.

'Hannah was his true love. He fell in love with her when he was Prince of Wales, trying to escape the clutches of his mother and

Lord Bute. My mother was well looked after, as were we all. She was installed in a country house and lived there until her death. One of the witnesses to the marriage was Lord Chatham, father of the British Prime Minister, William Pitt.'

At the mention of Pitt, the noblemen gasped. Clearly their knowledge of English was about as good as my knowledge of German – that is, very poor – but the word 'Pitt' was universal. The youthful underling of George III had outwitted all his rivals and was now, after ten years, the supreme leader of the British government, and ally of the Holy Roman Empire in the war against France.

'This is significant information,' von Starhemberg had reverted to French, which we could all understand. 'What you are saying seems truthful. The marriage you describe was of course morganatic and thus not recognised in the eyes of royalty. However, in the eyes of the Church, at least your Church in England, it was legal and you are therefore the legitimate son of King George.'

Hope fleetingly leapt in my heart but was dashed immediately.

'If you are indeed who you say you are. We have another guest coming to visit you. He is Graf Konstantin von Esterhazy. He served with the Imperial Ambassador to the Court of St James in London and has seen the King of England in the flesh many times. He will tell us whether or not you bear any resemblance to the man you believe is your father.'

As we waited, we drank more wine. The servants brought us cold meats and cheeses. It grew dark outside. The temptation to tell von Starhemberg and his companions the full story of my duel with Meadows and my mock execution was great, but if I told them that the King had ordered my trial to be conducted in secret so that I could be executed, then any sympathy I might receive from them would be lost. At last, after an aeon of silence, a horse cantered into the courtyard. A deep voice shouting for servants reached us in the drawing room, and von Starhemberg smiled.

'Von Esterhazy. I would recognise his voice anywhere.'

Motioning for me to remain where I was, von Starhemberg strode to the door and went to greet his guest. Only a minute later, the door reopened, and von Starhemberg ushered him in. I rose from my seat, and faced von Esterhazy with as much dignity as I could muster.

Von Esterhazy, a youngish, well-groomed man, stopped dead when he saw me. Nobody spoke. We were all waiting for von Esterhazy to speak. He did not move. Instead, I took three steps towards him, and gazed straight into his eyes. When at last von Esterhazy spoke, it was with the words I knew he would use, words Wilmot had uttered five years ago at Kew Palace when he stood alongside my father and myself:

'He is the King of England's son. I would swear my life on it.'

Nothing happened for several days after von Esterhazy's visit, and I was left by myself at the palace in Grinzing. Alone I may have been, but the presence of four armed soldiers at the gates left me in no doubt as to my new-found position. On the third day I had a visitor to confound my earlier pessimism: the Princess Augusta. Her carriage swept into the courtyard just as I was returning from my morning exercise in the park and so I was able to greet her as she stepped out. She had brought with her three ladies-in-waiting who were dismissed as we reached the entrance hall. Somewhat bemused by this unexpected opportunity for privacy with the girl, I showed her into the drawing room. Total privacy was never a reality, though; the butler and several footmen were in constant attendance upon us. But I was fast learning the etiquette of high society. Servants were not counted as people; they were seen but never heard.

'It is true?' the princess asked me, when we were seated. At the sight of my shocked expression, she added, 'von Starhemberg told me about the ring and explained how von Esterhazy recognised your features. I cannot say I am surprised, after what you were saying during the journey from France. You were delirious and we listened as you rambled about the King and your mother, Hannah, and their marriage.'

'My secrets are exposed then, Your Highness?'

The princess gave me a charming smile.

'Yes . . . George. I would like you to call me Augusta. Let us dispense with titles when we are together.'

This seemed to suggest that we would be alone together on future occasions. I was curious. I liked the girl very much but my mind was too full of my own difficulties to wonder how a relationship with Augusta would develop.

'I am so pleased,' the princess went on. 'I knew you were special. This means you are by birth a prince, though not in title, because your mother was a commoner. But in our country you would still be a Graf – how would you say in English?'

'A Count,' I said, endeared by her enthusiasm at my sudden elevation into the ranks of the nobility. 'Or, more correctly, an Earl, because in the English peerage we have no counts.'

'George, I have been longing to visit you since you were first lodged here, but von Starhemberg forbade it. I am sorry you have thought ill of me for not calling upon you.'

'Not at all.'

I was not going to let this beautiful girl know my doubts for one second.

'However, even this visit is only permitted because I bring with me a message.'

'Who is it from?' I took the sealed paper from her.

Augusta's answer was irrelevant after I had glanced at the double-headed eagle on the seal, for it was the imperial insignia of the Habsburg Holy Roman Emperor. The note was a summons to the presence of His Imperial Majesty.

The Emperor was not in Vienna that week; instead he was residing in his castle of Artstetten. A carriage was sent for me and I was provided with a new tailor-made outfit, including boots and a wig. The journey took most of the morning, but the carriage was one of the finest I had travelled in. I went alone, with four outriders posted to escort me – or to prevent any escape I might engineer – and as we passed through the delightful Austrian landscape, the peasants in the villages and fields had no doubt in their minds as to the grandeur of my passage.

On my arrival at the castle, high up in the mountains, I was accompanied into the main hallway, where von Starhemberg awaited me.

'His Imperial Majesty is very interested in you, George. Austria is currently allied to Britain in the war against France and your presence here in Austria could either be very beneficial to us, or . . .'

He left the words hanging in the air. Now my true identity had been uncovered, I could not live an ordinary existence. A chill went through me as the next thought entered my head: if I was allowed to live at all. There was little time to consider the alternative. Guards came to fetch us and we entered room after room filled with courtiers.

'It is more relaxed here than at the Hofburg,' von Starhemberg whispered to me. 'Most people here are the local nobility, here for the gossip and the shooting.'

When the guards halted at the next room, I sensed it was the private state room accommodating the Emperor. The doors opened, and we were led inside. The Emperor was seated on a throne though he was not dressed in full ceremonial imperial attire. He was flanked by sombrely dressed officials. Children played in the room, oblivious to our entrance.

I bowed deeply alongside von Starhemberg. The Emperor waved at me to come forward. He spoke to me in French in a voice little more than a whisper.

'So this is George of England's secret, then?' His eyes betrayed none of the mirth his voice offered. 'You claim to be the eldest and legitimate son of the king of England?'

I swallowed. Events had conspired against me to deny it.

'Yes, your Imperial Majesty, I am.'

The Emperor looked me up and down.

'You certainly have his looks. Von Esterhazy swears by it. But pretenders have appeared in the past and almost toppled thrones in Europe. How can we be certain?'

I waited, not sure whether his question was rhetorical or not. It was.

'We are allies with Great Britain against those revolutionary vermin who rule France and executed our aunt Marie-Antoinette. We do not wish to offend our ally. And yet you were in France. How so?'

'I was sent there by my father, your Imperial Majesty.'

I did not dare risk the whole truth. I still did not know whether the enmity my father bore me would work in my favour or not.

'To get you out of the way, yes?'

'Yes, your Imperial Majesty.'

187

'No doubt with an annuity and a warning to keep quiet and live an ordinary life? That is usually the way with these things. But then the Revolution came and things were too dangerous, and you found yourself helping to rescue my niece, Augusta.'

'Your niece, sire? I had no idea she was so closely related to you.'

'Of course not. You acted on impulse. You are a man of honour and integrity. For that you will be rewarded. However, your royal blood is not a simple affair. To inform His Majesty the King of Great Britain of your presence here in our realm might jeopardise his own security in these dark times, as well as your own.'

Silently, and fervently, I agreed with this last point, though for different reasons. If my father discovered I was alive and well in the Habsburg Empire, he would either request my presence in London or send assassins to deal with me here and now.

'We request you remain in Grinzing until we send you notice of our proposal. Everything you require will be provided for you.'

Except for my freedom, I almost said, but refrained from doing so.

'Thank you, sire.'

I made to step backwards, but not until he had me kiss his hand.

'I thank you, George Rex, for your heroic deed in assisting Graf von Starhemberg on his dangerous mission.'

With that, we were dismissed. I sat deep in thought in the carriage on the journey back to Grinzing, but von Starhemberg's parting handshake was accompanied by a friendly pat on the shoulder as I climbed out of the carriage. I brightened at this and reflected that at least the Emperor's view of me was a favourable one. It was a comforting thought and on the return journey to Grinzing, I convinced myself I was out of danger.

❖   ❖   ❖

I waited for many months at Grinzing for word from the emperor. Late summer became autumn and winter and the days grew shorter. My life was comfortable and I was permitted to go where I wished, by horse or by carriage, with the proviso that I was escorted at all times. Guest of the emperor though I undoubtedly was, my status was equally that of a prisoner. My chief occupation was looking out for the carriage of the Princess Augusta, whose visits became more and more frequent. With each visit, we grew to know each other and I convinced myself it was not the loneliness which persuaded me to fall in love with her. Her quick wit and intellect made her the best female company I had known for many years, better even than Catherine Meadows, the memory of whom was so dimmed by time as to be almost non-existent. Augusta's alabaster skin and large dark eyes stayed with me as I closed my eyes to sleep, and I saw her in my dreams so vividly that I sometimes awoke in the middle of the night fully expecting to see her standing in the room.

It could not last. Early in February, von Starhemberg paid me a visit. He had not been for many weeks – away, perhaps, on a mission – and I greeted his arrival with anticipation. He shook hands warmly and led me to his private drawing room. Again, he had sent word of his visit ahead and the fire was burning cheerfully. It reminded me I was very much his guest and that my residence in his castle was strictly conditional.

'Let's get to our business,' he said without preamble. 'The Emperor is making you an offer. He has decided that you are indeed the rightful son of His Majesty King George of England. He has deduced that you are too valuable to go off on your wanderings. Thanks to the French, the whole of Europe is ablaze with war. You will not be safe. Your presence in England would endanger the King there and possibly provoke rebellion. Do you play poker, Rex?'

Von Starhemberg's question was startling to say the least. What was he up to now? When I replied in the negative, he continued with a mischievous glint in his eye.

'We wish to maintain our alliance with Great Britain but at the same time, you are – in the words of a gambler – a bargaining chip which we can use in the great game of politics. We have you at our disposal to use as we wish whenever we need a strong hand. Putting it bluntly, Rex, the Emperor wishes you to remain in his realm. He will see you married and settled with an estate worthy of your royal rank.'

Did I have a choice? I was a prisoner in Grinzing and my birth made me a prisoner of the world. Considering that I had left France with nothing but the clothes I stood up in, my fortunes had changed dramatically. Indeed, this was the arrangement I had been half-expecting.

'It is an offer you would be foolish to refuse.' Von Starhemberg confirmed my thoughts. 'We would of course let you go . . .'

But my safety would not be guaranteed. In fact, they would hunt me down like a stag. To release a royal prince into revolutionary Europe was unthinkable. I was a pawn on the chessboard of Europe.

'Whom will I marry?'

Von Starhemberg inclined his head, gracefully acknowledging my acceptance.

'We have noted your growing relationship with the Princess Augusta. She is the youngest of five daughters and should your position as a royal prince ever be necessary to, er, call upon, then a marriage into the Habsburg royal line would reflect your status.'

It made sense to me now. The visits had been planned and encouraged. All these months, they had been watching us. Did Augusta know? Probably not, bless her. And should a revolution ever befall England and destroy the British monarchy as it had in

France, the Austrian Emperor had his own puppet ready to use on the political stage.

'It will be a morganatic marriage. Your children will have no claim whatsoever to the Habsburg throne. But they will of course continue the true descent of His Majesty King George.'

'Does Augusta know yet?'

'She will be told this afternoon. I am certain she will be happy.'

It was all so cleverly arranged I could not demur. I was very fond of the girl. My life would be comfortable and with luck, untouched by the wider vagaries of political affairs. The Emperor would never need to use me for his diplomatic games. In England, Fox had made a big splash with his radicals, but I doubted whether the English had the stomach to have a revolution like the French and execute their king. It was something I had fervently hoped for during my years in France, but not now. I prayed that my chances of being pushed to the foreground of world events were very slim.

'I accept.'

I shook von Starhemberg's hand and he flashed a smile at me, pleased to have accomplished his mission without any need for persuasion.

'Excellent. An estate will be provided for you, but not here, not near Vienna.'

'Where?'

'In Bohemia, up in the hills outside Prague. You will be safe there, and undisturbed.'

I understood. I would not be near enough to interfere or to make my presence known to anyone.

'You will be well cared for. You will have servants, several houses and a title. And the Princess is a truly lovely girl, no?'

With a roar of laughter, von Starhemberg clapped me on the back and strode from the room, leaving me to contemplate my future.

◈ ◈ ◈

Our wedding took place one month later. The quiet and private affair was not the event Augusta had anticipated as a young girl – even the Emperor declined to come – but she was radiant and I was filled with the growing realisation that I was wealthy and powerful in my own way. We rode to our new abode in the Bohemian hills, Hrad Jiri, escorted by dozens of armed guards, and our welcome at the castle was truly feudal. I sensed that some of our servants and the armed guards were employed by the Emperor to watch over us; but in time, their presence intruded less and less, until it was negligible. I grew to love the Princess deeply, and she me; I was content to bide my time, watching and waiting on world events from our home at Jiri. My desire for revenge had not lessened. Indeed, I felt my great fortunes afforded me possibilities to wreak that revenge when I chose.

Years passed. Augusta produced four sons for me, two of whom lived to reach a healthy adulthood, and four daughters, three of whom survived. In France, the unknown Napoleon had risen to command the Republican armies and the European wars took on a new dimension. Napoleon defeated the Austrian armies at both Marengo and Hohenlinden, and became Emperor. After France's crushing defeat of Austria at Austerlitz, it was only the victory of the British Royal Navy at Trafalgar that halted his progress to domination over the known world. These momentous events barely affected my family. We lived a happy life at Hrad Jiri whilst the great armies of Europe marched to and fro across the plains of Germany and Poland.

When our lives were finally intruded upon, it came not from Napoleon or from the Austrian emperor (I lived with half an ear trained to the castle gate, expecting von Starhemberg's arrival with a summons from the Emperor, but even this diminished when word of von Starhemberg's death at Marengo reached us), but from the place I thought I would never want to hear from again: England.

Pitt was dying. When the Third Coalition was crushed at Austerlitz, Pitt's health, never sound, worsened. I got word of this and it troubled my conscience so much that for the first time in so many years, I decided to travel to England and seek him out.

It was a hazardous mission, fraught with difficulties. I had to slip away from Jiri unnoticed, get across war-torn Europe, enter England and find Pitt. I would be arrested if caught. And what would Pitt make of my visit? Augusta begged and pleaded with me not to go, for the sake of the children if not for her own. But I became like a man possessed. I had to return. I had to see Pitt once more. Ever since his father, Lord Chatham, had witnessed the marriage of the King to my mother our lives had been intertwined. Pitt himself had played me like a puppet during my career at the Bar but his principles would not allow my execution, even in the interests of the King and, for that, I owed him.

I set out in the teeth of winter, in late December, and reached the English shore early in January. My wealth ensured me comfort and speed; my stealth ensured me security. Nobody in the Emperor's court would suspect me of leaving for a mission to England at Christmas time. I crossed Germany and took a ship to England from the Low Countries, docking at Felixstowe in fog and chilly gloom. I arrived in the darkening late afternoon, exactly seventeen years since I had been incarcerated at Newgate. It was my first visit to England, the land of my birth and the land that had cheated me of my birthright. I, the eternal exile, who should have been monarch, now returned like a despised thief in the night.

I knew Pitt would be at Downing Street, living in his own simple style. He had spent too much money on gambling and port to acquire a permanent country house where he could conduct government business, and the simplicity of Downing Street suited his style. I knocked on the door and was received by a nurse, who appeared to be exhausted. She agreed to let me in, on condition that I stayed for only a short time.

I followed her upstairs to Pitt's room. Pitt was sitting up in the bed, reading his newspaper. A half-empty bottle of port stood on the table. It occurred to me then that his liking for the stuff had undoubtedly hastened his end. His age could not have been greater than forty-six – my age, in fact – but he looked years older.

What little colour he had drained from his face when he saw me. So fixed had I been on getting to him that it had not occurred to me until then that my arrival might give him enough shock to send him to his maker.

'You!' he uttered, raising a limp hand at me. 'I thought never to see you again.'

I went to his side and took his hand. It was cold and damp.

'I had to come when I heard of your illness.'

'You came all the way from the Cape?'

'No, from Austria.'

I described the story of my escape and my life as an exile in Paris. When he learnt of my marriage to Augusta his eyes widened.

'My God! Do you have children?'

At my nod, he closed his eyes. Even now, in his dying days, his thoughts were for the politics of Britain and Europe. Any anxieties of the danger I had put myself in by coming to see him were put aside by the consuming admiration I had for the man.

'You saved me,' I said to him. 'You arranged for my mock execution and my freedom. You and Wilmot. The King wanted me dead.'

'And you come back to England to haunt me, putting all that into doubt.'

'I had to see you, to thank you for what you did.'

Pitt nodded, releasing my hand. 'I should have you arrested. Your very existence threatens European peace.'

'Napoleon seeks to destroy Europe and he has no knowledge of my existence.'

Pitt smiled wanly.

'He is a monster. I fear for the world when I am gone. Curse this liver!'

I met Pitt's jaundiced stare, and begged him not to report my presence in England.

'I will not betray you. There is enough grief in the world without adding you to it. You say you live quietly and happily in your castle? I envy you your wife and children.'

But you were the greatest politician of your age, I thought: greater even than your father.

'Go and find Wilmot.' Pitt spoke with an urgency that overrode his sickness. 'He will tell you things you have yet to learn. You will find him at Oxford. There are things you should know.'

'Thank y . . .'

Pitt cut me short and I had no chance to say more because the nurse bustled in and shooed me out of the room. My last sight of Pitt was of his slumped, sweating body in the bed, uttering groans of agony as the nurse turned him and plumped up the pillows.

I hired a private coach and ordered full speed to Oxford. We left before dawn and forced the horses hard. The weather was cold but dry and the mud had frozen in places, otherwise our progress would have taken another day. On enquiring at the porter's lodge at Trinity College I was informed that Wilmot, now very elderly, had retired but had the living of the parish of Barton-on-the-Heath in Warwickshire, by the gift of the College. It was too late to travel onwards, so I put up at the Mitre on the High Street.

I slept soundly and woke before the dawn. Chill, January light eked through the shutters. Pitt's twisted, dying body appeared before my eyes. Fate had set us together. His fortunes had been my misfortunes until he had seen fit to play the part of a Greek god and pluck me from the grip of death. And now it was I who had the wealth and the status. Pitt had played his part in the story of my life. He had done all he could for me. It was left to Wilmot, the man behind it all and the only person who knew our secrets, to have the final word.

We arrived at Barton-on-the-Heath at midday. The Rectory was the largest house in the village, a fine three-storey red-brick building on the green. I rapped on the door like a man possessed and demanded to see the Rector.

'You'll find him in the church.'

The housekeeper's peremptory reply cut through my demands. I thanked her – remembering some graces in my desperate urgency – and strode towards the church.

The door creaked open and as my eyes became accustomed to the light, I made out a figure seated on the front pew, seemingly in prayer. Advancing silently along the nave, I thought my approach was clandestine, but when I was three yards away, the figure twisted round.

Unlike Pitt, Wilmot showed no reaction at my presence in the church. Perhaps his life as a clergyman had given him a greater sense of patience than the meteor who was Pitt, whose trajectory soared above the rest of us but burnt out so much more quickly.

'You were instructed never to return.'

Wilmot's voice was cracked with age, his face lined and scored like the bark of a tree. I guessed his age to be over eighty.

'What ill wind blows you back to these shores?'

I ignored his hostility; my purpose overrode the need for good manners, on either behalf.

'I owe you a debt of thanks. You and Pitt saved my life . . .'

'. . . which you jeopardise by returning here to England. We are at war. There are government spies in every town. Napoleon talks of invasion. And you dare to come here?'

Wilmot wiped the spittle from the corner of his mouth and glared malevolently at me. How sad that fate should give this man such a great age and make him so bitter, and yet leave the inestimable Pitt so few years.

'I have seen Pitt. It was he who caused me to travel all this way. He told me you were here. He said there was more to know.'

'Did he?'

Wilmot's eyes widened. I sensed a change come over him.

'Pitt is dying. He is the greatest statesman of our age. Better Pitt than the Bonaparte ogre!'

I nodded, fearing to speak lest he revive his bad temper.

'More to know, eh?'

Wilmot patted the pew and I sat next to him.

'Yes, there is more for you to know. There is nothing that will alter your circumstances, but what I will tell you will confirm your worst suspicions of your father the King. You see, I married in secret to the sister of the King of Poland, Izabela. We were very young, and very much in love, and marriage was the only way to have each other. This was before I was elected to the College Fellowship. The grasping world of diplomacy and politics forced us apart before our love could continue. I took my Fellowship, without anyone being aware of my married status – which would have forbidden me the Fellowship – and Izabela returned to Poland and married again, to a Polish aristocrat. Our marriage was never known to the world. Her brother was Stanislaus, later king of Poland.'

I met the rector's unsteady gaze, unsure where this was leading us. It was another life built upon a lie, to be sure, but what had it got to do with me?

'We had a child.' Wilmot uttered the statement so quietly I almost did hear it. 'A girl. Olive, we called her. The Princess had to leave her in my care when she returned to Poland. She never returned and has not seen her daughter since that day. The child grew up cared for by others; I sent money, doing what I could to assist. What else could I do? The discovery of the child would have stripped me of my livelihood.'

Wilmot raised his shoulders, still angry at his own behaviour and the inequity of his situation over half a century later.

'Olive grew to be a beautiful woman and caught the eye of the younger brother of King George, marrying him.'

'Your daughter married the Duke of Cumberland?'

Wilmot smiled an uncharacteristically warm smile.

'Oh, yes. I officiated. Hannah's marriage was not the only secret marriage, for sure. Chatham witnessed that marriage and the King was present, though he did not witness it. But the Hanoverian perfidy did not end with the King's behaviour towards Hannah; the Duke of Cumberland was induced to put aside Olive and make a marriage more worthy of his royal origins. George III swiftly moved Olive and her child into private quarters and put it about that she was merely the mistress of the Duke.'

'There was a child?'

'Yes, also Olive. She is still living, and is the legitimate daughter of the Duke of Cumberland. The King panicked; the Royal Marriages

Act was passed by Parliament to prevent any future marriages occurring and to obliterate any signs of previous unions, including his own to Hannah Lightfoot. However, the Hanoverian habit of secret marriages knows no end. The King's other brother, the Duke of Gloucester, had secretly married Lady Maria Waldegrave, the illegitimate daughter of Horace Walpole's elder brother, several years before the Marriages Act. And the King's son, the Prince of Wales, married Mrs FitzHerbert, a Catholic. This secret marriage flouted not only the Marriages Act but also the Act of Settlement, which strictly forbids the heir to the throne to marry a Catholic, on pain of disbarment from the throne. Prince George has followed true to that dastardly Hanoverian strain, and married again, while Mrs FitzHerbert still lives, to Princess Caroline of Brunswick, who shall be his Queen one day.'

I was aghast. My mother was not the only casualty of the Hanoverian perfidy. Untold broken promises and betrayals cried out for justice; swift and deadly government concealments had crushed their victims.

'I knew all these secrets,' Wilmot continued, 'and so did Pitt. His father, Chatham, had told him everything. He had the King at his mercy, and so when the opportunity came for Pitt to take the highest office in the land he used this knowledge. Knowledge is power, so they say, and by God it worked for Pitt. My Fellowship was secured for life, and with it an annuity which allowed me to lead a comfortable life; I also prevailed upon the King to sign papers declaring that my daughter was legitimate and that her marriage to the Duke of Cumberland was also lawful. I have these papers stored safely and one day – perhaps not in my lifetime – Olive or her descendants will right the wrong which has been done. As will you, I sincerely hope.'

As Wilmot gripped my arm on that pew that wintry afternoon, I knew my destiny was as yet unfulfilled. I longed to tell him of my marriage to Augusta, and of the wealth and the power I possessed: that I had a son and heir who carried not only Hanoverian blood in him but Habsburg blood too; and that I harboured a careful and studied desire for revenge on my father and on his descendants. Our eyes locked and in that glance I knew I had no need to say anything. Our turn would come. History would yield up its secrets one day.

❖ ❖ ❖

I took my leave of Dr Wilmot soon after those words, though he had one last offering for me. We walked back to the Rectory together and he bade me wait in the drawing room whilst he fetched some documents from his study. I drank some hot grog with greedy gratitude, and read the contents of the documents. They included a copy of my parents' marriage certificate and I was grateful to have them. They are now stored with this memoir at Hrad Jiri, where one day they will, I am sure, be used to tell the world of my true heritage.

We shook hands, and I departed, travelling through the night to Felixstowe, where I took the first ship to the Low Countries and made my way back to my family at Hrad Jiri. I heard that Wilmot died just one year later. He took his secrets to the grave, confident that one day they would be revealed to the world.

❖ ❖ ❖

Our life at Hrad Jiri continued much as before. My absence had not been noticed and in February the news of Pitt's death reached us. I felt the visit to England had engendered me with a renewed sense of purpose. I began to use my wealth to train and employ a network of spies whom I sent to England to gain employment in the Court of St James. The King's health was erratic, and without Pitt's steady hand at the tiller of government, there was no knowing what might happen.

In August of 1806, the Holy Roman Empire was dissolved by Napoleon. It has been said that the empire was neither Holy, nor Roman, nor an Empire. The Emperor Francis assumed the title Francis I of Austria. Due to a series of damaging defeats inflicted on the Habsburgs by Napoleon, I became less and less of a royal puppet. Our family's wealth was secured; our privacy was assured when the last spies left the castle that summer. Francis was further humiliated when he was forced to send his daughter Marie-Louise to marry the Emperor Napoleon, as he now was. The English victory at Waterloo forced Napoleon into exile and has ensured peace in Europe for the last two and a half decades.

There is only one more episode to tell. My family prospered and when my eldest son William was twenty-one, I told him of his birthright. He was shocked, and understandably outraged, at the treatment meted out to me and his grandmother, Hannah. He vowed revenge, and I was satisfied that the secret had been passed on and with it, the seed of hatred which would find a fertile bed. When, at the age of eighty-one, my father the King died, I felt a great sorrow, coupled with disgust, as the Prince of Wales succeeded as King George IV. My spies wrote to me describing the sordid and pathetic details of his treatment of Queen Caroline, her exclusion from the coronation and of her subsequent trial for adultery. Ten years later, the throne passed to his feckless younger brother, William. It was obvious he too would have no heir; his daughters had died in infancy. I knew that God was cursing the Hanoverian line. My father had produced fifteen children with

Charlotte and yet had no living grandson to continue the royal line. Instead, it was the daughter of the Duke of Kent, Victoria, who inherited the throne in 1837 and sits on it this very day.

It was this succession that almost brought death to Hrad Jiri. My spies kept me well informed of the events at Court, and my son, William, had visited England on several occasions. During the summer of Victoria's accession I was resting in the gardens of the castle, my old bones no longer capable of over-exertion, watching my grandchildren play. I was content; my line was secure, and my son wealthy and invested in plotting our revenge, which I knew now would come after my lifetime.

'Mr Rex?'

The English voice stunned me, as did the use of the title. I had been known as Graf von Habsburg-Rex. He stood with his back to the sun, obliging me to shield my eyes. How he had got past the guards at the gate was a mystery.

'Who calls on me in this manner?'

'The Queen of England,' said the Englishman, moving so he blotted out the sun.

I saw then he was holding a pistol. The short, squat barrel was inches away from me.

'One of your spies became careless, and we took him in for questioning. He revealed a few things about you which we found very interesting.'

Shock had given way to fear now. If the British government knew of my whereabouts, my family, and all that I had worked for, would be in danger. One look at the hard-faced, determined gunman in front of me left me in no doubt of that.

'Interesting, yes,' I managed to regain my dignity and spoke with an imperious tone that belied my terror. 'Perhaps such knowledge would be very damaging to the Crown if it were widely known.'

'Do not fear on that account,' the agent said with a ruthless smile. 'Very few people know. It is in your interest to have it widely known, not ours.'

'It is said your Queen is illegitimate and that she was smuggled into the bedroom in a warming pan after decades of childless marriages,' I said trying to stall him.

'There are always rumours. Perhaps there is some truth to them. The truth is far too dangerous. It must be buried deep.'

As he raised the pistol, the crack of the musket was followed by another, and he dropped without a sound at my feet, his brains splashing close to my boots. Behind his corpse, I saw my son running with three of our guards, chasing two intruders out of the garden and into the orchard. A second body lay inert on the lawn. The grandchildren were screaming. Augusta came out of the hall, open-mouthed; the wet-nurse rushed to the infants.

'Get the children inside!' I shouted to my wife, climbing to my feet. 'Shut the doors!'

There was no need to take any further action, however. Moments later, my eldest son returned grim-faced, with the guards. His sword dripped with blood and his eyes exuded triumph.

'You caught them?'

'Yes, father.'

'Good. Bury them as far from here as possible. Do it tonight.'

I glanced down at the corpse at my feet.

'Let us hope that is the last we shall hear from Victoria of England.'

My darling Augusta died one year ago, a year after that intrusion, and so I sit here, in the study of the castle, writing my memoirs which will one day form the greatest weapon I can hope to devise. My revenge will be germinal; it may take several decades, but the seed has been sown. The British monarchy has a foundation of sand, each illegitimacy built on top of another. One day it will come crashing down. My life is almost at an end. I have outlived Pitt and Wilmot, the guardians of my secret, and I have outlived my half-brothers, the false kings George and William; I know a mere girl with no right to the throne rules England. My son and his sons will strive to unseat her and her descendants. I will have my revenge; the final battle for the truth will come like the Last Judgement, and these words I have written shall blast my enemies to nothing. The truth will reveal itself. My blood royal will one day triumph. Justice will be done.

George Rex
Hrad Jiri, August 1839

1914

22 June 1914

As soon as he spotted Septimus emerging from the vestry, clutching the second part of the memoir, Quayle diverted Unsworth's attention – which he did with aplomb. Septimus slipped the memoir under his jacket and they made their excuses and left, thanking him profusely.

'But it's theft!' Quayle exclaimed as they raced out of the churchyard, appalled but half-laughing.

'We're merely borrowing it,' was Septimus's retort. 'Anyway, it doesn't belong in a church. We're simply returning it to its rightful owner.'

They'd put up at the Great Western Hotel, with a room apiece alongside one another. Septimus's room had a balcony overlooking the gardens and it was here he sat, reading the memoir before passing it to Quayle, whose muttered exclamations mirrored his own thoughts. When the last remnants of the candles flickered and died and Septimus heard an owl hooting somewhere beyond the high wall he knew it was time for bed. The bottle on the table was empty – the last of three – but Septimus felt more awake than ever before. It was as if everything in his life had been in preparation for this. His senses were sharply focused; his mind was alert and it was now he could feel the energy and the power of the past surging through his veins. The memoir had been handed to him for a purpose. He was the one who would make the connection between Rex's oath of vengeance and Hahn's murder. It was left to Septimus – and Septimus alone – to reconcile those factors.

❖   ❖   ❖

Next morning, leaving Quayle at the breakfast table finishing the last of his bacon, Septimus went down to the lobby and asked them to put a call through to Christ's College. It was imperative to speak to Battiscombe and tell him about the discovery at St Peter's Church. Only he could authenticate the memoir. His expertise and authority would give sufficient weight to Septimus's claims.

'Christ's College. Porter's lodge.'

'This is Septimus Oates, Travers. Has Professor Battiscombe been into College this morning?'

'No, Mr Oates. His post is here ready for collection. He should be in for the College Council meeting at nine o'clock.'

Septimus checked the clock behind the hotel reception desk. It was half past eight.

'Could you ask him to put a call through to the Great Western Hotel, Carmarthen when he arrives, please? Tell him it is urgent. I must speak to him before the council meeting.'

Septimus returned to the breakfast table with an irritation he couldn't contain.

'Patience, my boy,' Quayle said, pouring more coffee. 'Leave it another half hour. Battiscombe's probably forgotten all about the memoir. I expect he's working in the Bodleian. He might not even be in College until lunchtime.'

'There's a College Council at nine. He has to be in for that.'

'In that case, we'll finish up here and settle the bill. Since your generous benefactor is paying I think I'll have another coffee. When we're on the train, I suggest you re-read the memoir.'

Septimus went to his room to pack his case. After smoking a couple of cigarettes, he got a call through to Christ's. It was gone nine now.

'He's still not here, Mr Oates.' Travers sounded concerned. 'It's the first time the Professor has missed College Council since he was elected in '64. I should know, my father was head porter then . . .'

Septimus didn't wait to hear Travers continue his reminiscences. What he heard was enough to tell him that something was very wrong. Septimus returned the receiver to the hook and accosted Quayle who was sitting in the hotel lounge reading *The Times*.

'Ireland again,' he said. 'It seems there's another imminent crisis and we're to send troops over to settle things once and for all.'

'Never mind that,' Septimus said bluntly, in a manner he'd never have used previously. 'Professor Battiscombe hasn't gone into College. Something's wrong, Quayle, very wrong. I'm going to Oxford.'

They parted at Reading, Quayle going south to Winchester for afternoon lessons, Septimus going north up to Oxford. Professor Battiscombe lived in one of the rambling four-storey redbrick Victorian houses off the Woodstock Road, half a mile north of the city centre. Septimus wasted no expense, taking a taxi from the railway station and up St Giles, promising a hefty tip for a speedy journey. Battiscombe had lived in College accommodation for twenty-five years before moving. Septimus had visited the house many times for research tutorials, which more often than not led to late-night sessions involving frequent visits to the wine cellar. Remembering those good times and how kind Battiscombe had been to him during his lonely years researching his dissertation, Septimus marched up to the front door and rang the bell. The authenticity of the memoir was not so important any more. What concerned him was the Professor's safety.

There was no reply. He waited and rang again. He stooped and peered through the letter box. There didn't appear to be anything unusual about the hallway: Battiscombe's coat and hat were on the peg and his umbrella in the stand. He walked along the side of the house to the back door and peered through the kitchen window.

'Can I help you?'

Septimus jumped. Spinning round he saw a formidable, matronly woman, almost as broad as she was tall, blocking the way to the door. A pair of angry eyes glared up at him from behind thick-rimmed glasses.

'I am looking for Professor Battiscombe.'

'And who might you be?'

'I'm one of his research students. Septimus Oates,' he explained, with a bright smile, hoping that charm might melt the frozen stare.

'And why are you poking around the Professor's house? Is he expecting you? He's normally out on Tuesdays. College Council.'

'Yes, he is expecting me,' Septimus lied. 'I telephoned him at the College earlier this morning and got no reply. He asked me to phone him there. It's rather important.'

'I see.' The stare relented a little. 'I'm Mrs Lobb, the Professor's housekeeper. I do one 'til three on Tuesdays. That's the way he likes it.' She pulled out a bunch of keys, adding in a softer tone, 'You'd better come inside if he's expecting you.'

Septimus knew something was wrong as soon as Mrs Lobb opened the door. The morning post lay untouched on the floor. The house was eerily quiet. Following the housekeeper through the hall and into the sitting room, Septimus resisted the urge to run upstairs and shout for the Professor.

'Dear, oh dear. Another long night in the senior common room,' said Mrs Lobb as she bustled into the kitchen and grabbed her apron.

Septimus glanced round the sitting room. Nothing was amiss. Perhaps Battiscombe had stayed too long in College and imbibed too much port after all? For a bachelor don, it was the habit of a lifetime and one not easily broken. No doubt he had found a room spare in College and stayed the night. But Septimus knew in his heart this was not the case. Battiscombe had been at home last night with the first part of the memoir. He was excited about the possibility of finding the second half. He would never allow a dinner in College to distract from an historical find of this magnitude. Septimus knew the Professor well enough to know that when it came to matters of such importance, nothing would have distracted him.

'May I go upstairs?'

Before Mrs Lobb could protest, Septimus leapt up the stairs two at a time and strode down the landing to the study. He knocked on the door, waited a second, then tried to open it but met with considerable resistance. He shoved hard and almost fell into the room.

A scene of devastation greeted him. The Professor's normally pristine, book-lined study had been savagely torn apart. Valuable, leather-bound books had been ripped from the shelves and hurled onto the floor with such ferocity that some of the spines had smashed. Papers from the desk were scattered all over the room; ink had spilled randomly across the desk. Even the Chesterfield had been savaged with a knife and hacked open. Battiscombe's rare Hogarth prints had been plucked from the wall and hurled to the floor; glass crunched under Septimus's feet as he entered the room.

211

It had all been done with deliberate, and calculated, brutality.

Septimus made his way through the room, absent-mindedly picking up books and clearing the floor. He knew what he had come for would have vanished with the Professor. He couldn't hope he would find the memoir, or any sign of it. His stomach lurched. If the intruders could do this to his study, what would they do to his friend? Septimus rushed out of the room, blindly stumbling back along the landing and into the bedroom.

The bed was made and the room was perfectly tidy. The Professor himself was sitting at his bureau by the window, with his back to Septimus. He was fully dressed, in tweed suit and gown.

'Professor?'

As he moved towards the window, he realised the chair was pushed tightly against the bureau, the Professor's arms placed on the surface as if writing. But it was a grotesque parody. Septimus placed a tentative hand on his shoulder; something in his brain still expected his friend to turn and greet him with an enthusiastic grin. Battiscombe fell forward onto his face, hitting the bureau with a dull thump. There was congealed blood on his neck where his throat had been cut. Septimus noticed a slew of blood across the curtains in front of the bureau, which had spurted from the Professor's throat. Septimus guessed Battiscombe had been dead a few hours, probably since yesterday evening. He had been taken by surprise, by an assassin using stealth and cunning. Perhaps they had ransacked the study in search of the memoir while the house was empty and, failing to find it, had lain in wait for the Professor.

Septimus recoiled, his thoughts whirling. He was in shock at the sight of another corpse in front of him – the second in eleven days – and he was overwhelmed with guilt. He should have kept the Professor out of this whole business. He'd never been a threat to anyone, never had a bad word or an evil thought. He was just a College man of devotion and genuine compassion. Who had

212

done this awful thing? It was beyond comprehension to think that a secret royal marriage could lead to this.

But it had. Battiscombe was dead, slaughtered in his own bedroom. The memoir was missing. Septimus was at the scene of another crime. He couldn't run away from this. And he knew whoever had killed Hahn had also murdered Battiscombe. As he turned to leave the room he noticed the Professor's right fist was clenched. Septimus reached forward, steeled himself, and eased something from his old friend's grasp. It was only a scrap of paper, and on it were three words written in the Professor's inimitable handwriting. Septimus looked at it quickly, but it appeared to have been written in some sort of code: *ujedinjenje ili smrt*.

Folding the paper into his waistcoat pocket, he went downstairs and steeled himself to ask Mrs Lobb to contact the police.

For the second time in eleven days, Police Inspector Albert Coppard studied Septimus Oates. Was he a murderer? Perhaps . . . Perhaps not. A fantasist? They had certainly thought so after the New College Lane hoax. But now they had a body and no doubt about that. Coppard couldn't rule anything out; the young don was writing his dissertation and the victim was his supervisor. Academe was no stranger to fits of jealous rage. This was outright murder, through and through. And the young man sitting opposite him was the first person to discover the murder victim. He may well have been the last to see the victim alive.

'How well did you know Professor Battiscombe?'

'Well enough,' said Septimus, his tone as measured as he could make it. He knew he wasn't a suspect, but once they made the link with Hahn's murder things would look very bad indeed. 'I have been a member of College for seven years and Professor Battiscombe has been acquainted with my progress during that period. We have been particularly close since I began my research.'

'Particularly close? What precisely do you mean?'

Septimus returned the Inspector's gaze. He saw in front of him a policeman of great experience, who had sent many people to gaol, and in all probability quite a few to the gallows. He quelled his panic. He might, just might, find himself charged with murder if the interview didn't go well, even though he had contacted the police with Mrs Lobb and had come voluntarily to the Police Station.

'We were close in a professional sense. We used to spend hours together talking through my research and, because this is Oxford, our work was often our private life also. We dined together – in College and at his house – and sat up late.'

'Just the two of you?'

'No, there's a group of us. All research graduates.'

Septimus thought of the others who would be devastated at the news of Battiscombe's violent death.

'But you were one of his favoured pupils?'

Septimus paused. Had he been? Possibly. Battiscombe always seemed to single him out at lectures and dinners, and it was Septimus who was invited back for port more frequently than the others.

'Yes, to be honest, I suppose I could be considered his favoured pupil. But not to the detriment of the others.'

'As far as you're aware.' Coppard leant forward and lit his pipe. 'There may have been others who were jealous and found his patronage of you intolerable.'

Septimus knew he couldn't dismiss the Inspector's theory, for he could hardly afford to anger the man. When would he be able to introduce the memoir as the motive for Battiscombe's murder?

A police constable entered the room silently, and presented Coppard with a sheet of paper. Coppard read it, looked at Septimus, and read it again, before dismissing his constable. He placed the paper on the table and folded his arms.

'Do you know what this is, Mr Oates?'

Septimus had no idea, but he guessed it was information that was going to make the situation either far worse or far better.

'This is the preliminary autopsy report. Professor Battiscombe was killed at least twelve hours ago. In that case, you couldn't have killed him this morning. However . . .' Coppard tapped his pencil against his teeth, '. . . where were you yesterday afternoon, Mr Oates?'

Septimus tried not to let the relief show on his face.

'Carmarthen, South Wales. On research business.'

'Can anyone confirm your whereabouts?'

'Yes. My companion was Captain Mordecai Quayle. He's a senior master at Winchester College. We met Reverend Thaddeus Unsworth, the curate of St Peter's Church while we were there and stayed at the Great Western Hotel last night.'

Coppard jotted the names down. Oxford dons, a Winchester master and a man of the cloth. He would have to tread carefully against this Trinity of the Establishment.

Flushed with increasing confidence, Septimus dug into his wallet and produced his train ticket to Carmarthen. Coppard took it, examined it closely, and placed it on the table.

'I'll keep that, if I may.'

A statement, not a request, but Septimus sensed he was on surer ground.

'The autopsy report states the deceased was knocked out by a blow to the back of the head and then his throat was cut. He would have felt no pain. In my opinion, this was a professional job. But why, I ask, did they kill him? Did he have any enemies? Were they looking for something? The state of his study certainly suggests they were.' Coppard's eyes narrowed. 'Would you know what they were looking for Mr Oates?'

Septimus had a split second to tell the Inspector about the memoir, and about the Rex family but something in Coppard's eyes warned him that if he did so, he wouldn't be leaving the confines of the police station for many more hours, if not days. The memoir was missing and his friend's death needed explaining, if not avenging. He had to get out of this building and find it, and in doing so, he would find Battiscombe's killers – and Hahn's.

'I have no idea what they were after, Inspector,' Septimus said looking Coppard straight in the eye. 'He was not wealthy as far as I know.'

'We are looking into his finances. I doubt that's an aspect of the Professor's life with which you are familiar.' Satisfied he had at least had the last word, Coppard rose from his chair. 'You're free to leave, Mr Oates. We have your College address.'

Relief washed over Septimus, but just as he reached the door, the Inspector said,

'One last thing . . .'

Septimus halted, holding his breath. Now they would charge him with Hahn's murder.

But Coppard merely said,

'Please leave the address of your friend, Mr Quayle, at the front desk.'

'How's Battiscombe?' Quayle asked. He was in his garden seat, enjoying the evening sunshine.

'He's been murdered.' The words came out harshly, but Septimus didn't know how to break it any other way.

'Good God,' Quayle exclaimed. 'Where did you find him?'

'When I got into the house it was clear Battiscombe hadn't been home the previous night, so I ran up to his study to see if I could find the memoir but there was no sign of it. The room had been ransacked. When I looked in his bedroom, there he was, with his throat cut. He was fully dressed and the Inspector thinks he was killed last night, on his return from College. I've just spent three hours at Oxford City Police station making my statement.'

'My God, you poor boy.'

Quayle gently guided Septimus to a neighbouring chair. When he returned from the house he carried whisky glasses and a bottle of single malt. He poured two generous measures and passed Septimus a glass, which the young man downed at a gulp. Quayle poured another measure and handed Septimus one of his slim Turkish cigars. He lit them and they puffed in silence for a moment.

'You would have been questioned closely over Battiscombe's murder.'

'I was.'

Septimus recalled the horror and the panic once he had told Mrs Lobb, which had set in train the whole process of police involvement. The housekeeper had been inconsolable, but even in her hysterical state she had managed to give a statement describing Septimus's arrival and the condition in which they'd found the house.

'The police suspect nothing of me. The autopsy report confirms Battiscombe was murdered last night. I explained we were in Carmarthen.'

'*We*? So I'm in on this now?'

'Of course. You're my alibi.'

Quayle grunted with exasperation.

'And the memoir?'

'I made no mention of it.'

'Good man. The last thing we want is some half-witted peeler stamping all over that and bringing me, Hargeaves and Rex in on the whole business. That is for us to investigate.'

'I found this.' Septimus handed him the scrap of paper he'd

prised from Battiscombe's fist. 'It appears to be a code of some sort.'

'Do you recognise the paper?' Quayle asked, turning it round in his hand and holding it up to the light.

'I think it's been torn from the memoir.'

Quayle placed the scrap on the garden table.

'Yes, you could be right. But it's not in code. It's in a Slavonic language. I'm not sure which one.'

Septimus took the scrap and read the strange words again. Battiscombe had made a discovery of sorts and in his haste had scribbled it on the manuscript itself, only for it to be wrenched violently from his hands. What had he done to deserve that? For a man of peace who had never left Oxford in his lifelong pursuit of learning, to be slain horribly was so unjust.

'Oates?' Quayle asked gently, placing his hand on his young friend's arm. 'Try not to think of it. You must put it behind you. I know you've had a shock but we have to go on. Have the police ventured anything about motive?'

Septimus took a deep breath.

'Nothing . . . yet. I gave them your address and told them I was lodging here for the foreseeable future.'

'Our fates are entwined, then.' Quayle said wryly as he poured more measures of whisky. 'Did they mention Hahn?'

'No. And I still don't understand why his murder wasn't reported. Do you think it is possible that he survived the attack?'

'Not from what you've said. But then I have seen many a dead man get up and walk away from gunshot wounds, so we shouldn't rule anything out. It is also possible that Hahn's killer returned to New College Lane and removed the body and that's why the crime has been overlooked. You're the sole witness.'

'It would explain the police ignorance of the whole matter.'

'Let it lie for now. The question is: what next? We have

a killer on the loose. Two people have lost their lives and the first part of the memoir has been stolen. Since we hold the remainder the killer will track us down next. What do you propose we do?'

Septimus picked up the scrap of paper and read the line again: *ujedinjenje ili smrt*. The clue to Battiscombe's murder lay in this obscure phrase.

'Well?' asked Quayle impatiently. 'What do you propose we do?'

Quayle had thought the language was Slavonic. That in itself was a clear directive.

'Prague. That's where I'm going. To find Charles Rex and get some answers. Battiscombe deserves as much, and so does Hahn.'

❖ ❖ ❖

Septimus had been instructed to contact the East India Club as soon as he had some information. He sent a telegram from the Swan Hotel, for the attention of William Rex:

MEMOIR FOUND. AWAIT FURTHER INSTRUCTIONS.

'That'll reel him in,' said Quayle, with satisfaction.

Sure enough, a boy from the Swan came round with a telegram within the hour which simply read:

TICKETS FOR PRAGUE AT CLUB. DEPART CHARING X 0900.

'Told you,' grinned Quayle.

Septimus realised, not for the first time, how much his old friend was relishing this whole business. He took his pen and copied the words onto a piece of paper.

'I want you to translate this and find out anything you can which may tell us more about the Professor's death. I'll keep the copy; you'll need to ensure that anything you have translated is identical to the words poor old Battiscombe wrote.'

Quayle took the scrap and folded it carefully into his waistcoat pocket.

'Consider it done. How will I know where to contact you in Prague?'

'Try the Golden Tree in Mala Strana.' He fished into his jacket pocket and brought out a small box of matches. 'Here's the full address.'

'If you need anything, I will come out as soon as I can.'

Septimus suppressed a smile at the thought of the schoolmaster – morning-coat, side-whiskers, cigars and all – arriving in Prague. He would be a welcome face, but would he be any use? It was a while since Quayle had served in Egypt and the Sudan.

'Thank you,' Septimus said, treating the offer with the respect it deserved. 'I shall not hesitate to call upon your services.' He put his hand on the memoir. 'If they want this, they'll have to give me some answers first.'

'That's the spirit,' Quayle said looking at his pocket watch. 'Let's get an early night. You'll be getting the first train up to town in the morning.'

He got up from the garden seat and blew out the candles. The darkness had settled around them and although it wasn't late, Septimus was exhausted by the discovery of Battiscombe's body and his subsequent interrogation by the police. He followed Quayle into the house, bade him goodnight and fell asleep immediately, confident that the solutions would be found in Prague.

The train drew into Franz Josef station on Thursday afternoon. Septimus was to report to the reception at the Grand Hotel adjacent to the station, where he would be given a telephone connection through to Rex.

'Mr Rex?' Septimus spoke urgently into the receiver.

'No, this is Charles. Who is calling?' The tone was typically abrupt and arrogant.

'This is Septimus Oates.'

'Do you have the manuscript?'

Septimus took a deep breath.

'Yes. I have the second part . . .'

The line went dead and for a moment Septimus thought he had been cut off, but then William Rex came on the line.

'Septimus. How delightful to hear from you. You have been successful, I gather?'

'Yes, Mr Rex, although not entirely. There is much I must tell you. When can we meet?'

'Stay where you are,' ordered Rex. 'I'll send a car for you. It will take an hour or so. We can talk properly then.'

The wait gave Septimus an opportunity to buy some tobacco

and enjoy a delicious Czech coffee. Precisely one hour later the car arrived, the same Daimler he'd seen parked outside the Blue Duckling, the restaurant where he'd met Rex. It was the same taciturn chauffeur who loaded his bag into the boot and held the door for him, saying nothing in response to his charge's cheerful greeting.

They sped out of the city, heading south. He registered the sign-posts as he tried to orientate himself – Říčany, Benešov, Sedlčany – but only when the looming Czech-Moravian highlands emerged in the far distance did he find his bearings. He remembered travelling through the hills by train to Vienna in the year before going up to Oxford. It had been winter and the mountains had been heavy with snow. Now the sun shone with dazzling intensity. The Daimler turned off the main road and drove through the town of Pelhřimov before climbing into the hills towards Křemešnik. Septimus enjoyed the breathtaking views but during the journey his unease grew. He was at Rex's mercy out here.

The road grew narrower as the Daimler climbed the steep hillside, and a castle topped with several tall towers lay before them. There was little time to appreciate the full extent of the fortress before the driver turned into the gateway. Just as he did so another car came towards them at speed and swerved around them. In a split second Septimus recognised Charles Rex behind the wheel. The Daimler braked sharply to let him pass and rolled to a halt across the cobbled courtyard alongside the steps up to the main doors.

'Where are we?' asked Septimus, noticing several armed men in the shadows under the gateway.

The chauffeur spoke for the first time since leaving Prague: 'This is Hrad Jiri.'

❖   ❖   ❖

Septimus followed the chauffeur up the steps and into the main entrance hall to where Rex was standing, a broad smile on his face.

'Welcome to Hrad Jiri, Mr Oates. It is a pleasure to welcome you to my home.'

Gone was any trace of the menace Septimus had detected on the telephone. Instead, it had been replaced by a great deal of charm.

'Thank you, Mr Rex. I am honoured to be here.'

'Let me show you round,' said Rex. 'We're in the Vysorina region and, more specifically, on the Křemešnik mountain. This was a traditional gathering place for pilgrims. You can see the church of the Holy Trinity from the north windows. Near the church is a spring, which has miraculous healing abilities.'

As he spoke, Rex led his guest through the Great Hall, a vast room with an open fireplace; the walls were adorned with carvings, tapestries and stags' heads.

'This castle was originally built in 1348 by the Czech King and Roman Emperor Charles IV and the castle was the stronghold for the royal treasures and coronation jewels during the Hussite wars. The chapel has a collection of rare fourteenth-century panel paintings.'

Climbing a winding stone staircase above the Great Hall they entered what appeared to be the private quarters of the Rex family. The views from the windows across the mountains were spectacular but Septimus couldn't help noticing several guards strolling along the battlements.

'Nice view,' he said dryly, gesturing to the guards.

He could see into the garden where, according to the memoir, the ageing George Rex had been sitting when Queen Victoria's assassins had come for him. He turned back to the living room. Here George Rex had ended his days, wealthy and titled, with a loving wife and heirs and his family line – and the secret emnity – assured.

'Come. Sit.'

Rex waved at an easy chair. A servant brought a tray of tea and cakes into the room. The tea set was exquisite, no doubt an eighteenth-century heirloom. Rex waited until the tea had been poured before continuing.

'My ancestors made a fortune in the late nineteenth century when the industrial revolution reached Bohemia. George Rex married a Habsburg princess, a union which in itself ensured great riches, but he devoted the rest of his life to increasing his wealth. His wife's dowry included estates located in some of the most prosperous coal regions. He became one of the richest men in Bohemia.'

Septimus sipped some tea and took a slice of cake.

'You said you had not entirely been successful. What did you mean?'

Caught off guard by the sudden interrogatory tone, Septimus struggled to remain calm, reminding himself he had the remainder of the memoir in his briefcase. Before relinquishing it he needed to find out what – if anything – his host knew about Battiscombe's murder and the scrap of paper.

'I have the second half of the memoir. However, we suffered a great loss in recovering it for you.'

He drew the memoir from his bag, taking care to hold it tightly to his chest. Rex glanced at it but betrayed no desire to take it.

'Professor Battiscombe, my tutor and friend, was in possession of the first part of the memoir when he . . . he . . .'

'Go on,' said Rex, not unkindly.

'. . . he was murdered. He was brutally slain in his own bedroom, his throat cut.'

The horror of the discovery threatened to overwhelm Septimus and he took a deep breath. Rex poured him a glass of water and he drank it greedily, grateful for Rex's silence. 'His study had been ransacked and the memoir has been taken.'

'How did the Professor come to be in possession of the memoir?' Rex's tone was no longer sympathetic.

Septimus replaced the glass on the table.

'I asked him to verify the story of George Rex, son of King George III.'

'And what did the Professor conclude?'

'That the tale is a mere fabrication. There is no evidence, other than the memoir, to support his existence. The sole George Rex in history – the son of a London distiller – emigrated to southern Africa in search of his fortune.'

Septimus waited for Rex's reaction, but his host was impassive, so he continued: 'I believe Battiscombe was murdered because he knew George Rex was not what legend purports him to be.'

'There are many who have dismissed the Rex story. None of them have been murdered. The reason your friend the Professor was killed is simple.'

'What do you suggest?'

'Battiscombe was murdered because you gave him the memoir.'

The words fell like an axe on Septimus's neck. He had known it was wrong to have allowed Quayle to take the memoir up to Oxford. Quayle may have delivered it, but he alone must take responsibility for Battiscombe's death. Septimus had known after Karl Hahn's murder that possession of the documents put the keeper at great risk, and he had failed to inform his old friend just how dangerous it was.

'But who would want to kill Battiscombe, other than someone with much to lose if they were unmasked as frauds or at least supporting a fraudulent cause?'

If Rex interpreted this as an accusation levelled against him, then he showed no indication of it.

'My son and I warned you that there are many unscrupulous bodies – Royalists, republicans, anarchists, Bolsheviks, government agencies – who stand to gain by either concealing or revealing the truth behind the story and who will stop at nothing to get their hands on the documents.' He spread his hands in a helpless gesture. 'I am at the mercy of the events and fear I cannot help you. Whoever killed Battiscombe is long gone and the authorities will have little success in catching a professional assassin.'

'Then perhaps you might understand this,' Septimus suggested as he unfolded the words found in Battiscombe's fist and passed them to Rex.

'I've never seen the words before,' he said, giving the paper a perfunctory glance before handing it back to Septimus.

There was an imperceptible change in his demeanour however. Septimus knew he was lying.

'Do you recognise the language?'

'I regret not. Now, we must conclude our business. I have a cheque here for the balance owed to you. I shall overlook the unfortunate loss of part one of the memoir, but we have copies of that. It is the second part – containing conclusive evidence – we require. We owe you a great debt. I shall inform you when you are free to publish your findings and make your name. It will be Professor Oates before too long, no doubt?'

The door opened and attendants entered the room and proceeded to clear the tea table. Rex escorted Septimus through the hallway to the main entrance.

'I wish you a safe journey. Thank you for your efforts.'

Septimus shook Rex's hand, knowing there was little else he could do. Just as he began to walk down the steps away, his host called softly after him.

'Where did you find the scrap of paper?'

'In the Professor's fist. I believe he was onto something when he was killed. There is more to it than just the George Rex story.'

For a moment, the mask slipped and Rex's shoulders seemed to slump a fraction before he regained his composure.

'Goodbye Septimus,' he said. 'Take very good care of yourself in these uncertain times.'

Despite the brilliant sunshine Septimus felt chilled to the bone. Rex may have settled the balance but the account was not yet closed.

The Daimler took Septimus back to Prague, where he asked to be dropped off at the Golden Tree. His train to England was scheduled to depart the following morning, so he had the rest of the afternoon and an evening to kill in Prague. He was determined to find out as much as he could about Charles. If Rex was not going to reveal anything, then perhaps another conversation with his son might open up new avenues. Rex's reaction to the scrap of paper nagged at Septimus; therein lay the clue to Battiscombe's murder. He couldn't rule out Rex's direct involvement in the Professor's murder. He had the motive – Battiscombe's insistence that the George Rex story was a fabrication would undermine Rex's credibility – and he had the means to hire thugs. And this meant Hahn's murder could also be laid at Rex's door.

It was risky to remain in Prague but he owed it to Battiscombe to find out whatever he could. The hotel manager, the ever-helpful Bruno, gave him directions to the University of Prague's administrative buildings, because it was there – where Charles had let slip that he was studying – Septimus had decided to begin his search.

Septimus had no letters of recommendation with him, but he knew Charles was a student in the Faculty of Politics, or at least had some association with that department. He approached the University offices, enquired as to the whereabouts of the Faculty. His British papers and youthful looks were seemingly enough to authenticate his claim that he was a visiting academic from the University of Oxford, which, in a sense, he was.

A noisy crowd of students was just leaving a lecture when he entered the building. They were no different to the energetic and confident young men who attended the lectures in Oxford. Septimus scanned the crowd carefully but couldn't see Charles.

'Can I help?'

Septimus turned to see a short, bespectacled man of slight build, with thinning hair. He was not as well dressed as the boisterous students milling around, and Septimus suspected he was a research scholar, living off his own merits, and warmed to him instantly.

'I'm looking for a student in the Political Faculty, name of Charles Rex. Do you know him?'

'We can't talk here,' he said nodding curtly. 'Come and buy me a coffee across the road, where I'll tell you more.'

They left the university square, the student walking rapidly along the pavement before darting between two trams, leaving Septimus running to keep up. The man ducked through a low door and Septimus found himself in a tiny smoke-filled bar, in semi-darkness but for the June sunlight which stabbed through the blinds. Dust and cigarette smoke swirled lazily in the beams of light and the room was large enough for no more than half a dozen people. As it was, there were two people there and one of them was serving behind the bar. Septimus's new-found acquaintance rattled out something in Czech in a way which suggested he was a regular customer, and two small glasses were placed on the bar.

'Schnapps,' he explained, downing his.

Septimus put the glass to his lips and caught a whiff of the sickly drink; he took it in one gulp, grateful for the coffee which had also been prepared.

'Oskar Horaček,' said his companion, by way of introduction, gesturing to a seat.

'Septimus Oates. Thank you for helping me.'

'It is no trouble,' said Horaček. 'I have something you need and maybe there is something you can offer me in return. It could be a valuable trade.'

Septimus swallowed his coffee, not entirely sure what Horaček meant, but presumably it involved money. His initial favourable impression of the man began to fade.

'You enquired about Charles Rex.' Horaček lit a cigarette. 'Yes, I know something of him. He is a final-year student at the university. He comes from the country – a wealthy estate to the south – and he has an apartment in the city. I am not sure where, but it wouldn't be difficult to find.'

'How much would this information cost me?'

Horaček lit another cigarette, this time offering one to Septimus.

'You have English pounds? That is good. Let us say one pound for the coffee and, for the information you require, another five pounds.'

Septimus drew on the cigarette, which was a foul, cheap local brand. It was a high price to pay, but William Rex had given him a great deal of money for the memoir.

'How can you be certain to locate Rex?'

Horaček grinned, pleased to have sparked interest from the Englishman. The money was sure to be forthcoming.

'In this city of spies, information is everywhere. You just have to know how to use it and, of course, have the resources to acquire it. I can find the information for you and you can afford it. It is a good partnership, I think.'

At this point, Septimus wondered whether Horaček was a student at the university at all. What was it Charles had said about this city? Something about the state of secrets and the Emperor knowing everything.

'Agreed,' said Septimus, finishing his coffee and reaching for his wallet. 'When will you have the details?'

With the transaction almost concluded Horaček assumed a brisk air. He needed to get to work.

'Permit me one hour. I'll meet you here at six.'

Septimus handed him the payment. He was sceptical as to whether he would ever see the man again, but since it was Rex's money, it didn't matter quite so much.

'I'll leave first,' Horaček said as he got up from the table. 'Wait five minutes before you come out. I'll see you later, my English friend.'

Septimus watched him leave. The barman behind the counter merely shrugged. When the time was up, he left some coins for the drinks and walked out of the café. Horaček was long gone, as he had intended, probably to the money exchange at the railway station with his pound, which would feed him for a week, leaving Septimus none the wiser.

Septimus wandered through the city to Old Town Square, where crowds of tourists were gathering around the clock to hear it strike the hour. It was another hot day and the city was bursting with energy. Troops were a frequent sight in this city, riding in groups of three abreast, sometimes with swords drawn in a rigid display of Habsburg Imperial prowess. Uniformed police were numerous too, and Septimus wondered what it was like for the native Czechs to be ruled by a foreign elite and by an ageing emperor in Vienna who refused to sanction any further independence. Secret police were another sinister feature of this city and Septimus had noticed at least three people having their papers inspected. Each time they were waved on, but people hurried by, averting their eyes, hoping they wouldn't be stopped as well. As a British citizen, Septimus felt he had nothing to fear, but even so, this was a city of secrets.

He walked through the narrow streets and across the Charles Bridge to the castle and cathedral, where he passed half an hour inside the cool ancient walls, pondering the defenestration of Prague and its ramifications for the genocidal religious wars that had ravaged the region for the following thirty years. England had had its own religious wars and had executed a King; Habsburg Europe had triumphed and with it, Catholicism, subsequently reimposed with a vengeance on Bohemia and Austria. And the Habsburgs ruled still, with Emperor Franz Josef's spidery web of power reaching into every household across the rambling Imperial domains. It was said his heir apparent, the Archduke Franz Ferdinand, wanted to devolve power to the regions – to allow the Czechs, Hungarians and Serbs more independence – but the old Emperor refused. Most people were waiting for him to die, and at eighty-four years of age it would be soon enough.

Septimus returned to the Golden Tree with time to spare before his rendezvous with Horaček. When he reported to the hotel reception to collect his room key, there was a telegram for him. He took it, tipped the porter, and read the message:

QUAYLE ARRIVING GOLDEN TREE 2100 HOURS. ATTEMPT NOTHING. WAIT IN HOTEL.

Septimus read the message twice to ensure he had understood it but there could be no mistake. Quayle was heading to Prague.

❖　❖　❖

Horaček was waiting for him at the café. He waved Septimus in, pulling out a chair, all smiles, wreathed in cigarette smoke. An empty schnapps glass sat at his elbow.

'Two more,' he signalled to the barman. 'I have good news for you, Mr Oates.'

Horaček took out a piece of paper from his greasy waistcoat and passed it to Septimus with a triumphant flourish. The schnapps arrived and Horaček put a finger to his lips, though Septimus doubted whether the barman would even acknowledge the arrival of the Emperor himself. Septimus unfolded the paper to discover an address: 136 Nebovidska.

'It's across the Charles Bridge, off Prokopská,' explained Horaček. 'Very fine houses, too,' he sniffed, finishing the schnapps.

Septimus pulled out the money he owed Horaček. This was excellent work and he only hoped the address was reliable. He had to take his chances, however, and Horaček was intelligent enough to know that if Septimus wanted more information, he would seek his assistance again. Horaček took the money, counted it, and slipped it into his pocket. Septimus shook his damp hand.

'Thank you,' he said. 'You have been most helpful.'

'If you require anything more, please don't hesitate to ask. You'll always find me here or in my absence, you can leave a message.' He jerked his head towards the bar. 'Tomáš may seem a simpleton but he has his uses.'

'There is one last thing,' Septimus said, as Horaček turned to go. He pulled out the paper with the Professor's scribbled words. 'Does this mean anything to you?'

As Horaček peered at the words, his grin vanished and the colour drained from his face.

'Where did you get this?' he hissed, flecks of spittle landing on Septimus's arm. 'You can't be found in this city with these words. My God . . .'

'What is it?' Septimus asked. 'What does it mean?'

'You honestly don't know? Then it is better for you that way, my friend. These words mean certain death for anyone discovered carrying them within the imperial domains.'

Horaček snatched the paper and before Septimus could stop him, he had lit a match. The scrap crumbled to ash.

'What are you doing?' Septimus looked on in horror. How dare the wretched little man do such a thing?

'We're safe, now,' said Horaček. 'I am sorry, my friend, but we can't afford to take risks. If a member of the state police stopped you, then they would eventually find their way to me and to Tomáš and that would be the end of us.'

The strength of feeling in Horaček's words was genuine, his fear palpable, and it made Septimus's indignation seem petty. He had witnessed the Habsburg troops on the streets, the state police, and seen people stopped and searched. Who knew how many secret policemen there were out there?

'Can't you tell me what the words mean? If they are so shocking, don't I have a right to know?'

'This isn't England,' Horaček sneered, his poise somewhat restored. 'There are no rights here. As I said, it is safer if you don't know. And, no matter what rewards you offer, I consider our acquaintance at an end.'

Septimus returned to the Golden Tree angry and frustrated with Horaček's impertinent and downright mischievous behaviour. Secret police or not, those words had been left for Septimus to find and now he had lost them. All he knew was that they were inflammatory, possibly some sort of call to arms, or the motto of a revolutionary movement. There were plenty of those in the seething underworlds of the Habsburg and Balkan dominions. But what was so special about this particular crowd?

Septimus changed and took supper in the hotel restaurant and then retired to his room to wait for Quayle. He must have fallen asleep, for when he answered a knock on the door, he found it was a quarter past nine. He took the message from the bell-boy and tipped him.

In hotel bar. Come now. Q.

He could see Quayle through the revolving doors. The school-master was seated at the bar, sipping a glass of schnapps, and reading a copy of *The Times*. His battered Gladstone leather travel bag was nestled at his feet like a pet dog.

'Oates. Where've you been?' Quayle grinned.

'I must have dozed off.'

Septimus ordered a beer. He felt bone-tired but was relieved to see Quayle. He took a long swallow from the glass.

'That's good. I needed that.'

'Long evening?'

Quayle was annoyingly cheerful and fresh-faced.

'It's been a long day. Perhaps you can tell me what the devil you're doing here? I'm due to return to England tomorrow.'

'Not yet, my boy, not yet. We've work to do here. Tell me, what have you discovered from Rex?'

'He's a hard-nosed sort, for starters.'

'Go on.'

'He didn't give a damn about Battiscombe. He blamed anarchists, Bolsheviks, republicans. You name it.'

'I take it you gave him the memoir?'

'Yes. There was little else I could do, Quayle. It was what was agreed, after all.'

'Anything else?'

'Yes. Those words clasped in Battiscombe's fingers. They really disturbed him.'

Septimus recounted his encounter with Horaček, the discovery of Charles's address and Horaček's reaction to the paper fragment.

'Sheer terror. His jaw almost hit the floor and he destroyed the scrap in front of my eyes.'

'I'm not surprised, given the translation.'

'What does it mean?'

'It's Serbian and it stands for "union" or "death",' explained Quayle. 'It is the motto of the Black Hand, a Serbian terror group. There are many secret societies in Prague, Vienna and Budapest dedicated to assaulting Habsburg rule, but this is a determined group. They attempted to assassinate the Emperor three years ago. One of the leaders is the famous Dragutin Dimitrijević. Some of my old army chums at Horse Guards rate him very highly. Brilliant graduate of the Belgrade Military Academy and one of the top strategists during the wars a couple of years ago in the Balkans. The name will mean little to you,' Quayle continued gently, 'but eleven years ago, Dimitrijević was a young officer who participated in the assassination of the King of Serbia. It was he who stormed the palace in Belgrade and assisted in the killing of the King and his Queen, Draga.'

' . . .and the death of my parents,' Septimus heard himself saying, numb with shock.

'Your parents were mown down by the getaway car which included Dimitrijević, yes. A terrible tragedy which embraced innocent bystanders. The assassins found the King hiding in the wardrobe and they filled him with bullets. Dimitrijević was badly wounded, but survived. It is unlikely he was driving the car but he became a Serbian hero. The "Saviour of the Fatherland" is how the Serbian parliament described him. He was Professor of Tactics at the Military Academy and is now Chief of Serbian Intelligence.'

Septimus stared at his empty glass. A dim memory of his parents surfaced before his eyes. Father playing cricket with him in the garden; a sunny afternoon, father home from work, dressed in shirtsleeves and slacks, mother bringing a jug of lemonade with glasses onto the lawn; laughter, a dog barking, the smell of mown grass. Gone in that moment when the motor car hit them. His father had died instantly but his mother had lain unconscious for several hours before passing away. Such was the chaos and confusion in the aftermath of the assassination that two dead foreigners had been accorded little importance. Septimus had learned about his mother's lingering death years later. She might have been saved, he thought, again and again, in lonely moments at school and university. And now, just when it seemed the ghosts had been lain to rest, they were unexpectedly dragged up again.

'Oates?'

Quayle's expression was full of concern but Septimus's thoughts were racing, moving beyond grief and memories, back to the present.

'So Dimitrijević murdered my parents and he's the leader of the Black Hand group whose motto Battiscombe stumbled across before he was killed. Therefore, the Black Hand must be responsible for his murder.'

'The Black Hand may not be responsible for the Professor's murder. He was killed because he was convinced that the memoir is a fake which means the story of George Rex is a fabrication.'

Septimus wasn't convinced.

'I saw it, Quayle. The destruction of his study, the desecration of his beloved books and prints. I found the fragment in his fist. It is as if he wanted me to find it.'

238

'Possibly,' Quayle nodded.

'Do you recall the other documents in the bundle? There was a reference to the death of the Crown Prince Rudolf at Mayerling and the assassination of the Empress Elisabeth in Italy.'

'But what is their connection to George Rex and his memoir?'

'Don't you remember the final words he wrote, Quayle? "My blood royal will one day triumph. Justice will be done".'

'Rex is seeking vengeance.'

'He is. And he's using Dimitrijević and the Black Hand to achieve this.'

'Something Battiscombe stumbled upon during his enquiries.' Quayle paused. 'Where did you say Charles has his apartment?'

'Nebovidska Street.'

'Well, then,' Quayle finished his schnapps and banged the glass down on the bar. 'Let's go!'

'Now?'

'Why not?' Quayle's face lit up with mischievous energy. 'We've got to establish the link between the Rex memoir and the Black Hand. Hahn is dead and so is Battiscombe. Why wait?'

Septimus thought of the long trail which led from his parents' deaths eleven years ago to Battiscombe's murder. He thought of Hahn gunned down in front of him. It was time for a reckoning.

'I don't have any objections. Let's go and find him.'

Except for a few late-night theatre-goers and courting couples, the Charles Bridge was deserted at that time of night. A full moon reflected off the Vltava River and the statues on the bridge loomed above them like sentinels. Quayle and Septimus had no time for the scenery though. Septimus walked hurriedly with his head bowed, furiously thinking of Dimitrijević, the Black Hand and the possible connections with the Rex family's desire for vengeance after its betrayal over one hundred and fifty years ago. Whichever way he looked at it, it all came back to the death of his parents. Wounds he thought had healed long ago were still as raw as the dark days when the news had first reached him. The numbing shock, the anger and grief came flooding back. What could be done? What could he do?

A uniformed figure appeared from the darkness at the end of the bridge. He rasped something in Czech, then German, and when the pair didn't respond, English.

'Your papers, if you please.'

Quayle and Septimus fumbled for their passports. The police officer studied the papers and handed them back, waving his lamp in acknowledgement of their authenticity. The men hurried towards the end of the bridge where Septimus turned left, spotting the street to which Bruno at the Golden Tree had directed him. They walked on in silence, with Quayle letting his young companion set the pace as he turned right up a narrow road. The sign above them indicated that they had reached Nebovidska Street. It was a long, cobbled street, crowded with majestic nineteenth-century buildings.

'It's number 136. That's number nineteen, so it's a little further ahead, yet.'

They walked on, their footsteps the only sound in the otherwise deathly silent street.

'Look – 100,' said Quayle. 'We're almost there.'

'Here,' he said, but then the triumph in his voice died.

The two men stood facing an imposing late-nineteenth-century building with a massive arched doorway displaying the number 136. Built into it was a smaller door, and to the side a list of names with the numbers of apartments. Septimus peered at the list in the light of the street lamps and the moon. With a sense of inevitable dread, he realised Charles's name didn't appear on the list.

'So, which apartment belongs to Rex?' whispered Quayle.

'Damned if I know.' Septimus was at a loss. 'It doesn't say on the paper the man gave me.'

Had Horaček cheated him? Impossible to say. Very probably. He had found the details requested and taken his payment. Nothing was said about which apartment belonged to their quarry. The address was correct. Horaček had fulfilled his promise but had succeeded in not betraying Charles's whereabouts too easily.

'That's a problem,' said Quayle. 'Looks like we'll be paying Rex a visit in the morning after all.'

Septimus shook his head impatiently. He would not countenance any further delay. Charles might leave at any time in the night or early morning, if indeed he hadn't already departed. He looked up and down the street but there was little sign of life. They couldn't stand there all night. It was highly likely an inquisitive policeman would turn up at some point. Quayle pointed to one of the buildings that had a few more lights than the others.

'That looks like a bar over there. Let's have a drink and think about our options. Something will turn up.'

'You're right, let's do that,' Septimus agreed.

The alternative was to knock on every door in the building until they found Charles's apartment, thus announcing their intentions to all the inhabitants.

It was a small, single-roomed bar, with a handful of late-night customers. The barman gave them a weary look as they entered. Quayle ordered brandies and, after he had taken an appreciative swallow, said,

'So, what we are dealing with is a minor branch of the Habsburg royal family which claims to have direct – and legitimate – descent from the British royal family. This is a decades-old story of gathering grievances and grudges. The memoir is just one aspect of it. The connection with the Black Hand makes it deadly.'

'And unexpectedly personal.'

Septimus gulped his brandy. William Rex had played him for a fool. Then the thought occurred to him; was Rex aware of the circumstances surrounding his parents' deaths in Belgrade? If he knew about that, then it made his offer to Septimus a thousand times more cynical.

'We don't have evidence to link the Black Hand with William Rex, yet,' Quayle said, reading his thoughts. 'It's possible that

Battiscombe could have stumbled upon something else, unrelated to this Rex business.'

'Then why scribble those words on a scrap of the memoir? Why die holding them?' Septimus was convinced that Rex, Dimitrijević and the Black Hand were one and the same.

Quayle made to reply but before he could do so pointed to the other side of the street, where a large motor car had pulled up. Charles got out of the car.

'That's him, isn't it?' said Quayle, finding his voice.

'Yes, it's him all right.'

Quayle drained his glass. 'Let's follow him in.'

'Wait!' hissed Septimus, grabbing his friend's arm.

A dark-suited figure crossed the street and was advancing towards Charles. By now Rex had disappeared inside, without a backwards glance. His pursuer waited until the door was almost closed, then skilfully caught it. He waited a few seconds and then slipped inside furtively.

'Good Lord, did you see that?' Quayle whispered. 'What the hell's going on?'

Septimus threw some money on the bar. 'Come on, follow me!'

The street was dimly lit, which had enabled the intruder to approach unseen. Septimus was banking on doing exactly the same. Quayle was surprisingly nimble and reached the door first, wedging his foot on the step just before it caught the latch.

'Got it,' he breathed.

Septimus looked anxiously down the street. They hadn't been spotted.

'Shall we go in?'

'Yes. Slowly.'

The heavy door swung open to reveal a spacious, brightly lit, communal hall with a wide staircase. Septimus glanced at Quayle as they cautiously ascended the stairs. On the first floor, there was no sign of life, so they continued to climb to the second floor. Quayle held up a hand.

'Can you hear something?'

'Yes. Voices. Next floor up. Let's keep going.'

Septimus eased himself in front and, as the exchange grew louder, he could distinguish Charles's voice. He was speaking, in German, in a low, urgent tone.

Carefully, they crept up the stairs to the third floor, where one of the apartment doors was slightly ajar, casting light onto the landing. Slowly, Septimus and Quayle edged along the wall towards the apartment. The intruder was speaking slowly in German, occasionally breaking into another language much more rapidly. The menace was unmistakable, however. He was getting louder, banging something to make his point. Septimus strained to hear what was going on. His schoolboy German had improved during his travels and researches and he understood a few words. He had to know more. As if drawn by an irresistible force, Septimus found himself surreptitiously peering into Charles Rex's apartment.

He saw a spacious room, luxuriously furnished with sofas, a grand piano, prints and bookcases. Above the mantelpiece was a vast oil painting which Septimus recognised instantly and which made his blood curdle: it was George III, and if Septimus hadn't been distracted by the people in the room he would have bet a hundred pounds on it being an original Gainsborough. The intruder had his back to the door, but Septimus could see he was armed. Septimus opened the door a fraction and, as he did so, Charles caught sight of him.

'*Ich weiss est nicht, Gudelj,*' he said, pointedly. He was standing next to a small bureau, dressed for dinner. He looked shaken.

His eyes flicked imperceptibly to Septimus and away again.

'*Natürlich!*' sneered Gudelj who moved further into the room and raised his pistol. He was a broad-shouldered, squat figure of a man. Then he swore in a language Septimus didn't recognise, but which seemed familiar all the same.

'*Nein!*' Charles shrank away from his advance, looking over his shoulder directly at Septimus, his eyes widening, this time holding the stare.

'*Was ist das . . .?*' Gudelj turned round and saw Septimus. His oafish face registered surprise for a second before the pistol arm swung upwards.

In that second, Charles pulled a large revolver from the bureau drawer and shot Gudelj in the head. Bone, gristle and brain splattered the ceiling and wall behind Septimus, a mist of blood catching him in the face. Gudelj crashed to the floor, like a puppet with its strings cut, stone dead, his eyes and mouth wide open, forever frozen in time.

'Jesus Christ,' Septimus swore, as he had never done in his life, not even when informed of his parents' deaths.

Charles calmly replaced the gun in the desk drawer. There was no sign of nerves, no evidence he felt any compassion for the man he had just executed.

'Who . . . who was that?'

'Never you mind.'

'Of course I mind! You just blew his brains out in front of me, damn your eyes.'

Septimus wiped blood from his cheek. There was something else – some sort of gore – on the handkerchief too. Then the familiarity of the other language the intruder had used struck him. Septimus was no linguist, but it sounded not unlike the words Battiscombe had scrawled on the memoir: Serbian.

'Was he a member of the Black Hand?'

Charles turned sharply from the bureau.

'What do you know of the Black Hand?'

'More than is good for me I suspect, judging by your reaction.'

Septimus sensed he had Charles at a disadvantage. The supercilious smile had disappeared from his face. His demeanour echoed his father's expression earlier that day. It didn't last long. Charles wasn't to be drawn any further by Septimus's questioning.

'Forget about him,' he jerked his head at the body on the floor. 'My fellow Horaček warned me to expect you.'

So locating Charles had been too easy, after all. Horaček's appearance outside the lecture theatre had seemed too good to be true. In this city of spies it was unrealistic to expect he would have been able to locate Charles without being observed himself.

'Every man has his price,' Charles continued. 'You didn't believe my father would allow you to wander freely in the city, did you?' Then he added: 'Are you alone?'

Charles's query was rapped out in a tone which confirmed he had the advantage now. Still half shielded by the door, Septimus put a hand out behind him to where Quayle had been standing and felt . . . nothing. Where had he gone? Not for the police, please, no. This was far too complicated for them.

'Yes, I'm alone.'

Septimus hoped the tremor in his voice wouldn't betray his true fears, but Charles was too confident of his position now to notice it.

'Good.' Charles's face was hard and for the first time Septimus became aware of how cold his eyes could be. 'Now you're here, you'd better come with me.'

'Where?'

'Where do you think? Hrad Jiri.'

Charles's tone suggested no alternative. It was clear that they were going to Hrad Jiri whether Septimus wished to or not. As they descended the stairs, Septimus initially hoped Quayle would reappear and confront Charles, but given the ruthlessness with which Gudelj had been despatched, Septimus willed his friend to stay in the shadows. The Winchester schoolmaster – British Army officer or not – would be no match for this cold-blooded killer.

'Why was Professor Battiscombe murdered?' Septimus asked, as Charles opened the door to the car.

'I don't know. Now get in.'

'Did the Black Hand kill him?'

'Get in.'

Septimus felt the barrel of the pistol nudge into his ribs. This was no time to push Rex any further. Perhaps some answers would be found at Hrad Jiri, where Septimus could confront Rex. He had nothing to lose. But where in God's name *was* Quayle?

Few words were exchanged as Charles drove out of the city and back onto the main highway.

'We've fought to stay alive for so long now that we'll do anything.'

Charles spoke so quietly in the dark that Septimus thought he was talking to himself. Thankfully, the gun had been removed from his ribs when they left the suburbs of Prague.

'We've always had enemies. We've always struggled. And in our quest for revenge and for the truth, we've accrued new enemies.'

'Including the Black Hand?'

'Yes.'

Septimus sensed it was the closest he would get to an admission of the identity of the corpse in the flat. Charles didn't speak again and when the road began to wind up into the mountains towards Hrad Jiri, it was Septimus who broke the long silence.

'They killed my parents, you know. After the assassination of the King and Queen of Serbia in 1903.'

Charles looked genuinely surprised.

'I was not aware of that.'

'Were you not?' Septimus spoke sharply.

'No. That is to be regretted.'

'They were knocked down by the getaway car. It was pure bad luck. Wrong time, wrong place.'

'Everything happens for a reason.'

Charles steered the car up to the castle gatehouse, slowed as the guards acknowledged him, and accelerated into the courtyard.

'You think I'm here for a reason?'

Charles switched the engine off. When he looked across at Septimus his expression was one of intense purposefulness, yet not devoid of kindness.

'Septimus, there are wheels within wheels in this business. What does Shakespeare say? "All the world's a stage, and all the men and women merely players . . ." You're involved in something graver than you can possibly comprehend, way beyond the security of the dreaming spires and quadrangles of Oxford. My advice to you is to lie very low indeed, and keep your counsel.' Charles climbed out of the car, adding, 'In any case, there will be nothing you can do, because it will all be over in the next few days.'

Leaving his guest to ponder the significance of those words, Charles disappeared into the castle. Two men in hunting clothes with rifles slung over their shoulders appeared. The foremost one opened the door.

'Out, please.'

Septimus accompanied them into the hallway.

'In here,' the attendant gestured, indicating a side-room. 'Wait here.'

The door closed. Septimus didn't hear a key turn but he was as good as imprisoned; he knew the guard would be stationed outside. As his eyes became accustomed to the gloom, he found the switches and turned on some more lights. It was a large room, with a fire burning brightly, and wall-to-wall shelving, containing thousands of leather-bound tomes – Descartes, Racine, Hobbes, Milton, Newton, Voltaire, and so on – as far as the eye could make out. A thought struck him and he took Newton's *Philosophiae Naturalis Principia Mathematica* down from the shelf. On opening it, he could see that it was a first edition.

'These should be in a library,' he whispered.

'They are,' said William Rex, appearing from the shadows. 'Mine.'

'A collection created by George Rex no doubt?'

'Yes. But we have no time for pleasantries. Charles has informed me of the . . . er . . . unfortunate incident at his apartment earlier this evening.'

'It was certainly unfortunate for his visitor.' Septimus decided to take a bullish line. He'd had enough of being given the runaround by the Rex family. 'And it's a pity that you denied any knowledge of those words I showed you. The Black Hand motto, meaning "union" or "death", it seems.'

A smile crept into the corner of Rex's mouth but vanished as soon as it arrived.

'Your visit here earlier today was rather sudden. I did not wish to tell you anything you had no need to know.'

'Had no need to know? When my friend has been brutally murdered?'

Something in Rex's manner encouraged Septimus to probe further and push his luck.

'Perhaps you can tell me why the Black Hand is trying to locate George Rex's memoir?'

'The Black Hand is not the least bit interested in the memoir. Do you really suppose that a few Serbian students or such like would actually travel to Oxford and murder Battiscombe? No, the secrets of the memoir are worth more than one dead Oxford Professor. Your King George V is a prime target. I intend to publish the memoir and the marriage certificates as widely as I can; indeed, all across Europe and beyond, to the United States of America, that young republic. As I told you, any number of interested parties are after that evidence.'

'I hardly think the Bolsheviks would be bothered to make off with it.'

'You are mistaken, then, Septimus. They are committed to the sort of violent and radical change that will bring down monarchies and landowners. And where do you think the Bolshevik leaders are skulking as I speak?'

'Exiled somewhere, as they normally are, and living off dubious means, no doubt.'

'Absolutely. Lenin and Trotsky are currently residing in Vienna, the imperial city, or at least that was the last I heard. They are waiting.'

'Waiting for what?'

'An opportunity. A chance to have their revolution whenever chaos and havoc present themselves.'

Septimus thought about the crowned heads of Europe; Wilhem II, George V, Tsar Nicholas, Emperor Franz Josef. All of them were well established and firmly in control of their various realms. True, the late king of England, Edward VII, had declared the Kaiser 'Satan' and formed an entente with France, which Russia had joined. Germany had formed an alliance with Austria but these understandings were decades old and formed part of the pattern of centuries of diplomatic manoeuvring. Nobody took any notice.

'I don't see how this violent change will occur. England has not fought a war in Europe since Waterloo. Things will not change.'

Rex sat on the sofa, gesturing to Septimus to sit opposite him.

'The reign of Victoria – the girl who should never have been Queen – was an insult to my father and grandfather,' Rex began, his eyes gleaming with intent. 'And yet Victoria's reign was supreme. She was Queen-Empress of India and of the British Empire. Her marriage to Albert of Saxe-Coburg-Gotha spawned an entirely new ruling dynasty in Europe. My father and I wished to put an end to what he saw as this domination by the House of Saxe-Coburg-Gotha.'

'What did you do?' asked Septimus. 'What could you do?'

'We had many opportunities.' Rex smiled. 'The end of the last century was a boiling cauldron of change. Revolution was in the air, whatever you may think. You as an Englishman have little experience of political upheaval. Emperor Franz Joseph's own brother, Emperor Maximilian of Mexico, was executed by revolutionaries. His son, Rudolf shot himself. His wife, Empress Elisabeth was assassinated. As well as this, the Tsar of all the Russians, Alexander II, was assassinated in St Petersburg. A new world is dawning, a world of the common man where the power of the many, not the few, will hold sway.'

'But you and your father are descended from both British and Austrian Royal houses. You're hardly a common man.'

'We were by the middle of the last century. Our name was simply Rex. We had no titles and we had taken measures to conceal our ancestry. The British Royal Family had flourished successfully because of the many children of Victoria and Albert and their European marriages, and the Rex family no longer posed a threat to the British Establishment. The Ryves trial is a distant memory, and, as you know, the authorities ruthlessly quashed the evidence, taking steps to impound it at Windsor Castle. But I had a purpose to my life.'

'And what was that?'

William Rex leant forward on the chair, his manner no longer cordial. Septimus was chilled to the bone by the expression in his eyes.

'Revenge. George Rex pledged to hound the British Royal Family to the ends of the earth to secure his revenge. You know that. You've read the memoir. His son was brought up to do the same but I, the grandson of George Rex, have far greater ambitions. I intend to bring about the destruction of all the crowned heads of Europe.'

It was preposterous but the look on William Rex's face suggested absolute sincerity. He rose from his chair and went to a cabinet, producing two brandy glasses and a bottle. He poured two generous measures and handed Septimus a glass. They both drank, and Rex opened a cigar box, offering one to his guest.

'You believe I am living a fantasy here in this castle, do you not, Septimus? Well, let me put you "in the picture" as the wonderful English language has it. I mentioned the murder of Empress Elisabeth – "Sisi" as she was fondly known – the darling of the Hungarians. She was hugely popular – far more so than that old autocrat who sits in the Hofburg from five in the morning until eight at night signing his letters and reading his secret police reports – and was regarded as their saviour, someone who could reason with the Emperor and persuade him to reinstate their power. This, for some, was not good news. Gradual change in the empire will lead to progress and reform. This is not what the radicals need. They require rigid resistance so they can preach violence. Therefore, Sisi had to go.'

'Had to go?'

Septimus disliked the self-satisfied tone of Rex's statement.

'Yes. Do you think she was just the victim of a crazed Italian assassin who had lost his senses? Well, you would not be mistaken because that is what we wanted everyone to think. A random attack by a lone killer. Our people in the press sold it very well and were paid for their services.'

Septimus remembered the newspaper cutting recounting the assassination of Empress Elisabeth. There was another report too, which he couldn't quite place . . .

'Sisi's demise brought an end to the Hungarians' hopes. They still boil with resentment. But there is more, Septimus, which will demonstrate our deadly intentions. I also mentioned the suicide of Rudolf, the Emperor's son and heir, at his Mayerling hunting lodge.'

Mayerling. Now he remembered: the second newspaper report he and Quayle had glanced at, but dismissed, in their excitement at discovering the secret marriage of Prince George and Hannah Lightfoot. Too late, the pieces fell into place. Septimus's pulse quickened. He reached for the brandy and took a large swallow.

'Crown Prince Rudolf was conducting an affair with the Baroness Mary Vatsera, an affair which was widely known of in court circles. The Emperor demanded that Rudolf end the affair, which he refused to do and instead the pair formed a suicide pact. Rudolf shot his mistress in the head and then turned the gun on himself. The Pope granted a dispensation so the Crown Prince could be buried in the family vault in Vienna.

'So much for the official version. The reality was this: the Crown Prince and the Baroness had finished supper in the hunting lodge that cold night in January when his deerhound alerted them to an intruder. The dog stopped baying abruptly when it was slain. At this, the Crown Prince went to the door, pushing aside his ineffectual guard. Three assailants burst in, the first pinning the guard to the wall, another seizing a champagne bottle and smashing it over the

Prince's head with such force it killed him instantly, crushing his skull. The Baroness was shot in the head with a stutzen – a hunting gun – and the guard was stabbed through the chest and another was also shot and killed. The assassins escaped into the night and have yet to be apprehended.

'You may ask how I know this? I will tell you why. Because I was the person who wielded the bottle which crushed the Crown Prince's skull, that is why. The Prince had to die for the same reason as his mother. He was a liberal, a reformer, one who would give the Hungarians, Czechs and various peoples throughout the Empire a greater measure of independence. Peaceful reform will not allow for radical, violent and total change. The Emperor did not wish stories of murder to circulate since it would weaken his rule, so our role was covered up, which suited my purposes very well.'

Septimus stared into the fire. He was petrified. And Rex's next words did nothing to allay his fears.

'The game has yet to play itself out. It must reach its final, inevitable conclusion.'

'Which is . . .?' Septimus felt the words on his lips like iron.

Numbed by the revelation of Dimitrijević's part in his parents' deaths and the murders of Empress Elisabeth and the Crown Prince, he could not anticipate what William Rex might have planned next.

'You will find out soon enough.' Rex rose from his chair and moved to the door.

'Why not kill me like the rest of them?' Bitterness crept into Septimus's voice.

'I am not a monster. My vengeance is reserved for those who have stood in the path of my family. You will be my witness. You can tell the world I am the true king of Great Britain, by direct descent from George III. And when the collapse of Old Europe occurs, I will step forward. History will call me onto the stage. By the way . . .' Rex smiled, entirely without mirth, '. . . thank you for helping me. You are to remain here for now however, where you will be safe.'

'Safe? You mean captive.'

'Nonsense. You are my guest. You will be shown to your room. It is late, and you must need your rest.'

He had no choice but to comply with William Rex's invitation. He followed one of the guards out of the library and up three flights of the wide, stone staircase and along a narrow panelled floor where an unobtrusive door opened to reveal a tower with a spiral staircase. After a few minutes climbing up, they reached another doorway which led into a small room, furnished sparsely with a single bed and sink in the corner. There was a tiny window. It was a drop of at least a hundred feet to the courtyard below.

'Don't think of it,' grunted the guard, in broken English, drawing a finger across his throat. 'Stay here. Yes?' Laughing, he shuffled off down the steps and then the distant echo of the door slamming at the foot of the tower could be heard.

Septimus climbed into bed. When he blew out the last candle, the initial darkness of the room brightened as a shaft of moonlight shone through the unshuttered window. As he lay there, exhaustion sank through the layers of panic, grief and shock which the events of the day had brought. He drifted into a deep sleep, the bed drawing him in to its embrace. His last thoughts were of George Rex, the master of this castle and begetter of the web of deceit, murder and conspiracies which had led him to this place. The question in his head, unanswered by Rex but promised soon: what was coming next?

❖ ❖ ❖

He awoke with a hand clutching his mouth so tightly he could scarcely breathe. He struggled to get upright, panic threatening to overwhelm him, but also giving him the strength to force the hand away. He took a deep breath, unsure yet whether he had been dreaming. Day was breaking outside – a watery pink light was seeping through the windows – but it was not yet light enough to see who was in the room. Then he saw the figure move into the shadows.

'Who's there?' he gasped, managing to sit up in the bed.

'You blasted idiot, Oates,' came a hoarse whisper. 'Wake up!'

A match flared and light flickered into the room. Septimus's eyes widened in recognition and astonishment: crouching over him in the darkened room was Mordecai Quayle.

Septimus rolled out of bed so suddenly he almost tipped onto the floor.

'How the hell did you get in here?'

'As soon as I heard that murderous swine Charles kill his visitor I raced down the steps and hid in the back of his car. He'd spotted you so there was little point in both of us getting embroiled. I stayed out of sight until it was safe. I watched you through the windows talking to Rex and saw you being led up here. There was a handy set of keys left on the hook at the base of the stairs.'

'But how are we going to get out of here? You're not Houdini.'

'I'll explain while you get dressed,' Quayle said as he flung Septimus's clothes on the bed. 'It's getting light and we've got to move fast.'

Septimus was still indignant.

'He could have finished me off, too. You left me alone with a killer.'

'True. It was a calculated risk. I knew Charles wouldn't just let you walk away but I was confident he wouldn't harm you.'

'Why not? How did you know? After all, I'd just witnessed a murder.'

'It was a chance I took.' Quayle's face was uncharacteristically hard. 'You know this is a dangerous business.'

'I do know that. William Rex has told me things you could never imagine. The depth of his malevolence knows no limits.'

'Save it for later. We've got to get out of here. Follow me.'

❖ ❖ ❖

Walking in just their socks, Septimus and Quayle were able to negotiate the spiral stairs and the landing in complete silence.

'There aren't any guards along here at all,' whispered Quayle. 'I came in through the back door to the kitchens which I've left open.'

It was not easy to navigate the main rooms downstairs. In the gloom Septimus could almost make out various obstacles – suits of armour, oak chests, huge candelabras and other feudal relics – but one false step would raise the alarm and set the guards onto them.

'This way,' Quayle mouthed, at the back of the main hall, leading them down the stairs and into the kitchens. It was made easier by the breaking daylight shining through the double French doors at the end of the room.

'That light's a problem. We'll be easy to spot when we drive out.'

'You think we can just get in the car and leave?'

'Have you got a better plan?'

Quayle eased open the kitchen door and they slipped through. Septimus could see the car at the other side of the courtyard where Charles had left it.

'Stick close to the walls of the house. If they spot us, freeze and put your hands up. They won't hesitate to shoot, I reckon.'

With great care and agonising slowness, they inched their way along the wall towards the car, reaching it after what seemed like an age. From the rooms above, there was no sound.

Just as they were almost in touching distance of the vehicle, a thickset guard with a rifle slung over his shoulder came into view. Quayle and Septimus ducked behind the driver's door, crouching on the cobbles, praying that the guard would walk on the other side of the car. A minute or two passed. Septimus exhaled slowly as soon as he realised the guard had indeed gone past the other side.

'Don't move,' Quayle whispered between gritted teeth.

They waited by the side of Charles's car. He eased open the driver's door and reached for the starting handle.

'You'll need to turn the engine over. All hell will break loose when it starts. Get in and keep your head down. The main gate is open, thank God, but we'll have to drive through the front gate further down the track. I spotted it when we came in.'

Septimus nodded, wondering where Quayle had acquired the driving skills to control this vehicle, but there was no time to argue. Gingerly, he took the starter handle and crept to the front of the car.

'Ready?' he whispered.

At Quayle's nod, Septimus grabbed the handle with both hands and gave it a violent wrench, praying it would start. Nothing happened.

'Again!'

Gripping the handle even tighter, Septimus tried again, and this time the engine roared into life.

'Get in!' Quayle bellowed.

This time his voice was almost drowned out by the engine. Septimus dived into the passenger seat and the car leapt backwards. Quayle skilfully spun the wheel, selected a forward gear and slammed his foot down. They flashed through the gateway and out of the courtyard in seconds. Septimus glanced back and saw rooms lighting up across the courtyard and half-dressed figures stumbling out onto the cobbles shouting. He could hear dogs barking and men shouting.

'Hold on!' Quayle shouted. 'Keep your head down!'

Up ahead, in the gradually strengthening daylight, Septimus could see the main gates which were firmly shut against them. Three figures barred the route, rifles unslung.

'We'll never get through! They're wrought iron!'

'You're quite right!' Quayle replied. 'Hang on!'

Just as they neared the lodge, he swung the wheel again. The car careered off the lane and bounced across the open field, Quayle swerving alongside the low wall which surrounded the estate.

'There's got to be a gateway down here.'

'I hope you're right.'

Septimus looked back again and wished he hadn't. Mounted riflemen were in hot pursuit, and a car was coming after them, at speed.

'There!' Quayle shouted breathlessly in triumph.

In the lights Septimus saw a five-bar gate up ahead.

'Put your foot down – they're gaining on us!'

The car roared and shot forward, smashing through the gate. Trees loomed large around them, scratching the sides of the car. The track was full of deep potholes. Quayle slowed the car and pressed on, cautiously. A few minutes later, the trees around them cleared, and they joined the road.

'They'll have gone through the main gate. Go as fast as you can before they catch us,' Septimus shouted, the terror in his voice piercing the dawn air.

Quayle put his foot flat to the floor and they raced down the mountain road at a terrifying speed; Septimus held the door-handle and prayed, not daring to look to his right, which he knew from the journey up with Charles was a sheer drop. The road eventually levelled off and reached a junction.

'Anything behind us?'

Septimus glanced over his shoulder. Some way up the hillside was the motor car, its headlights swinging wildly as the driver negotiated the sharp bends. It was descending rapidly.

'There's a car still on our tail. Keep going!'

'Take a look in my bag.' Quayle motioned to the Gladstone at Septimus's feet. 'You'll find my revolver.'

Septimus opened the clasps of the bag and fumbled around. Quayle had packed a spare shirt, his Continental Bradshaw and his gun.

'It's a .455 Webley-Fosbery and it's fully loaded. Take a pot shot at those bounders.'

As he spoke, Quayle spun the car onto the main road to Prague. Clutching the door, Septimus cocked the revolver and leant out of the window. As the car straightened up, Quayle accelerated.

'I would expect young Rex to have a fast car!' he shouted, grinning with excitement.

But the car chasing them was just as fast and was gaining on them. Septimus levelled the pistol and took a shot. Their pursuers skidded, corrected and continued after them. One of the occupants was about to shoot when Septimus fired again, this time shattering the windscreen, causing the car to swerve violently onto the roadside and come to a halt.

'Bull's eye!'

Septimus sat back and dropped the Webley into the Gladstone, his terror giving way to exhilaration.

'That'll slow them up a bit.'

'Capital shooting, Oates. Couldn't have done better myself.'

❖　❖　❖

It was daylight when they arrived at the outskirts of Prague. Quayle followed the signs to the railway station and parked in the forecourt.

'We need to get to a place called Dürnstein,' he said, taking out a hipflask and passing it to Septimus who took a pull on the flask.

'How so?'

'When I was in the back of Charles Rex's car I overheard some of the guards talking about a rendezvous there with the Black Hand. It seems like Rex is cooking up some sort of devilish deed.'

Septimus handed back the flask.

'That settles it. He's already up to his neck in it. Rex confessed to murdering Crown Prince Rudolf with his own hands and to hiring an assassin to murder Empress Elisabeth.'

Quayle gave a low whistle.

'He means to kill again,' Septimus added. 'It could be the Emperor himself, this time.'

'It's almost six now,' Quayle said consulting his pocket watch. 'Dürnstein's on the outskirts of Vienna.' He reached into the Gladstone and thumbed his Bradshaw. 'Here we are. There's a train leaving Prague for Vienna at ten to seven, arriving just before one. Splendid. We can take luncheon on the train.'

Septimus bought first class tickets and sat at the end of the platform while Quayle took himself off to the cloakrooms. The station was quiet at that time of the morning, with only a few seasoned travellers about. Septimus kept an eye on the ticket office entrance, wondering how long it would take Charles Rex and his men to trace them to the station. Perhaps they should have parked the car in the town centre to throw them off the scent? It was too late to move it now, however. They would have to sit tight. Where had

Quayle gone? He'd been an age. They might need that Webley again if Charles had repaired his car and came looking for them.

'We'll need to ascertain the whereabouts of the Emperor when we get to Vienna,' said Quayle.

'The Emperor will surely be at his summer residence in the Schönbrunn Palace,' Septimus observed.

'Or in the mountains at Bad Ischl.'

'There are Court Circulars which are widely published. They'll prove informative. Rex made it clear something spectacular is planned to happen in the next couple of days, so we don't have much time.'

'Do you really think there will be another assassination?'

Septimus met Quayle's red-eyed stare and remembered that the schoolmaster had spent the night awake in the back of Charles's car while he had lain in a bed fast asleep.

'Yes,' he said. 'I believe there is another assassination planned.'

The train pulled in right on time and, as they boarded, Septimus surveyed the station quickly.

'Breakfast is served in half an hour. We have a private compartment.'

'Excellent,' said Quayle. 'Once we've eaten I can get some sleep.'

Doors slammed, the whistle blew and the train lurched forward, gathering speed. Just then, there was a commotion on the platform. Septimus looked out of the window and hastily ducked back in again.

'What is it?'

'Charles and some of his henchmen. They were trying to board the train.'

Quick as a flash, Quayle whipped out the Webley from the Gladstone bag and cocked it. He got up from his seat and leant out of the window, the gun at his side. The train was now moving at speed. He sat back down, a smile on his face.

'They didn't make it.'

The two friends breakfasted, retired to their compartment to sleep, waking in time to take lunch in the restaurant car. Suitably refreshed, they prepared to disembark as the train drew into Vienna. Septimus bought a newspaper at a platform news-stand and leafed through it quickly.

'What news?' asked Quayle from over his shoulder.

'You were right. The Emperor is at Bad Ischl.'

Septimus folded the newspaper and examined the timetables in Bradshaw.

'There's a train leaving here for Dürnstein within the hour. I think we'll have more information then. Why don't we have a stroll through the imperial city and take in the sights?'

It took five minutes to travel by tram from the railway station to Stephansplatz, in the centre of Vienna. The heat was almost unbearable on the packed tram, busy as it was with sightseers. The great clock on the Stephansdom struck the half hour just as they walked past, scattering a small flock of pigeons. Crowds of tourists drifted aimlessly across the square, photographing one another and stopping to admire the jugglers and entertainers plying their trade. Hundreds more sat in the shady cafés on the perimeter of the square, taking afternoon coffee and cake, the famous Viennese refreshment.

'Did you know,' asked Quayle in his mild-mannered school-masterly way which usually indicated he was about to impart a piece of superfluous information, 'that the Viennese invented the croissant when the Ottomans withdrew from the last great siege of Vienna in 1687?'

'I did know.' For once, Septimus felt quite pleased with himself. 'They baked them in celebration in the shape of the crescent.'

The cool, cavernous interior of the vast cathedral of Stephansdom offered a welcome respite from the heat, and they spent ten minutes inside before they re-emerged into the bright sunshine.

'Let's have some coffee and cake,' suggested Quayle. 'It's what the city is famous for, amongst other things. There's a patisserie over there.'

As they walked down the street, Septimus noticed a small church with a nondescript door. Curious as ever, he peered through the entrance. An attendant dressed in imperial blue uniform waved him in, speaking in German and then English.

'It is open today,' he said. 'You may enter.'

'We haven't time for diversion, Oates.'

'This,' said the little man drawing himself up to his full height, 'is the *Kaisergruft*, and it is here, on the site of the Capuchins' Church, where the imperial emperors, empresses, princesses, archdukes, archduchesses, counts, countesses and bishops of the Habsburg dynasty have been interred since 1633. It is the last resting place of eleven emperors and eighteen empresses.'

Intrigued to have stumbled upon such a place, Septimus and Quayle wandered amongst the tombs. The large crypt was lined with tombs of varying sizes, many of them extraordinarily ornate. Chief amongst them was that of Empress Maria Theresa. Wreaths and messages were arranged in their dozens by the bronze and copper castings, and judging by the number of people milling about, it was a popular tourist attraction.

Septimus caught up with his friend by the stone sarcophagus of the Empress Elisabeth and her son Rudolf.

'And we know who put them here,' murmured Quayle.

'Careful,' muttered Septimus.

Others around them had bowed their heads in deference.

When people moved on, he added, 'Yes, and this is where the old Emperor will be lain to rest.'

They walked on, past many other tombs until they reached the last in the row. It was a plain tomb which had neither wreaths or ribbons. There was a simple inscription carved into the stone, which read PRINCESS AUGUSTA MARIA ELIZABETH HABSBURG-LOTHRINGEN 1787–1795.

'Princess Augusta,' Septimus mused. 'That name rings a bell.'

'Is she mentioned in the memoir?'

'Yes, this is her. Look, there's the tomb of her uncle, Francis II, the last Holy Roman Emperor.' Septimus spoke with mounting excitement as he went on. 'You haven't read the second part of the memoir, Quayle, but believe me. Rex describes how he married Princess Augusta, niece of the Emperor. He was a prisoner, exploited by the Emperor as useful diplomatic bait; due to Napoleon's invasion and the abolition of the Holy Roman Empire, Rex and his imperial wife weren't needed.'

'But look at the dates, Oates. This Augusta died at the age of eight. There must have been another Augusta. The death rate was so high that they often repeated the names of the children . . .'

'. . . and if this is the correct princess? If there was no second Augusta?'

'Then . . . George Rex must have been lying about his marriage in the memoir.'

'There's one way to settle this. We'll ask the attendant what he knows.'

The uniformed attendant on the front desk was very helpful, disappearing into his office and returning with a huge rolled genealogy of the full Habsburg-Lothringen family which he spread across his table, placing a paperweight on each corner.

'These are the names here,' he said, 'including all the minor branches of the family.'

Septimus and Quayle pored over the sheet, eventually locating Emperor Francis II after several minutes, so complicated was the genealogy.

'There.' Septimus found Augusta first. 'Just the one Princess Augusta.'

Quayle crouched over and nodded.

'You're right. And she died aged eight. I can't see another Augusta within that branch of the family.'

'Which means George Rex never married a princess called Augusta.'

'Assuming this genealogy is accurate. After all, not all the Habsburgs are buried here in Vienna; they have burial spots in Prague, Graz and Munich. The chances are Augusta is in the family mausoleum at Hrad Jiri.'

Septimus shook his head. He couldn't let wishful thinking get in the way of his historical senses.

'The fact remains no other Augusta appears on this detailed genealogy.'

'But where does that leave us? Perhaps he lied about his marriage, and made his money by other means. The Habsburg connection is just an affectation.'

'And doesn't that bring into question the authenticity of the entire memoir?'

Septimus almost choked on his words. How could it be? He had lived Rex's life, breathed his innermost fears and ambitions, shared his journey from England to France and to the Bohemian Mountains, travelled with the young prince, exile and husband of an imperial princess.

'Battiscombe was right all along. There was never a George Rex, son of George III and Hannah Lightfoot. His research was accurate. The George Rex he described to me was the son of a London merchant. That is why he was killed, no doubt about it.'

'But William Rex needs the memoir for something, Oates,' said Quayle. 'He needs it to convince people of his false identity as the grandson of George Rex and direct descendant of George III.'

The two friends wandered slowly out of the crypt, absorbing the revelations. They stood in the busy street, in the shadow of the Stephansdom, and it was Septimus who voiced the thoughts they both shared:

'In that case, if the memoir is a forgery and William Rex needs it to conceal his true identity, then the question is: who is Rex?'

Septimus said very little during the journey to Dürnstein. Just two weeks ago, he had been putting the finishing touches to his dissertation for his College Fellowship. Since then he'd learned more from George Rex's memoir than four years of research had taught him. That knowledge had brought with it danger, risk and uncertainty. Never again would Septimus sit in a library surrounded by books and not be aware of the possibilities and the unknowns which the past presented. History was no longer a reassuring series of facts which could be arranged like butterflies in a glass case. Instead, it was a mass of half-hidden events, anonymous people, threads of secrets and lies, untold stories and deadly conspiracies. He recalled the conversation at High Table at Christ's, when Herbert Gilbert had declared history to be a science, and the past there to be mapped with precision. He had believed Gilbert was misguided and now he knew it to be so. The past was a living space, yet to be explored. In that sense, it wasn't the past at all. It was the future waiting to be discovered.

But there was something else, too, about this whole business which Septimus couldn't quite put his finger on. As the train slowed at Dürnstein, Septimus realised what it was. He was enjoying it. He relished the exploration of new territory, the unpredictability and liberation which came with the lack of facts. He thrived on the thrill of finding the unknowns which lay outside the sphere of scholarly, bookish research: the past was future knowledge. Rather than discovering all about what had happened, the question was: what would happen next?

Septimus was chilled to the bone after their visit to the *Kaisergruft*, even though it was a hot June day and the afternoon sun remained high in the sky. Both men had their jackets over their shoulders as they walked into the tiny village of Dürnstein. Far above them, on a rocky outcrop jutting out over the river, lay the castle ruins. There was a single main street running alongside the river.

'Keep with the crowds,' muttered Quayle. 'It's a small place and we don't want to run into Rex and his pals just yet do we?'

'If he caught the next train from Prague that gives us at least an hour's headstart.'

'Assume nothing with these people,' Quayle mopped his brow. 'He may have driven down in one of his fancy sports cars. He might even have flown, in one of those new-fangled aeroplanes, though God knows where he would land around here.'

'There's the sign to the castle over there.'

Septimus pointed to an alleyway leading off the main street.

'Stop pointing,' hissed Quayle. 'Just follow those people up ahead. They look as though they're going up.'

The path led steeply up dozens of steps carved into the hillside and within minutes they found themselves high above the village.

'Speed up a bit, now,' huffed Quayle. 'Let's get ahead of these folks.'

The ascent was so steep there was no opportunity to talk. The castle walls were circular, and as they entered them, Septimus paused to look at the magnificent view down to the Danube and across the Wachau region.

'Marvellous,' he breathed, before Quayle's impatient grunt summoned him on.

Further up lay the remains of the tower, and it was there, along the winding path, where Quayle headed. When the two men reached the top of the tower there was no one there.

'Look at that view. How wonderful.'

Quayle shielded his eyes from the glare of the sun. Stretching for miles and miles, the rolling Austrian countryside unfurled before them and, far below, the mighty Danube glistened as it snaked through the valley, its two-thousand-mile journey to the Black Sea barely underway. Clouds scudded along the horizon, the sun glinting off distant towers, and down in the village a river boat sounded its horn and began to pull away.

'Day trippers from Vienna,' Quayle said, pointing to the small dots of people basking in the sunshine. 'Just like us. Entirely innocent, of course,' he grinned wolfishly.

Septimus glanced at the tower walls. They had crumbled to a height of only three feet. The sheer drop down the cliff-face was fenced off by only the flimsiest of bars. The wind was strong up here: too strong to light a cigarette. Still, given the way his chest was thumping after the climb, it was perhaps wise not to attempt it.

'What now?'

'We wait.'

Septimus perched on part of the ruined wall on the perimeter of the keep.

'There's a good story about this castle, you know.'

'Really? Do tell, Oates. It will help pass the time.' Quayle sat next to him, looking across to the Wachau.

'It's just a legend, really. The story goes that when Richard the Lionheart left the Holy Land after the Third Crusade he was shipwrecked on the Adriatic coast. Word got round of this and he was handed over to the Duke of Austria, who had fallen foul of him in the Holy Land. Old scores were settled and Richard was thrown into a dungeon. Legend says it was here, at Dürnstein. Richard's minstrel, a cove named Blondel — who some say was his lover — went round all the castles in Austria, singing Richard's favourite song, until one day he arrived here, and Richard apparently sang the refrain. A ransom was raised and Richard was freed.'

Quayle clapped his hands in a little show of appreciation. 'It's a nice story. One hopes ours will end just as happily.'

'Perhaps it will, gentlemen but I very much doubt it.'

Neither Septimus nor Quayle had heard the approach of their companion and when Septimus turned to see who it was, his stomach lurched. There, standing alongside them in the ruins of the tower, was Charles Rex.

Charles had a gun trained on them. His face was white with controlled anger. How he had climbed up so quickly and quietly without being observed, Septimus didn't know, and he was furious with himself for allowing Rex to catch them out.

'Don't move,' he said. 'I won't hesitate to shoot you both, one after the other. Up here, nobody will here the shots.'

'You're insane,' uttered Quayle. 'You'll never get down without being seen. There are day trippers further down the hillside.'

'*Schnauze!*' Rex waved his pistol at Quayle. 'My patience has ended.' He turned to Septimus. 'First, you come to my apartment in Prague and then you escape from Hrad Jiri. Your insolence is breathtaking. I advised you to keep your counsel. I warned you this was more dangerous than you could ever have known. My father . . .'

'Your father?' Quayle sneered. 'Would that be William Rex, great-grandson of King George III? Do you truly expect us to believe that?'

'Quayle, keep your temper,' Septimus hissed.

He had seen Charles blow Gudelj's brains out with as much compunction as he would squash a spider. Quayle's Webley was firmly in the Gladstone, well out of reach. They would have to try to reason with Charles.

'Who I am is of no concern,' Charles continued. 'Your time is up. My men have done what we came here to do, and the plan will proceed. I saw you walking down the street, bold as brass, and I followed you up here. You're too late and now you must be dealt with.'

'Wait!'

Septimus held up his hand to stall Charles. There was something he had to know amidst all the uncertainties, before their captor took the action he threatened.

'Who killed Professor Battiscombe?'

Charles's slow smile told Septimus all he needed to know.

'That old fool knew more than was good for him. Not only did he suspect the memoir was a forgery but he was also onto the Black Hand. His life was over.'

Septimus had hoped, deep down, that William Rex's smooth words about Bolsheviks, anarchists and others with a motive to seize the memoir and murder Battiscombe had been right, but now he saw the truth for what it was. Charles had slain Battiscombe because Septimus had handed over the memoir. They were both culpable – but Septimus hadn't pulled the trigger.

Charles raised his revolver.

'Time is running out, gentlemen. I . . .'

Gunfire broke out in the valley. Charles whirled round and fired three shots into the walls below them. Quayle pulled Septimus to the ground and they crouched behind a low wall as more shots were fired. Charles leant over and fired three more shots before crouching, breathlessly, to reload his revolver. He was cursing furiously, in German. Charles stood above the wall and fired again, but this time a bullet hit him in the chest and he collapsed to the ground, groaning. Quayle jumped forward, kicked the gun away from him, and pinned him down. It soon became evident that Charles was seriously wounded. Quayle released him from his grasp and reached for the revolver. More shots came from below as Quayle returned and crouched next to Septimus.

'Stay down,' he said, checking the chamber for the number of rounds left. 'Just stay down.'

Several yards away, Charles was breathing in short gasps. Blood poured through his fingers as he scrabbled to staunch the wound in his chest.

'Listen to me,' Charles said, between breaths. 'You . . . are . . . too . . . late. The money . . . and weapons . . . have been despatched. The assassins are . . . on their way.'

He managed a grin, devilishly pale, then fixed Septimus with a stare, uttering with forceful clarity.

'*Vidovdan*. You must remember that . . . *Vidovdan*. You will be . . . a witness to . . . history itself.'

As the life-blood ebbed out of Charles, Septimus was dimly aware that Quayle had begun to search his pockets.

'Here take this. It might be useful,' he said to Septimus, thrusting a folded map at him. 'He's not going to need it now.'

Charles had lost consciousness, but was still breathing.

'What can we do for him?' asked Septimus.

'Nothing,' said Quayle, his voice cracking with a severity Septimus had never heard from him. 'He knew the risks and now we must take our own chance.'

They remained huddled on the ground at the top of the ruined fortress for what seemed like an age. Quayle guarded the entrance with his pistol, and Septimus lost hope. Apart from the wind whistling across the Wachau valley, they had nothing but silence for company.

There was another series of shots below them. More gunfire followed, accompanied by shouts and screams. Some unwitting tourists had stumbled upon the gunmen. Quayle and Septimus stayed where they were, not even daring to look up from the low wall. They could hear footsteps coming towards them. Septimus crouched closer to the ground, his breathing contracting. The footsteps stopped just short of the entrance to the tower. Quayle raised his pistol. How many rounds had he got left? Not enough, that was for sure. A face peered round the wall. Quayle lowered his pistol.

It was Karl Hahn.

'Come quickly . . . follow me,' he said. 'I will take you to a place of safety.'

He led the two men down the path, past the bodies of Rex's gunmen, past the shocked day trippers, away from the ruined tower and Charles's body. They descended further and further until they reached a fork in the twisting steep, bramble-strewn path and diverted from the main path to the side of the hill.

'Here, he said, pointing to a battered Audi parked at the end of the rough track.

'Get in.'

They clambered into the vehicle. Hahn put the car into gear and drove at breakneck speed to the bottom of the hill where the track joined the main road out of Dürnstein.

'I take it we're heading to Vienna?' asked Septimus, breaking the long silence.

'Yes,' said Hahn, 'we are.'

'Perhaps you could tell me who you are and what the hell's going on?'

'Not now.'

Hahn glanced at Septimus, whose face, which had been white with shock at the castle, had regained some colour.

'When we get there.'

❖ ❖ ❖

The little Audi took them into the centre of Vienna's Old Town, where Hahn parked alongside a small hotel on a cobbled side street. Quayle had pocketed Charles's pistol and Hahn stowed his weapon as he led them into the lobby, retrieved some room keys and started up three flights to the top floor.

'We're safe here,' Hahn said, panting slightly.

He threw the keys onto a small dining table and placed his weapon next to them.

The attic room was simply furnished with a wicker chair, another easy chair and a single bed. Septimus walked across to the window and opened the blinds. He wrenched it open, disturbing a pair of roosting pigeons. Afternoon sunlight flooded into the room. Septimus looked across to the Cathedral of St Stephen and to Heldenplatz. It was an impressive vista of the old imperial city.

'Nice eh?' Hahn said at his shoulder. 'Whisky, if you'd care for some.'

Septimus took it in one gulp. Hahn replenished his own glass and sat on the wicker chair.

Hahn cleared his throat.

'I owe you an explanation.'

Septimus sat in the easy chair, lit a cigarette and inhaled deeply. Quayle stood by the door.

'Yes, you most certainly do. For someone who's dead you're looking rather well. Where do you want to begin? Oxford? Dürnstein?'

He couldn't contain his anger any longer. It bubbled over into

278

rage. Septimus wanted answers and at last he was going to get some.

'Let's begin with New College Lane,' Hahn smiled, but without humour.

He glanced at Quayle who seemed unmoved by the exchange.

'We needed to get close to William Rex. He had commissioned me to research the George Rex story to prove his lineage was authentic. He gave me the first part of the memoir and I found the marriage certificates. As soon as I realised Rex was beginning to grow suspicious of me, my murder was arranged. That was where you came in.'

'You needed me to take over the research so that Rex would use me? And when your cover with Rex was about to be blown, you thought you would use me to get to them?'

'Correct. My . . . er . . . assassination in New College Lane was observed by one of Rex's men, who had been following me. Once they saw me hand over the papers I knew Rex would approach you to continue the research. Which you did, admirably, if I may say so. With me dead, we could still get closer to Rex without fear of discovery, because of your undoubted authority as a young Oxford don.'

Septimus was unmoved by the flattery.

'Tell me who "we" is and why do you need to get close to Rex?'

'My name is not "Karl Hahn". You may know me as Sidney Reilly. I work for His Majesty's Secret Intelligence Service. William Rex, as you know, is posing as the legitimate descendant of George III to lend credence to his plans to undermine and ultimately unseat the monarchies of Europe. This alone makes him a threat – it is treason, if nothing else – and that is a capital offence. However, he is not William Rex, grandson of George Rex. That is merely one of his many false identities.'

'Who is he then?'

Hahn, or Reilly as he now was, took a small photograph from his wallet and passed it to Septimus, who recognised immediately the distinguished, bearded William Rex complete with pince-nez.

'His name is Basil Zaharoff, international arms dealer and financier,' Reilly smiled grimly. 'Of Turko-Greek origin, now with French citizenship, he sells arms to Britain, France, Spain, Russia, Germany and Austria, and many other countries, no doubt. He specialises in sabotage and misinformation. As a director of Vickers, he has made millions of pounds through arms sales. He has achieved this by convincing the governments of Europe that the others are re-arming. He owns newspapers and controls press releases which engender panic in the parliaments of London, Paris, Berlin, Vienna and St Petersburg. Each is led to believe the other has more weapons so they increase their own. It is simple, brilliant . . . and deadly.

'However, he manages his friends very well indeed, and has gained much respectability. He owns the Union Bank in Paris, has established a retirement home for French sailors and endowed a Chair in Aerodynamics at the University of Paris. He has covered his tracks so successfully it is impossible to touch him. Instead, we watch him and try to get close to him to establish what his next move will be.'

'You used me. And you did this knowing I would be in danger?'

'The risk was a calculated one. The danger would be minimised.'

'How? Anything could have happened to me. Battiscombe's been murdered. I witnessed a man shot dead in a flat in Prague. We got embroiled in a gunfight at Dürnstein.'

'Battiscombe's murder took us by surprise, I admit.' Reilly had the grace to look shamefaced. 'But we were watching you at all times. You were covered.'

'Covered? By whom?'

'Me.'

For the first time since they arrived at the hotel, Quayle spoke.

Nobody said anything for a moment. Quayle stood in the centre of the room. Outside, a pigeon settled on the window ledge. Car horns hooted in the streets below and the clock towers chimed the quarter hour.

'You?' Septimus finally broke the silence. 'But . . .'

'Yes, me, Oates.'

Quayle had a smile on his face but it wasn't the easy going smile Septimus was familiar with. His eyes were hard and flat.

'Captain in His Majesty's Armed Forces, don't forget,' said Reilly. 'Survivor of many a tricky situation with Kitchener at Khartoum, proficient with arms and cool under fire. We hoped you would go to Winchester after witnessing my murder. If not, we would have engineered a chance meeting between the two of you. Where we needed your intellect we needed Quayle's professional experience. And we knew you would trust him implicitly.'

'Is this true, Quayle?' Septimus asked.

'It is. When the intelligence bureau was formed five years ago I was sought out to serve, periodically, as an agent for His Majesty's Government. We live in changing times. There are constantly shifting sands of international allegiances; we have an Empire to protect and there are others who would bring us down in order to build up their own. And Reilly has spoken of the arms race which has significantly increased the military capacity of the major European states.'

'But you seemed so . . . so surprised when I arrived at Spurlings that evening.'

'Reilly telephoned from Oxford and told me you were on the train.'

'You didn't seem to care too much about the murder I'd witnessed. And you did your best to prevent me from meeting Charles that evening in Winchester and you were vehemently against me travelling to Prague alone.'

'There were calculated risks involved but they were minimal since you were meeting Rex himself. I insisted on coming to Carmarthen with you if you remember. We weren't sure what – or who – you'd encounter there.'

'And following me to Prague this time? You must have been on my train . . .'

'I left Victoria an hour later. I had to make sure I was in Prague with you. It was too dangerous to leave you alone with Zaharoff and Charles Rex – whoever he is – on their home territory once you'd handed over the memoir.'

'And Inspector Coppard? Was he in on this as well? He seemed to give up on Hahn's – Reilly's – murder easily enough.'

Quayle glanced at Reilly.

'Our jurisdiction doesn't run to battening down the local peelers. At least not yet. The Chief doesn't have enough weight in Whitehall. We're a young outfit and the bureaucrats regard this cloak-and-dagger stuff as all very well for the tuppenny thrillers. This'll put them right.'

'You've succeeded beyond our expectations, Septimus,' Reilly concluded. 'You've taken us to the very core of Zaharoff's conspiracy. He's determined to engineer a war between Austria and Serbia. He's sold arms to both countries and stands to profit enormously from a war because both governments will, inevitably, wish to secure more arms. Charles was in the process of paying off the Black Hand so they can attempt their latest, murderous plan.'

'Which is to assassinate the Emperor himself?' Septimus asked.

'What would be achieved by that? The Emperor has ruled for sixty-six years and almost died of pneumonia in April.' Reilly shook his head. 'He's eighty-four. It's a matter of when, not if.'

'His nephew and heir then, Archduke Franz Ferdinand.'

'The Archduke? Very likely, yes. The heir apparent.'

'He's a reformer who's sworn to grant autonomy to the Hungarians, Bohemians, Croatians, Slovenians and Bosnian-Serbs. This will make way for peaceful transition.'

'Not what the revolutionaries want at all,' said Reilly, warming to Septimus's theory. 'The Archduke has promised to remove Tisza, the hard-line Hungarian prime minister, within twenty-four hours of his accession.'

'He's promised all manner of reform once he accedes,' Quayle added.

'The Black Hand's violent behaviour won't be tolerated if that happens,' said Septimus.

'And Zaharoff won't get his war,' Reilly explained as he lit his cigarette. 'It's what he's been plotting since the murders of Empress Elisabeth and Crown Prince Rudolf. It'll all be for nothing if the Archduke succeeds to the throne.'

There was no doubt left in their minds about Zaharoff's intentions. Archduke Franz Ferdinand was unpopular in court circles. His marriage to Countess Sophie Chotek had been made for love and had disbarred their offspring from the succession because of her low birth. The Archduke's furious temper and his rows with his uncle, the Emperor, were well known. Countess Sophie was forbidden from attending court as the Archduke's equal, walk alongside him or sit in an open carriage through Vienna. The Archduke even had to request permission from the Emperor for his wife and their children to sleep in an imperial residence. The moment he succeeded as Emperor everything would change.

If Zaharoff wanted war, it was now or never.

'But what is different this time,' Reilly continued, 'is the involvement of the Black Hand, which we now realise Zaharoff is financing. Using a Serbian terror group raises the stakes immeasurably. This won't be an isolated killing by a lone madman or indeed a murder masquerading as a suicide as at Mayerling. This will be an audacious public assassination perpetrated by a Serbian national. And Serbia itself is torn in half, between the intelligence chief, Dimitrijevic´ and the prime minister, Nikola Pašic´. We believe the Black Hand seeks to stage a coup and seize power in Serbia.'

That name again. Dimitrijević, the hitherto nameless killer of Septimus's parents, who now wanted to despatch death and destruction into the Balkans and achieve his ultimate ambition: rule over Serbia.

'It could go a great deal further than that,' Quayle interjected. 'I doubt whether the Archduke would be much mourned in Austria, but there are those at the Imperial court who would not overlook an opportunity to punish the Serbs. Behind Serbia, lies the support and the might of Russia.'

'And behind Austria lies the might of Kaiser Wilhelm's Germany,' said Septimus.

'The Kaiser visited the Archduke just two weeks ago at his castle at Konopiště for what was, by all accounts, a very successful visit,' Reilly explained.

'But if Zaharoff is planning to assassinate a member of the Habsburg Royal Family, you must have informed London and therefore something will be done?' Septimus asked.

Reilly gave a wry smile.

'I have indeed despatched the information back to London by telegram where it has been noted and filed.'

'Filed? When we have irrefutable evidence that Black Hand killers have been paid to assassinate the heir apparent to the Austro-Hungarian throne?'

'Parliament is in recess, Septimus. Government officials in Whitehall are on holiday. The foreign secretary, Sir Edward Grey, is trout fishing on the Itchen in Hampshire. We're on our own.'

'You mean we're not receiving any support from the government?'

Septimus could hardly believe what Reilly had just said.

'Yes. That's about the sum of it.'

'What about the Austrian police?'

'Not a chance. Don't even think about it,' Reilly said. 'I'll be in enough trouble over Dürnstein as it is.'

Septimus still had with him the newspaper he had bought at the railway station. He opened it at the Court Circular pages.

'We know that the Emperor is at Bad Ischl.'

He scanned the heavy Germanic typeface anxiously.

'And the Archduke?' asked Reilly.

'There's no mention of him in the Court Circular.'

'Try elsewhere in the paper. He may be on a visit in which case it would be considered news.'

Septimus turned the pages. There must be some information.

'Here!' He jabbed the page, peering at it. 'He appears to be in . . .'

'Where, damnation?' rasped Quayle.

'It mentions a city called Sarajevo. He's conducting some sort of military review. And Countess Sophie has accompanied him.'

'Sarajevo?' queried Quayle.

'A town in Bosnia,' explained Reilly. 'It's in the far reaches of the Empire and shouldn't be in the Empire at all. It was annexed by the Austrians a few years ago.'

'Perhaps he and Countess Sophie will have a chance to escape the court etiquette down there,' Quayle grunted. 'Can we be sure the target is the Archduke? If not, where should we go? Bad Ischl or Sarajevo? We need more information before we proceed.'

'We already have it,' said Septimus.

'Do we?'

Septimus unfolded the bloodied map Quayle had retrieved from Charles Rex's pocket.

'It's a street map of Sarajevo.'

'With the route of the official entourage marked,' Reilly explained as he studied the map. 'Good. If Charles had this on him then that would appear to confirm the location. The question is when, exactly?'

'I can answer that,' said Septimus. 'The clue is in the last word Charles uttered at Dürnstein, as he lay dying. "*Vidovdan*," he said. He seemed pleased to be telling us. He was laughing at us.'

'*Vidovdan*?' Reilly snapped, his eyes twinkling with delight. 'Well done, Septimus! *Vidovdan* is the Serb religious day, St Vitus's day. But it's much more significant for the Serbs. It's a day of immense historical importance because it commemorates the Battle of Kosovo in 1389, when the Serbian Prince Lazar and the Holy Martyrs were killed. After the Battle, legends continued to flourish about fairies who gathered during the night next to forest streams to light fires around which they danced naked. If a young Serb were to accidentally run into the fairies during this ritual, they would give him red wine to drink and turn him into a dragon, wanting him to avenge the death of Prince Lazar and his Knights and to free the God of Vido, the Sun.'

'So the Serbs take *Vidovdan* seriously?' Quayle asked.

'Yes. It's their most sacred day of the year.'

'When is it celebrated?' asked Septimus.

Reilly picked up his revolver, hefting it from one hand to the other.

'*Vidovdan* is celebrated on June 28th.'

'But that's . . .' Quayle started to say.

'. . . the day after tomorrow,' Septimus interjected.

When the mist lifted from the valleys, it was obvious it was going to be a bright, warm midsummer's morning after a week of rain. It was a Sunday, a day of rest for the hard-working Sarajevans, a time of prayer for the Christians, a day off work for the many Muslims who had lived peacefully alongside the Bosnian-Christians for many centuries now. Even so, because it was *Vidovdan*, the Serb Holy Day of Martyrs, it was sensible for the Muslims to remain indoors and not provoke any conflict. Violence had always simmered in these Balkan valleys and, beneath the charming villages, church towers and minarets of the mosques, there was always the potential for discord to bubble to the surface.

Today, there was a different reason to feel anger. It was a reminder that the ancient cultures and religions could indeed unite in the face of a common foe if they wished.

The Archduke Franz Ferdinand, heir apparent to the crown which ruled over them, was visiting the city.

Most people had no desire to oppose the visit; indeed, the streets were decorated with the black and yellow of the Habsburg flags. It was a celebration, a chance to dress up in Sunday best, wave the flag and have a good dinner. The Mayor had ordered

287

the town to celebrate; houses had been repainted, streets swept, hanging baskets attached to the lamp posts and the main road into town renamed Franz Ferdinand Strasse in honour of the visit. A map of the route the Archduke would take through the town had been published. Hundreds were expected to line the avenues of the ancient town. And the Archduke had specifically requested no soldiers were to be stationed on the streets, as a sign of his goodwill and trust in the populace. Instead, the local police would wander amongst the crowds, assisting the public and answering any enquiries as to the movements of the royal party. Even those who were opposed to the Archduke's visit would not turn away from the entourage. They were curious to see the ceremonial finery and pomp and his poor wife, the duchess, who was not allowed in Vienna to sit alongside him. She would do so today however, and on their wedding anniversary. It would be a joyful occasion; a time to put aside differences and cheer them on, the happy couple. And didn't the Archduke wish to grant the Bosnians a measure of independence when he became emperor?

So for most people, it was a pleasant diversion on a sunny Sunday. Why not let the Archduke have his place in the newspapers for once? When he had gone, families could sit down for Sunday lunch and discuss the merits of Habsburg rule and the future at leisure. After a few glasses of wine no doubt, the debate might get heated, but at least it would remain civilised. Who needed violence? There was too much in the world already. Better to talk, bang the table, despatch the women for more wine from the cellars and wake up with a sore head tomorrow. Who looked forward to going back to work with a clear head anyway?

The Archduke and his wife, Duchess Sophie Chotek, were staying at the Hotel Bosna in Ilidža, a suburb of Sarajevo, and a grand dinner had been held in their honour on the evening of their arrival. Forty guests from Sarajevo's high society dined on a main course of potage régence, soufflés délicieux, blanquette de truite à la gelée, chicken, lamb and beef with asparagus, salad and sherbet. Desserts, cheeses and chocolate followed; wine was German and Hungarian with a nod to Bosnian culture, including Žilavka before the brandy. The Archduke led the toasts, carefully omitting any mention of his wife, whose lower status than his own caused such controversy in Viennese courtly circles, but as he spoke, he thought of his words to her when they had left Konopiště: *in Sarajevo we will be equals. You shall sit at my side and be my wife and the world will know it!*

The words were still echoing in his ears when a group of diners attempted to persuade the Archduke not to travel into Sarajevo the next day. News of assassination threats had been received from Vienna. It would be tempting fate to go into the town. He had reviewed the troop manoeuvres in the mountains and Sophie had spent the day in the town, mobbed by crowds of well-wishers, which would surely satisfy the popular press? The Archduke was on the point of agreeing to amend his plans when Count Erich von Merizzi pointed out that his itinerary had been published and an early departure would offend people, especially the Croats. This decided it: the Archduke would go after all. He sat up drinking cognac until midnight. The more he drank, the more he decried the rumours of assassination. Hadn't the people shouted *Živio! Živio!* on his return from reviewing the troops today?

The Archduke and his wife started the next day with prayers in a room converted for their use in the hotel. The Archduke returned to his suite to practise the speech he was going to deliver at the town hall in Sarajevo, some of it in Serbo-Croat. When he saw his wife after breakfast she gave him two pieces of good news:

a telegram from Vienna informed them that their eldest son had scored very highly in his examinations at the Schotten Academy. The second piece of news was for the Archduke's ears only: Sophie was expecting their fourth child.

The Archduke was dressed in a fine blue tunic, woven with special cloth said to have life-saving properties which would prevent any assassination attempts. With such wonderful news and with his wife by his side, there could be no success in any attempt. Anyone who dared threaten him would be dealt with ruthlessly.

❖   ❖   ❖

Septimus awoke to sunlight streaming through the curtains of the train compartment, and had to take a moment to remember where exactly he was. The train swayed and jolted abruptly as it crossed several sets of points. He reached out of the bunk and pulled the curtains open. He saw buildings, waggons, sidings: the usual accoutrements of the outskirts of an urban railway station.

Where were they?

Hrad Jiri, Dürnstein, Vienna . . .

'Sarajevo. We're here. Right on time.'

Sarajevo.

Quayle was sitting on the lower bunk. Septimus leaned over and noticed he was drinking tea. He poured another cup and passed it up. He was wearing a dressing gown embroidered at the edges with the Hungarian railway company colours. Septimus too, was dressed in company pyjamas.

They had caught the train from Vienna to Budapest just after nine o'clock yesterday morning and then taken the night-train through the Balkan towns of Szabadka, Brod and Doboj. Septimus had sufficient funds left, and this furnished them with first-class compartments and a splendid dinner. The conversation was spare, the wine abundant and their thoughts plenty. An early night was unanimously decided upon, their clothes sent for laundering, and to Septimus's surprise, he slept soundly.

He fumbled for his pocket watch. Ten to eight. He'd slept for almost eight hours, the best night's sleep for days. As he stared out of the window at the maze of railways lines converging and diverging on the approach to Sarajevo junction, he likened them to the course of history, which was never a smooth, single railway line progressing in a direct line from past to present; instead, it was a multitude of tracks, some main lines, some branch lines, with many alternative routes, some circular, and some dead-ends. And at this moment, he wondered whether the railway lines of the past were on a collision course with those of the present? Had the secret marriage of George III to Hannah Lightfoot sown a seed that would flower – not with the sweet scent of summertime, rather the stench of death and bloody murder – today? Was this ancient marriage about to give birth to a perverse evil which would witness the downfall of the crowned heads of Europe in a conflagration the like of which the world had never seen? And could he, Septimus Oates, armed with the knowledge that events were set upon such a deadly path, dispel the curse?

The three assassins had left Belgrade by steamer on the river Sava. Each carried two bombs tied under the waist, a revolver, ammunition and cyanide. They were going to be martyrs. On the night before their departure, in a darkened room lit by a single candle, they had sworn an oath by their ancestors' blood, by the preciousness of liberty and as true as they were Serbs and men, that they would suffer and die for the cause. This oath was sworn before an unsheathed dagger, a skull, a crucifix, a revolver and a bottle with a death's head label, in the presence of three hooded men.

They were going to be martyrs.

Ujedinjenje ili smrt!

❖ ❖ ❖

The door to the railway compartment opened and Quayle and Septimus's clothes – cleaned and pressed – were brought in by an attendant. The two men dressed quickly. There was another knock on the door. It was Sidney Reilly.

'I trust you slept well, my friends?'

Reilly certainly seemed to be enjoying himself. Without waiting for an answer – though Quayle uttered a sardonic grunt – he brandished his newspaper.

'Very helpful these Bosnians. We have here a map of the route the Archduke is due to take this morning. Let me see . . .' He unfolded the paper and turned the pages with a flourish, and it was then Septimus noticed that his humour was forced. 'The royal party will leave on a special train from the Hotel Bosna in Ilidža at 09.25 and by 09.50 will be at Sarajevo station – that's here – and then into a fleet of cars to travel to the military barracks near the station for a brief inspection, followed by a ten-minute drive down the Appel Quay to the town hall – passing the garrison, post office, gendarmerie and so forth – for a reception, leaving at 10.30 to drive back down the Appel Quay, down Franz Josef Strasse to open a new museum, receive a tour of the exhibits and at 11.30 return to the Governor's palace for lunch, leaving at two o'clock to visit a carpet factory on the way back to the station, then back to Ilidža and Hotel Bosna.'

As he finished, Reilly hurled the newspaper onto the floor, his face flushed with anger and frustration.

'Therefore, gentlemen, he could be a target at any time during the day, and at numerous points along this highly publicised route. I am open to suggestions as to what we do.'

'We should alert the police in Sarajevo,' said Septimus, aghast at the lack of security. Plots against the Habsburgs were a frequent occurrence, and yet the newspapers had been foolhardy enough to publish the itinerary!

'Yes, yes.' Reilly tapped a cigarette impatiently against his silver case. 'They will do nothing. Local peelers drafted in on their day off. All they're good for is helping old ladies to cross the road. No doubt they'll tell the assassins which car the Archduke is travelling in!'

'Well then, we'll have to intercept the Archduke and advise him to his face to get out of town before Dimitrijević's Black Hand killers nab him?'

Septimus half-thought Quayle was being facetious. Reilly drew pensively on his cigarette and blew out a stream of smoke.

'It might work, Quayle. It might just work. Let's make sure we're at the town hall by . . .' he picked up the paper from the floor and consulted it, '. . . ten o'clock. We'll wait for the Archduke and try to get through to him. He'll have his retinue around him but we can do our best.'

Reilly smiled. It was settled. They would interrupt the royal itinerary and persuade the Archduke to leave town. They had indisputable evidence; they were British and there was none of the distrust between Austria and Great Britain that existed between Britain and Germany. Before Septimus or Quayle could add anything, the train lurched to a standstill. They had arrived at Sarajevo station. Porters and guards started shouting and the sound of doors opening and slamming echoed down the platform.

Quayle lifted his Gladstone bag and checked his watch.

'I think at a time like this, a damned good breakfast is required.

We have plenty of time. One shouldn't deal with assassins on an empty stomach.'

Just after nine o'clock, the train carrying the Archduke and the Duchess of Hohenberg, and their retinue, steamed away from Ilidža and arrived at Sarajevo station twenty minutes later. A band of the 15th Army Corps played the imperial anthem as they disembarked and walked to their motor car, a Graft & Stift convertible. The sun was shining brightly, the air was warm and it promised to be a hot day. The Duchess was wearing a long, white silk dress with an ermine stole across her shoulders. Her head was covered with a veiled hat.

The first engagement for the six-car entourage was the inspection of the honour guard at Filippovič Barracks. Here Sophie – equals at last, side by side – accompanied the Archduke, his hand on hers as the rifles were presented. Here was a foretaste of what was to come when he was Emperor; supreme happiness with his beloved wife, benevolence for his people, peace throughout Europe.

As the entourage moved on, the cannons in the hilltop fortress began to fire a twenty-four gun salute. The guns echoed around the valley as the Imperial party drove steadily into the town, along the newly named Franz Ferdinand Strasse and into Appel Quay along the Miljacka River. Black and yellow Habsburg flags fluttered from the houses and some open windows displayed portraits of the Archduke.

The gathering crowds were shouting, vying with the cannons. '*Živio! Živio!*'

It was going to be a wonderful day.

There were now six of them. More bombs, pistols and cyanide had been delivered and had been passed round to the new assassins. The leader spent the evening of 27th June at Semitz wine shop with students and acquaintances. They sang Serbian songs and drank Mostar wine.

That morning – the morning of *Vidovdan* – some of them met at Vlajnič's pastry shop, where the remaining bombs were distributed. They said nothing, ate some fresh pastries and, leaving the café alone or in pairs, made way to their assigned positions along the route everyone knew the Archduke would take.

It wouldn't be long now.

There was plenty of time for Septimus and Quayle to enjoy a large breakfast of cold meats, cheeses, freshly baked bread, hard-boiled eggs, coffee and pastries at the outside table of one of the smarter cafés near the main town square. Septimus ate well. He had an appetite whetted by the long sleep and nervous exhaustion of the events at Hrad Jiri and Dürnstein. Quayle attacked the menu with gusto, but Reilly picked at his croissants and smoked incessantly between slurps of coffee.

'This is ridiculous,' he snapped, stubbing out another cigarette. 'For months we have been trying to trace Zaharoff's movements in the Balkans. We get the lead on his masquerade as William Rex, we succeed in planting Septimus close to him and we confirm the link with the Black Hand. We have firm proof of funding for the weapons and clear signs of a planned assassination. And for what? *Nothing!*'

As his voice rose to a shout, the pigeons pecking at their feet fluttered away and a couple seated next to them – young lovers enjoying their day off – turned round, startled at Reilly's exclamation.

'Can't you get Whitehall to act?' murmured Quayle, folding the newspaper.

Reilly grimaced.

'I could send another wire, I suppose. I'll try the hotel over there.'

Energised by Quayle's suggestion he seized his hat and got up from his chair.

'Wait for me here, gentlemen.'

The two men watched him push his way through the gathering crowds. It was hot already, at only half past nine, and Septimus's neck was damp with sweat. He mopped his brow and wondered what more they could do.

Quayle was on his feet.

'Come on,' he said, simply. 'Let's do a reconnaissance now that Reilly's out of the way for a few moments. That hotel opposite has opened its front rooms for viewing. Let's go and see what we can find out.'

As they pushed through the crowds and into the cool hotel lobby, Septimus didn't detect any hostility. There was an atmosphere of celebration and intense anticipation. They followed the crowds as they climbed the staircase to the upper rooms, which were filling up rapidly. Several people around them carried black and yellow flags, some decorated with a picture of the stern-faced Archduke, others that of his attractive wife, Sophie.

Quayle heaved his way to the balcony in the first room they entered, Septimus close behind him, and together they peered down onto the square. The town hall was decked out with flags and a band was playing. A red carpet cascaded down the steps. The Mayor and his welcoming committee of Serbs, Muslims and Catholic dignitaries were nervously pacing up and down, the Mayor referring to his notes, consciously rehearsing his welcome speech. The view from the hotel balcony of the church towers, minarets and red-tiled rooftops of Sarajevo was spectacular. The crowds below were now swelling into their hundreds. Septimus strained to see anything suspicious, but in truth he wasn't sure what he was looking for.

'We can't expect to see men waving guns, running around and shouting,' Quayle said from behind. 'Look for an inconspicuous, nonchalent type of chap, leaning against a lamp post or reading a newspaper. They'll bide their time. They'll be waiting for the imperial entourage to drive past, holding their bombs close in their pockets, watching for their chance. They won't be the sort to wave flags or cheer like most people.'

The security was lamentable. A few dozen policemen milled about amongst the crowds, chatting to people, pointing down the Appel Quay to where the Imperial party would first appear. The welcome party consisted of a few soldiers who were dressed in the gaudy colours of the ceremonial, armed with blunt, shiny swords to hold aloft in the Archduke's honour. They wouldn't stop any bullets.

'Let's go down. There's nothing to help us up here.'

Quayle led the way down the stairs but halted, abruptly, mid-way down. Septimus almost careered into the back of him.

'Take this,' Quayle said.

Septimus's hand closed automatically around the handle of the Webley and he slipped it quickly into his jacket-pocket.

'I kept Charles's Mauser, so you have this one. Don't use it unless absolutely necessary. These people will shoot to kill. Best to give 'em a swift whack on the head if you get close enough.'

The two men continued down the staircase. People were swarming up towards them, bemused to see them coming down at such a time as this. The entire exchange had taken less than thirty seconds and Septimus wondered when Quayle had decided to give him the weapon. During breakfast when it was obvious their mission to intercept Dimitijrevic's assassins was nigh on impossible? Was this his chance to avenge the deaths of his parents at long last?

The town square was packed. There was little hope of finding Reilly in the crush. It was too late to get anywhere near the front of the crowd – which was over ten deep – so the two men worked their way along the edge, contenting themselves with standing on the doorstep of a delicatessen to see over the throng. Septimus scanned the festive mass of people anxiously, but there was nothing untoward about the ice-cream sellers capitalising on the sunny weather, children in uniform waving flags and folk of all ages eagerly discussing the arrival of the royal party in a dozen different languages.

Septimus glanced at Quayle, who was squashed up against the wall looking intently into the crowd, the sweat dripping from his forehead.

'What can we do?' Septimus asked.

'Nothing – yet,' Quayle answered without taking his gaze away from the crowd. 'We just wait.'

As the minutes passed more and more people packed into the square, but the mood was good humoured and calm; those at the back seemed content to stand on tiptoe and raise their little children onto their shoulders so they could see. The few policemen on duty stood guard by the bollards without any concern.

Septimus continued to scan the area. It was impossible to tell if anyone was armed, so tightly packed was the crowd. The weapon Quayle had given him had fitted within the inside pocket of his jacket and there was little opportunity of him retrieving it out in a hurry. He looked up at the windows of the large nineteenth-century buildings adjacent to the town hall. A marksman up there would have a good view of the royal party but would he get a clear shot? Leaning out to shoot, people would see him, the alarm would be raised and the Archduke would be dragged away to safety and a baying mob would tear the assassin from limb to limb. So it would be a figure in the crowd, waiting, watching . . .

At that moment, the Archduke's entourage arrived. Several dignitaries waved to the crowds whose murmured chatter rose to a frenzied roar. Septimus strained to see over the heads of those in front of him; several fathers had placed their toddlers on their shoulders, obscuring his view further. Flags, babies and endless well-wishers waved in a sea of colour and movement.

Then the crowd fell silent.

Something was not right. Two cars had arrived but the Archduke and his wife were not in either. Moments later a third car, carrying the royal couple, drew up. Straining to see, Septimus watched the Archduke walk up the town hall steps. He was moving quickly, his wife struggling to keep up with him, her restraining hand on his arm. The Archduke's feathered hat bobbed and shook as he spoke, and he was not uttering any words of greeting. He was shouting, in German, and the mayor was grinning nervously, shrugging his shoulders, and reading from his prepared speech in return.

'What is it?' muttered Quayle to nobody in particular. 'What's going on?'

'It was a bomb,' someone said near them, translating the Archduke's words. 'There was an attack on the Appel Quay. Assassins threw a bomb at the Archduke and his wife. They missed.'

'Evidently,' said Quayle.

'Thank God,' said Septimus. So it had happened already. An unsuccessful attempt. A relief.

The news soon spread through the crowds. A low murmur rippled across the square like a breeze and a woman screamed. But the Archduke appeared to have steadied his legendary fury, thanks to his wife's calming influence, and was reading his prepared speech to the mayor, this time in Serbo-Croat. He finished, the Mayor smiled again and the royal party were led upstairs into the town hall for the official reception.

For a few moments the crowd remained locked in a current of electric shock and then dispersed, numb with anticlimax. People drifted towards the cafés and restaurants, women laughed with relief; hot, thirsty babies cried and men slapped each other on the back.

'One of them threw a bomb on the avenue,' said Reilly, appearing unexpectedly alongside Septimus and Quayle. 'He forgot it was on a timer and threw it immediately after he struck the cap. It bounced off the imperial car and exploded twenty yards further back.'

'Any casualties?' asked Quayle.

'Only a few onlookers with superficial wounds. It seems Dimitrijević and Zaharoff's plans have come to naught. The Archduke will be keen to leave as soon as possible and security will be tightened. They've missed their opportunity. There will be no assassination now.'

Septimus felt the pressure of the revolver in his pocket and wondered when he would be able to replace it in Quayle's bag. He wanted to take his jacket off and sit down. It was very warm and he was parched.

They found themselves walking towards the river Miljacka, where it was cooler and the crowds had thinned. The lime trees along the river front provided welcome shade and they walked for some minutes towards one of the bridges.

'Well then,' said Quayle, 'let's have a drink at that café over there and make plans to return home to England.'

They sat outside Schiller's café, situated on a corner close to the Appel Quay, off the Latin Bridge. The street was busy. People around them chattered about the failed bombing.

Septimus sipped his coffee and took a bite of cake. He closed his eyes. Home. Oxford. Here amongst these crowded, sweating, unfamiliar streets and the babble of a dozen languages, the cool quadrangles of Oxford seemed a million miles away. It would be good to sink back into the bosky glades along the banks of the Cherwell, take a punt and a picnic tea in the shade of the willows. There lay peace – of a sort. But the questions remained unanswered. George Rex was no more the son of George III than he, Septimus Oates. And somewhere out there was Basil Zaharoff, who would no doubt be placing as much distance between himself and the Black Hand as his international wealth and reputation would permit.

'Oates!'

Septimus opened his eyes and became aware of Quayle gripping his shoulder. The schoolmaster's expression was contorted with puzzlement. He was pointing to where the road turned into Appel Quay.

There, twenty yards away, was the Archduke's car, turning into the street towards them.

'What's this?' asked Reilly in disbelief. 'What are they doing coming up here? He'll never get that car up this street. It's far too narrow.'

The Archduke's chauffeur had clearly drawn the same conclusion, because the motor car came to a halt. People stopped to look, surprised and delighted to see the Archduke in their midst. One of the Archduke's retinue was standing on the running board, waving at them to get back. The gears of the car crunched and crashed as the chauffeur struggled to manoeuvre the large car. Then the car moved forward, the decision obviously to continue down the street after all, rather than to turn around.

Septimus and Quayle were standing up now, eager to catch a glimpse of the royal couple. Just as the car began to accelerate, a slight young man dressed in a crumpled dark suit and collarless shirt stepped from the crowd, arm outstretched, gun in hand. He was several feet from the couple in the car.

The assassin fired two shots and then put the revolver to his own head, but the crowds seized the weapon before punching and kicking him to the ground.

Septimus stepped forward. The final words of George Rex's memoir hammered into his brain:

The truth will reveal itself. My blood royal will one day triumph. Justice will be done. My revenge will be germinal; it may take several decades, but the seed has been sown.

The assassin and his assailants were just yards away from Septimus. The Archduke's car was barely moving. The royal couple seemed unharmed. But then the Duchess slumped forward across her husband's lap and he held his hand to his throat. Blood spurted down his tunic.

'*Sopherl! Sopherl! Sterbe nicht! Bleibe am Leben für unsere Kinder!*' Septimus heard the Archduke gasp before the car drove past him.

He drew out the Webley. So Dimitrjević had succeeded after all. Zaharoff had won. Septimus had dutifully discovered the story of George Rex and his descendants had now rewritten history. Septimus's parents' death remained unavenged.

What was it Charles Rex had said? *War has its casualties.* Septimus levelled the Webley at the young assassin who stared with piteous eyes back up him.

'Oates, no!'

He was dimly aware of Quayle shouting at him. And then something struck him on the back of the head. Pain ravaged through him and he opened his mouth to scream but no sound came out. The air roared in his ears. He noticed, with a detached interest, the sky beginning to spin above him before he hit the ground, face-first, without even putting his arms out to protect himself.

❖ ❖ ❖

Falling. He was falling. He couldn't see the ground but he was aware that he was spiralling downwards through the air, gasping great gulps in terror, a dreadful pain wracking his skull.

He awoke. He was lying on a bed, staring at a white-washed ceiling. He could hear distant voices – in the corridor outside – and shortly afterwards a doctor entered with a nurse.

'Hold still now,' said the nurse, inserting a needle into his arm. He passed out.

It was dark when he came round, and he was thirsty. It took a while for his eyes to adjust. After a few minutes he realised somebody was sitting next to the bed. He could hear steady breathing.

'Who's there?' he asked, but there was no reply.

A match flared, and the figure became apparent. A pale, sad face stared at him through the gloom. He recognised it from somewhere: the sloped shoulders, the dirty collarless shirt and the dark workman's suit. It was the young man who had shot the Archduke.

'Why did you do it?' Septimus asked him, but there was no reply. 'Who helped you? Was it Zaharoff?'

Septimus reached out to him but the searing agony in his head and neck made him gasp. Blinking back the tears, he realised the assassin had gone. He was alone in the room. Only the lingering smell of cheap tobacco remained.

28 July 1914

In his office in Whitehall Court, Mansfield Smith-Cumming, sometime captain in the Royal Navy, sat at a large desk with his back to the window, absorbed in a document. It was a report regarding the manufacturing of howitzers by Krupp, a German arms company.

Krupp is making a very large howitzer, 29.3cm, firing a projectile weighing 300 kilos, with a muzzle velocity of 450 metres per second, which pierces a nickel steel 'deck armour' plate of 10cm at an angle of 55 degrees . . . It is stated that the new 30.5 gun is to throw a projectile weighing over 500 kilos, with a muzzle velocity of 2800ft, and which will penetrate a 12in Krupp plate at 1600 feet per second . . .

Smith-Cumming sat back and let out a long sigh. The report was dated January 1910 and was over four years old. *Four years old.* The warning signs were all there; repeatedly they had tried to alert the government, but time and time again excuses had been found – Ireland, the colonies, expense, always expense. Nobody in Whitehall had listened.

They would have to now.

Smith-Cumming turned to his diary. He had entered one word for the 23rd July: '*Mobilmachung*'. Mobilisation. It summed up his worst fears, founded now upon fact: a report from Hector Bywater's agents in the northern ports of Germany, where the Imperial Navy's ships were the first to be mobilised. No public decree had been announced by the Kaiser, but all the evidence pointed to one single fact; Germany was mobilising to assist its ally, Austria.

Smith-Cumming's thoughts were interrupted by a brisk rap on the door.

'Come,' he said, absent-mindedly, shuffling the papers into a tidy pile.

His secretary entered the room.

'The gentleman from Oxford to see you, sir.'

Smith-Cumming's face registered surprise.

'Who, exactly?'

'The Zaharoff case, sir.'

Smith-Cumming's doubt cleared like sun breaking through a cloud. He smiled, his large head inclining to one side.

'Show him in.'

As Septimus entered the office the first thing he noticed was a large steel safe, painted green. There were maps and charts on the walls. By the window and seated behind a desk was a stout, grey-haired man wearing a monocle and dressed in a naval uniform. He stood up and extended a hand. Septimus met the grey eyes, took in the weather-beaten square face and surmised that this was man of immense authority. He sat in the proffered chair immediately opposite him.

'Do smoke if you so wish,' said Smith-Cumming, lighting his pipe.

Septimus shook a cigarette from his packet and accepted the lighted match.

'Are you indeed one of seven children or is the name just a flight of fancy?'

As this was spoken through a cloud of pipe smoke Septimus was not sure he had heard correctly. Flame flickered from the bowl as Smith-Cumming sucked furiously on the stem.

'I am referring to your name. Septimus. Curious, isn't it?'

'I see what you mean. No, in fact I'm an only child. My father's favourite novel was *The Warden*. Trollope, you know. Septimus Harding is the main character.'

'Can't say I do know it.' Smith-Cumming set the pipe down. 'Not a bookish sort, myself. Boats and ships and all things seaworthy are my bag. How's the head?'

'Fine now. Throbs a bit if I stand up quickly,' Septimus smiled, patting his crown. He'd needed stitches where the Mauser had cut into the back of his head. It was just as well Quayle hadn't used the heavy Webley on him.

Smith-Cumming nodded.

'It will hurt a bit. I hear Captain Quayle fetched you one hell of a wallop.'

'He saved my life.'

'Indeed. Which is more than we can say for the Archduke and his wife, may they rest in peace. What a total disaster.' Smith-Cumming must have seen Septimus flinch, as he added quickly, 'Not that it was your fault, dear boy, not at all. You were quite brilliant in leading us to Zaharoff. We just didn't have the authority we required to proceed any further. At least . . . not officially. Reilly had full backing from me to do whatever it took to ensure the plot failed. One might almost think . . .'

Smith-Cumming's voice tailed off.

'What, exactly?' Septimus prompted gently, when it became apparent that he was not going to continue.

Smith-Cumming looked his visitor in the eye, as if sizing him up to see whether he could divulge his thoughts on the matter. He decided he could.

'These agents, you know, some of them work for more than one employer.'

'I see.'

Septimus certainly thought that it might well be the case with Reilly, remembering his increasingly shifty behaviour on the morning of the assassination.

'Now then, to business.' Smith-Cumming shuffled his papers, stacking them needlessly to one side. 'I gather you are about to be offered a College Fellowship. Congratulations are in order.'

'Has it been confirmed? How did . . .'

'That is no matter,' Smith-Cumming brushed the question aside with a wave of his arm. 'The question is what do we do about George Rex?'

'George Rex? You mean the son of George III, the subject of the memoir which Zaharoff forged?'

'Ah, that is the question we must ask, Septimus. Is it a forgery?'

'Professor Battiscombe believed it was.'

'Did he consider the memoir to be a forgery or did he merely suggest that the only George Rex we know of was a simple London merchant? That does not necessarily make the memoir a forgery.'

Septimus thought about the tomb of the eight-year-old Princess Augusta in Vienna. But hadn't he and Quayle wondered about the existence of another Augusta, buried far away in some other Habsburg mausoleum? And hadn't they found the second part of the memoir in the crypt at Carmarthen church, hidden alongside the tombs of George III's granddaughters by the secret marriage? And the certificates – they were genuine enough.

But Zaharoff had them all.

'Zaharoff could indeed publish his evidence,' said Smith-Cumming, reading Septimus's thoughts. 'But he won't.'

'He won't?'

Smith-Cumming shook his head.

'No, he will not. He does not need to now. There is going to be a war. It will be a war to end all wars. A conflict not imagined by all the arms dealers in their wildest hopes and dreams. Two hours ago, at one o'clock this afternoon, the Austrian government declared war on the Serbian government by cable. How charming. That's the modern world for you.' Smith-Cumming permitted himself a grim smile. 'In Berlin, the Kaiser has promised anything to the Habsburgs and in St Petersburg, the Tsar will offer support to the Serbs. France will support Russia and we will support France. All shore leave has been cancelled. The stage is set. Zaharoff has got his war. He has no need of the memoir now. Indeed, we will need his armaments on a scale never envisaged before and he will need a strong Britain to pay him. But in the wrong hands, the memoir would cause immeasurable damage to our royal family at a time of national crisis. No mention must ever be made of it.'

Septimus lit a cigarette. It was too much to take in. And Hannah's story would have to vanish back into the dust of the crypt whence it came, untold; the secret marriage would always be that: secret.

That may be, but Battiscombe was an innocent bystander in this game of plot and counter-plot. He had lost his life: that was no game.

'But Zaharoff had Battiscombe murdered. He can't get away with that, even if you need his weapons for this war.'

Smith-Cumming nodded.

'He can't get away with it. He won't – at least, not in the next life. In this life, though, I am afraid Basil Zaharoff has too many powerful friends. In France, they are about to make him commander of the Légion d'honneur. He is untouchable – at present.'

Battiscombe's murder would never be avenged. The powers that be had decided it. And Dimitrijević: he had his war, too. His part in the accidental killing of Septimus's parents remained beyond the realm of justice.

'At least Zaharoff's hired help, the chap calling himself Charles Rex, hasn't escaped with his life.'

Smith-Cumming gave Septimus what he hoped was a look of sympathy.

'An unmarked grave at the foot of Dürnstein castle is all he has. I imagine he was the one who killed Battiscombe.'

'Why is it that those who give the orders always seem to come away purer than driven snow?' Septimus tried but failed to keep the bitterness from his voice.

'And what is it that makes you think that Battiscombe was such an innocent in all of this? There is much you do not know – and cannot know.'

'Professor Battiscombe knew about Zaharoff?'

Smith-Cumming inclined his head a fraction.

'So that was why he was killed, not because he declared George Rex to be an imposter. He knew what Zaharoff was up to and he made the connection between Rex and the Black Hand.'

'Which confirmed what we needed to know.'

Smith-Cumming rose from the desk and stood by the window.

'Battiscombe was more than simply an eminent Oxford don, Septimus. I need men of intellect, men in positions of influence and power to report back to me any titbits they may deem trivial but which for me form part of the larger picture. Battiscombe dined at All Souls; he was a member of several London clubs – White's, Boodle's, the Garrick, you name it - and he spent weekends in some of the great houses of England. Such a profile, apparently so absent-minded, could fool many people. And he did. Believe me, he did. Battiscombe's reports were pure gold.'

It didn't bring Battiscombe back or take away the pain of his dreadful murder for Septimus, but it explained why he died; and it gave Battiscombe back a stronger identity. No longer the ageing, innocent academic, slaughtered like a lamb. Rather a fighter dying for his cause.

'Battiscombe spoke very highly of you, Septimus,' Smith-Cumming continued, 'which is why you were chosen for this mission. Captain Quayle confirmed your integrity. Your background is impeccable. The country will need brilliant young men like you to work for the intelligence service. It isn't necessary to throw away your life in battle. You can fight different battles, different wars. Silent, secret combat, where death comes unannounced, heroes are never mentioned in dispatches and glory . . .. well, there is no glory. You would make an excellent addition to the Service. I'll leave it with you to think about it.

'In the meantime, you young chaps are wont to make your name with a splash in the newspapers. Take Churchill, for example. That's how he started out. Writing over-excited pieces for the Daily Mail and such like. His escape from the Boers made his name. Now look at him: First Lord of the Admiralty.'

Smith-Cumming leant towards Septimus.

'We wouldn't want you to think you could bring up any sort of over-excited story, would we? Not with the Fellowship pending. Wouldn't you agree?'

The threat was more than implicit. It was absolute.

In his mind's eye Septimus saw the view across the quad at Christ's to where his rooms were, and he knew what his answer would be. Brilliant afternoon sunlight had turned the stone to a glorious mellow colour. Soon, the bells would toll for dinner, and the Fellows would be gathering up their gowns to go to hall, where the steward and his staff had laid out the silver and prepared the wines in time-honoured fashion. The routine of academe continued day in and day out, undisturbed by the rise and fall of empires, the outbreak of wars and the foibles of kings. Assassinations and abdications may threaten peace, but the world of an Oxford college never changed.

George Rex had come into Septimus's cloistered life only a few weeks ago, turning it inside out – and nearly ending it. George Rex was still there; his story was waiting to be told one day. That day would come, Septimus thought as he turned to Smith-Cumming to give his answer, but not just yet.

1767

The woman sits on the window seat high above the market street of the little town of Bruton. From the window she can see across to the ruined abbey and the ancient hospital and to the far distant dovecote on the hill directly opposite her. To her left, the road snakes away sharply up the hill, and she knows that it is the road to London.

Every day, without fail, she sits by the window, waiting for him to come. She will sit for at least an hour, until the morning post has thundered in from Frome, just to see whether there will be a message for her. Every night, after she has kissed the children, she will sit for a few minutes, hoping fervently that he will come in secret, to see her.

He has not visited for three years now. She waits in vain, knowing that each month that passes without word from him means that his visit grows less and less likely.

Downstairs, in the nursery, the children play. There are three of them: two boys and a girl. She loves them deeply, as much as she loves him. Their future is assured, so long as she maintains her silence and endures the suspicious looks of her neighbours.

He will not come again and in her heart she knows this. What has been has been; she must look forward now, for her children's sake. Her past, and her shared past with him, is now their future.

That future, like the blank page of a manuscript, was theirs to fill; and they would, in time, have a story to tell.

Historical note

King George III reigned from 1760 to 1820. His marriage to Charlotte of Mecklenberg produced fifteen children, from whom were descended the ruling families of Germany, Britain and many European monarchies in the nineteenth century, including the future George IV and William IV. He famously went mad for a short time in 1788 (it is thought he suffered from porphyria, a hereditary disease carried by his descendants into the twentieth century). His younger son, the Duke of Kent, fathered Victoria, who reigned as Queen of Great Britain from 1837 to 1901, succeeded by her son Edward VII (reigned 1901–11) and his son George V (reigned 1911–36). Her Majesty Queen Elizabeth II is therefore directly descended from George III through Victoria.

The secret marriage to Hannah Lightfoot is recorded in several marriage certificates dated 1759, lodged in the Public Record Office, Kew, London (Reference J77/44). These documents were examined in a court of law in 1866 and impounded. The marriage was witnessed by William Pitt, later created the Earl of Chatham, and was conducted by Dr John Wilmot, Fellow of Trinity College, Oxford and rector of Barton-on-the-Heath, Warwickshire. The documents also suggest there were children from the secret marriage.

There is no memoir of George Rex. Professor I. R. Christie suggested long ago that George Rex of South Africa favoured in legend to be George III's son, was in fact the son of a Whitechapel wine distiller, John Rex. The Royal Marriages Act of 1772 ensured that members of the royal family married with proper permission from the sovereign, but George III's brothers and his son, the Prince of Wales, all had secret marriages – obviously a family trait.

However, in the summer of 2000, the ornate tombs of Charlotte Dalton and her niece, Margaret Augusta, were discovered underneath the tiled floor of the church of St Peter's, Carmarthen, South Wales. No mention of these tombs exists in any church guides. Charlotte may have been the daughter of Sarah, the second of the children of Prince George and Hannah Lightfoot. The large and ornate organ in St Peter's was originally destined for the royal chapel at St George's, Windsor, but for reasons perhaps linked with George III's putative granddaughter, Charlotte, it was installed at Carmarthen.

The Black Hand Society existed. The guns and bombs supplied to them enabled the assassination of Archduke Franz Ferdinand in Sarajevo on 28th June 1914 – the day when *Vidovdan*, a Serbian holy day is celebrated. The assassination led directly to the outbreak of the First World War, which ultimately caused the downfall of the Hohernzollern, Romanov and Habsburg monarchies as well as the deaths of many millions.

The following books and articles, among others, were useful:

'The Family Origins of George Rex of Knysna,' by I. R. Christie, Notes and Queries, pp.18–23 (January 1975)

'Charlotte Dalton, St Peter's Church, Carmarthen,' by S Mitchell, Notes and Queries, pp.384–6 (September 2003)

Aristocrats: Caroline, Emily, Louisa and Sarah Lennox 1740–1832 by S Tillyard (1995)

Bradshaw's Continental Railway Guide (1913 facsimile)

Decisions for War, 1914 by Keith Wilson (ed.) (1995)

The French Revolution by Christopher Hibbert (1980)

George III: A Personal History by Christopher Hibbert (1999)

Hannah Regina: Britain's Quaker Queen by Michael Kreps (2003)

One Morning in Sarajevo – 28 June 1914 by David James Smith (2009)

The Quest for C: Mansfield Cumming and the Founding of the Secret Service by Alan Judd (1999)

Six: A History of Britain's Secret Intelligence Service by Michael Smith (2010)

Thunder at Twilight by Frederic Morton (1989)

William Pitt the Younger by William Hague (2004)

Key Historical Characters

King George III (1738–1820, King of Great Britain & Hanover 1760–1820).

Secretly married Hannah Lightfoot, purportedly a Quaker's daughter, whilst Prince of Wales, in 1759. There is no record of any children or of what happened to her. Married secondly Charlotte of Mecklenberg-Strelitz, with whom he had fifteen children.

William Pitt (1759–1806)

Son of the famous William Pitt, 1st Earl of Chatham, Pitt 'the Younger' entered Cambridge at 14 and became Prime Minister aged 24. Against all odds, he remained in office until 1801, and was again prime minister from 1804 until his death in 1806. His meteoric rise to power was astonishing. A possible explanation for this might be that Pitt used the secret marriage his father had witnessed to force the King into giving his patronage and thus avoid knowledge of the royal bigamy entering the public domain, a threat not to be taken lightly coming as it did at the height of the American War of Independence. George III's bout of insanity in 1788, the French Revolution and fall of the French monarchy secured Pitt's grip even further.

Crown Prince Rudolf (1858–89)

Son and heir apparent to Emperor Franz Josef I (1830–1916); found dead at his hunting lodge on 30th January 1889 with his mistress Baroness Mary Vetsera (1871–89). Officially, Rudolf had suffered heart failure, but stories about a suicide pact quickly circulated. However, the last Habsburg Empress, Zita, gave an interview in 1988, claiming that Rudolf had been murdered by foreign agents; the true answer is not known.

Empress Elisabeth of Austria ['Sisi'] (1837–98)

Married, unhappily, to Emperor Franz Josef, who kept numerous mistresses. Her popularity with the Hungarians, who sought separation from the Austrians, only served to isolate her further. Whilst touring Italy in the early autumn of 1898, Sisi was stabbed and killed by an Italian anarchist, Luigi Lucheni, whose motives remain unknown to this day.

Basil Zaharoff ['The Mystery man of Europe'] (1849–1936)

Arms dealer and financier, of Greek origin, whose life of double-dealing began as child-arsonist setting fires for the Constantinople firefighters, who would rescue the treasured possessions of the rich for a commission. Zaharoff became a dealer for Nordenfelt, adept at sabotaging weapons demonstrations and famously selling a submarine to the Greeks, then persuading the Turks that they needed two to counter the threat, and selling two more to the Russians. None of the submarines were efficient. Nordenfelt merged with Maxim and was then bought out by Vickers; Zaharoff became a director. Vickers had secret plants inside Germany and issued press releases which encouraged the French to re-arm, which in turn pushed the German government to order more weapons. Zaharoff owned the Paris Union Bank and a daily newspaper which he used to foster the European arms race.

There is no evidence that he funded the Black Hand, however, or that he was involved in any way with the deaths of Crown Prince Rudolf or Empress 'Sisi'. He died in 1936, after burning his memoirs, which would have incriminated numerous individuals and countless governments.

Sidney Reilly ['Ace of Spies'] (1873–1925)

Real name Sigmund Rosenblum, of Jewish-Russian origin, who reportedly spied for four nations and was Ian Fleming's model for James Bond. He arrived in England in 1896 and set up a business selling miracle cures; by 1899 he was spying for the British government in Russia and then in Japan. In 1909 he was sent to Germany to spy on the Baltic shipping as part of the British Secret Service intelligence gathering. 'Karl Hahn' was one of Sidney Reilly's many disguises. In 1918 he was sent to Russia by the British government in a plot to overthrow the Bolshevik government. He was executed by the Bolsheviks outside Moscow in 1925, though rumours spread that he had survived and joined the White Russians.

Mansfield Smith-Cumming ['C'] (1859–1923)

Unassuming naval captain who became the first Chief ('C') of British Intelligence, which was founded in 1909, Cumming developed a network of thousands of agents and informants from Oxford and Cambridge Colleges to the backstreets of St Petersburg, many of whom worked for more than one government. He employed linguists, businessmen, academics and artists in any capacity he could establish, to spy for him across Europe and beyond.

Dragutin Dimitrijević ['Colonel Apis'] (1876–1917)

One of the young men who assassinated the King of Serbia in 1903, he rose to become chief of Serbian Intelligence and leader of the 'Black Hand' under the codename 'Apis' ('bee'). The Black Hand was a terrorist group committed to removing Habsburg rule from Serbian territory. He failed to murder the Emperor Franz Josef in 1911 but succeeded with Archduke Franz Ferdinand in 1914. He was executed in 1917 for complicity in another plot.

Archduke Franz Ferdinand (1863–1914)

Heir apparent and nephew to Emperor Franz Josef, a reformer who hated his uncle and was disliked by Viennese society. His wife was considered lowly in status – a mere Countess – but his visit to Sarajevo was their one chance to enjoy equality in public. His death caused little concern in Vienna but young diplomats persuaded the ageing Emperor to declare war on Serbia, backed by the militant Kaiser Wilhelm II of Germany. This triggered the alliance system and European war. The car which Franz Ferdinand and his wife Sophie were travelling in when they were assassinated can be seen in the Museum of Military History in Vienna, along with the bloodstained tunic he was wearing. They were buried at his castle in Artstetten Castle in Austria. Most of the Habsburgs are interred in the imperial crypt (*Kaisergruft*) in the Capuchin Church in Vienna.

Gavrilo Princip (1894–1918)

Nineteen-year-old student assassin of Archduke Franz Ferdinand whose two pistol shots killed the Archduke and his wife and set in motion the First World War. Disappointed by the failed bombing of the royal entourage, Princip bought a sandwich at Schiller's cafe in Sarajevo, only to be confronted with the royal car that had taken a wrong turn. Princip was too young to hang, but died most unpleasantly of tuberculosis whilst incarcerated in the Habsburg fortress of Theresienstadt (now Terezin, in the Czech Republic), in the spring of 1918.